All That I Got Is You

All That I Got Is You

By

The, oc

All That I Got Is You

Copyright © 2008 by The, oc

All That I Got Is You may be ordered at Lulu.com and other major booksellers.

Printed in the United States of America

ISBN: 978-0-615-23711-4

Library of Congress Control Number: **To be determined.**

This book is dedicated to Quincy, 'Q', Desroaches. Knowing a strong, courageous brother like you is what put courage within me. Rest in peace, brother. Special dedication to Martin Anderson, a 13-year old black male that was brutally beaten by guards at a Florida boot camp, and died shortly after. Those guards were acquitted of murder, but their hearts will punish them for their indifference to the life of a defenseless child against four adults. And we will continue to stand for beautiful black souls like you, Martin, because you are worth it. Rest in peace, young brother.

Contents

Acknowledgements

F irst off, I have to thank the creator for all of his blessings, and instilling within me the gift to create. Words cannot explain how thankful I am to you. To my beautiful wife, Demetria, and children, James, Jazmine, and Destyni. I am nothing without you. To all of my family, Mom, Dad, brothers and sisters, aunts and uncles, and cousins. Thank you all four your support. I know I haven't been the most social family member, but I pray that you all understand and bear with me while I strive to fulfill my purpose. I love all of you for your care and patience with me. To my extended family, my homeboys, Ralph, Anthony, Corey, Antonio, and Sukari. I could not ask for a better set of homies. We ride together 4 life. And I will ride 4 y'all for whatever, whenever. To all of my homies and homegirls throughout school, my homies from the service, and all the coworkers that were, and still are true friends to me. A lot of you gave your heart just for me to make it to another day, and I can never 4get that. I am more than grateful, and hope nothing but the best for all of y'all. To my genius editor, teacher, mentor, and good friend, Preston Allen. It was truly a blessing for me to go to Miami-Dade College and meet you. Everything that you gain from this game will be well deserved because you are truly an artist and teacher. Your time has been invaluable to my career, and I hope I can do the same for other young authors that are hungry to perfect their craft.

My cover was designed by a super-talented photographer and artist named Jackson Innocent of Zoe Images in Ft. Lauderdale, FL. Thank you brother for you diligence with the cover, your patience with me, and all that you put into making the cover hot, and my life a bit easier. Keep doing your thing. Haitians, represent.

To my publicist and good friend, Joy Farrington. Thank you for your hard work, giving heart, and patience with a perfectionist like me. You too make my life easier, and I'm grateful to have a sister like you in my corner.

I give thanks to all of my peers in the literary industry. Not only do you all keep me on my toes, but you give life to one of the greatest art forms ever seen by man. Let's keep doing our thing and show the world that there is nothing like books. God bless.

Shout out to my hometeam authors, Momowilly, Trista Russell, Preston Allen, all of the great authors out of Florida, and all that will be coming out. Florida will be known as a hot spot for literature and great authors because of you.

Thanks to all of the book clubs across the country, agents, editors, publishers, book stores, the reviewers and review sites, online magazines, and all of the literary industry outlets. Thank you for your continued support with our careers, your love for books, and your dedication to want us to remain great. We stand on your shoulders and the world sees how great we are. Let's keep it moving and give the world the best stories that they could ever ask for.

If I forgot anyone, please don't curse me. You are still in my heart, and I recognize that, even if these pages don't reflect it.

Much Blessings,
The, oc

I pray I'm forgiven for every bad decision I made,

every sister I played, cause I'm still paranoid to this day.

And it's nobody's fault. I made the decisions I made.

This is the life I chose, or rather the life that chose me.

by Jay-Z

from the Black Album's *December 4th*

Prologue

The urgency in the news reporter's voice sounded as if this tragedy had somehow affected her personally. Her tongue was razor-sharp, emotional, emphasizing on words like gangster, murderer, prime suspect, and the name, Parish 'Panther' Coles.

Panther thought back to everything that went down last night. The man's Spanish accent was as sharp as his tailor-made suit. His slicked back hair shined from the lone street lamp overlooking the empty parking lot. His six-foot frame was well defined, and he appeared to be in great shape, like a pro boxer in his prime. He and Panther stood a few feet from each other, as if ready to face off in the middle of a ring. The man asked Panther for a truce.

Panther laughed. He said, "I doubt there's a need for it. I don't want this life anymore, Mr. Colon. You can have it."

"And why should I believe this?" Mr. Colon said. "You're at the top of the game, Mr. Coles."

"And I want to stay there. Even more of a reason to get out."

Mr. Colon folded his arms. "Still, why should I believe this? What is the great Panther Coles going to do if he is no longer a part of the game?"

Panther could sense the tension in Mr. Colon's voice. He said, "First thing I will do is allow you to do your thing."

"That's good to here," Mr. Colon said as he smiled. "Because I was tired of you getting in my way." Mr. Colon let out a big laugh.

Panther reluctantly shook the man's hands, smiling inside about not having to deal with guys like this anymore.

A few hours later, Mr. Colon was dead, but other than Mr. Colon, Panther was the only big fish out there. And Panther had not ordered the hit.

Panther's problems were only just beginning. The news about what happened to Patrick Alden yesterday was on every radio station in South Florida. There was no time to waste.

Like any intelligent man, Panther knew when the pressure came, that was the time to be relaxed. It was the only way to focus. And music had always been his escape. An ally that he counted on whenever the pressure became too much to bear.

As he popped in a CD of Charlie Parker's Greatest Hits, zooming down I-95 South, a revelation came over Panther. How could he protect his loved ones if he was running? If he was always hiding, how could he obtain that peace that he so dearly craved? The ones setting him up had to hide from the truth, but Panther grew tired of the lies. He refused to allow all the games to dictate the outcome of his life. Just like the music that spoke to him, Panther wanted to be true. Like Charlie Parker, a.k.a Bird, Panther was determined to be free.

ಹ 1 ಆ

Deidra

I don't know what had me shook, but I almost burned myself when Panther came busting through the door. I was hooking up Shakita's hair, reached for the curling iron, and the surround sound on the T.V. had drowned out the click from the door when it unlocked. Shakita was just as shook and damn near jumped in my lap when Panther walked pass. Luckily for her, I wasn't holding that hot ass curling iron to her head. Our friendship would've singed away as fast as the skin on the back of her neck.

But now I was concentrated on Panther. I was worried about how he came in sweating puddles underneath his University of Miami basketball jersey. Still, he looked good doing it, the sweat glistening off the veins in his dark forearms. The print in the front of his matching, green shorts said more Panther did. That arrogant fucker didn't even acknowledge me when he passed. Just went straight to one of the rooms in the back as if I was some chickenhead. As if I was nobody to him. But it was all right. He would try getting into the pussy later on, but he was going to have to work for it.

I was glad that Panther didn't stay out front with us. Shakita was eyeing him so hard that if he was any closer he would've stepped on her tongue. I checked her about that shit before. She denied it then, just like every other bitch that I almost put a hurting on for attempting to overstep that line called Deidra. I couldn't help that my man was fine. But I could help to put a cap in a bitch's ass for trying to take him.

And Panther knew it. That's why he's with me, and not these other dick-hungry females, like Shakita. I yanked the shit out of that nappy head.

"Ahh," she screamed. "Goddamn, Dee. Watch my head."

"Ooh, my bad, girl. Maybe if you wasn't breaking your neck trying to peep out Panther, I wouldn't have pulled so hard."

Shakita sucked her teeth. "Whatever, girl. Don't start it."

"I start whatever I want to start," I told her. "And I finish it, too. Don't you forget it, either."

"Yeah, yeah. Anyway, are you about done?"

"Hell yes. And you better have all my dough. You already $50 in the hole. Do I look like a credit card company?"

Shakita waived my complaint down. "All right, girl. But it's a damn shame that you're charging your best friend."

"And it's a shame that you still owe me after six months."

Shakita tried icing me with her nasty Big Bird laugh, but I was dead serious. I liked getting my money. I hustled too hard to have bitches moochin' off of me. Yeah, Shakita was my girl and all, but business and friends didn't mix like two clits and no dick. Find yourself in serious shit. I made that one up myself, y'all.

So I snatched up my bread from Shakita and practically pushed her out the door. I had to see what was up with Panther. We've been together for two years now, and I didn't keep it that way by entertaining other hoes. Panther and I had gotten each other out of all types of shit in the past two years, some things that may have incriminated us both. But because of it, I was living the way I wanted. There was nothing I wouldn't do for that nigga, and he felt the same about me. For example, the three-bedroom house in Coral Springs that I was lounging in, he helped to get it. It may have been the quietest area in Florida, and the police rolled around like twenty-five-eight, but at least I wasn't in the projects anymore.

I went to the room where the noise was coming from, found Panther grabbing some clothes out the closet, rushing, stuffing them into a duffle bag. Instincts told me something was crucial with my man right now. It wasn't unusual for him to pack clothes in a rush. He was always going up the road on business. Still, he wasn't the type to walk by me like I wasn't even there.

"Panther, baby." I asked, "Is everything all right?"

"No, Baby-Dee," he said as he continued packing socks and boxers. "Everything is not all right."

I was more spooked than concerned. "Okay," I said. "What's going on?"

Panther stopped and turned to me. His sleepy, brown eyes were soaked with tension. Slowly he approached, pulled me close, and wrapped his mighty hands around my waist. A tingle shot straight through my body. I hadn't seen him in two days and I missed him like hell. I touched his face gently. I tried to look as cool as an ice cream pop. I just wanted him to know that I was there for him.

I said, "Talk to me, baby."

Panther took my hand and guided me to our heart-shaped waterbed. I rested on my side facing Panther while he sat on the edge of the bed. He placed his hand on my hip.

Panther's face was disturbed. "There's a lot going down right now," he said, "and I'm going to need you to represent."

I knew when something was up with my man. I said, "Baby, you know I'm always here. Whatever it is, just tell me. Is it money, cause you know I can get—

"No, it's not money."

"Then it's beef. Is it some beef, because I can holla at my—"

"Now since when have I ever involved you in my beefs? You are my woman. I put my energy into protecting you, not the other way around."

His words were sweet as Hershey's Kisses, but I wanted him to take me seriously. "All I'm saying is you know even though Eric is locked down, he still got your back. And all I need is the word from you and he'll have them boys ready to get them choppers—"

Panther signaled me to stop with a finger to his lips. He then moved his hand and calmed me with a kiss. Panther humbled me in a way that no one else was able to. Made me think before I acted a fool.

But not to get it twisted, Panther was my man because he was the only man that could handle me. At five-foot-nine, thick like maple syrup, and equipped with a healthy supply of tits, ass, and attitude, Panther was the only man for me.

He placed his hand back on my hip, stared at me as if I was the only person in the world that mattered right now.

He said, "I'm being framed for killing this rich, white man yesterday. I got a murder charge over my head so big, that CNN is even talking about it."

For a second it felt as if I had forgotten how to breathe. I wanted to say something, anything, but I couldn't find the words. "But—but how... Why," I finally said. I didn't want to believe it.

Panther clapped his hands together, leaned over and directed the fire in his eyes towards the hallway. "They're saying I'm a suspect," he said, "yet my name and face are all over the news. I'll be on the front page of every newspaper in the country, and by tomorrow morning the world is gonna want to convict Parish Coles of this murder. Fuck being just a suspect. Once the media tells their side of the story, I'm as guilty as a signed confession."

I felt my shoulders tighten. But before the fear set in, Panther turned to me and grabbed my hand.

He said, "Are you down to ride for me?"

The question was meant to test me. Even though Panther knew what type of girl I was, he could see the fear in my eyes and he needed to be sure that he could count on me. I got up, took a spot next to him and grabbed both of his hands. I said, "As far as you need me to, baby."

He gave me his magical smile before he stood up and guided me to the front of the closet. While snatching up some more street clothes, he said, "I need your word, baby. I need you to be my alibi. There's a chance that the police will find their way here. And if they do, I need you to say that I was here around four in the afternoon yesterday. I stayed until six and you don't know where I went. If they ask what we did, say we spent quality time watching T.V. and had something to eat. What did you eat yesterday about this time?"

I ran through my mind. "Some fried fish from the Haitian restaurant on Miramar Parkway."

"Good, then that's what we ate." He went on to pack his shoes. "Were you by yourself?"

"Yes."

"Perfect. So that's the way it went down. What did we do? Watched Rap City. Did we talk about anything in particular? No. How long was I there? Two hours. I left around six o'clock. And that's it. That's all they need to know. Can you ride with that, baby?"

He stopped packing and stared at me.

I nodded with a straight face, but on the real, I was shaking like a bowl of jello. I fought it off though. Growing up around my way, I learned how to numb those scary feelings. A big heart and a gangster mouthpiece pulled me out of a lot of crazy situations. But right now, it was all about Panther. And so was I.

He threw on a fitted cap, slung a couple duffel bags over his broad shoulders. I followed him to the front. I couldn't believe this was really happening. Next to my little sister and my business, Panther was like my world. And it felt good having my own place with my man here with me. I couldn't picture him being taken away from me for life. But those thoughts, I quickly shook away. The more I entertained them, the more they would try to control me. If Panther was going to beat this rap, he needed my help, so I had to get it together.

He stopped at the front door and just looked around for a moment. I knew he was thinking about not seeing me or this house anymore. We made a good amount of memories in the four months here. Some bitches might think I'm exaggerating, but every minute of every day spent with Panther made it memorable. Good and bad things, of course, but that's life. Everything that Panther has been to me and everything that I had because of him was worth it.

He pulled me close and I thought I was going to melt. My heart pounded against his chest. I didn't want him to leave. I prayed that I would wake from this nightmare. But if I had to be a part of this nightmare then I'd be the little angel hovering over my man's shoulder. We would navigate our way through these dark clouds together. That's just the way I was, down for my peoples for whatever. And I was down for Panther just the same.

He walked out and I stood at the door nervously biting at my nails. Could this be the last time I'd see Panther living as a free man. He jumped into a midnight blue Benz, a car that I had never seen him in before. He was already making moves to help us beat this murder rap.

I watched Panther drive off, thinking that I was crazy for being so shook. Panther would win. There was no doubt in my mind. It didn't matter what those fuckers had on him. He had never come up short. He had never had a losing hand. And I was ready to play my part as the queen at his side.

It was five o'clock now. I turned from the music videos and tuned into the evening news. Waited to see what lies were being spread about Panther. I was ready for those assholes, too. They didn't know who Deidra was. Nothing or no one was going to come between me holding down the man that I loved.

ಐ 2 ಜಃ

Sandra

It had been five days. Five whole fucking days since I last saw Panther. He had driven me restless. But I almost jumped out of my panties when I heard the door unlock. He came in the apartment wearing a basketball jersey and matching hat. Beads of sweat showed on his face while more sweat trickled down his bulging biceps. That chocolate wonder looked so tasty I could feel my mouth and other parts of my body grow moist. I couldn't help it. I was horny as hell. Just yesterday, I thought about pulling my plastic friend from out the closet and getting familiar with him again. It's not something that I normally did, but then again, Panther didn't normally go off for a week without me hearing from him. I made sure I was the first thing he saw when he came in.

"Parish, where were you?" I asked.

Panther studied me for a second. He locked the door then walked past as if I was a bum on a corner.

I followed him to the living room. "Panther, did you hear me? I haven't seen you in days. What's going on?"

He went over to the couch and grabbed the remote. He asked, "Have you seen the news today?"

I laughed under my breath. Did this nigga blatantly ignore me? I said. "Are you gonna tell me why I haven't heard from you? A call, e-mail, something to tell me that you were all right. You know I can't stand not knowing where—"

Panther told me to stop with his hand while he switched channels. What was so important on the damn T.V. that he couldn't pay me any attention? I held my ground, arms folded, bounced my foot, blew out a frustrated breath to let him know that I wanted an answer.

"Hel—lo," I said. "Parish Coles. Is that all that you see? What is it? I'm not interesting anymore. CNN has more to offer?"

Again with his hand, he told me to stop.

What the hell was this about? First, I don't hear from Panther in a week. Then I get ignored and pushed to the side like dust in a corner. I was sick of this shit. Sick of trying all that I could to be closer to Panther. I had asked him like twenty dozen times why couldn't he be here more often. I suspected that it was another woman that he lived with. I was even delusional enough to believe that he was already married. Smart, powerful men like Panther always had secrets.

Panther patted the spot next to him. I acted as if I didn't know what that meant. Rolled my head away, wondering why I constantly took myself through this torture. I mean Panther was a good man, but I deserved more. More than two nights a week. He could call it business, but business wasn't necessary all the time. I wanted him when I wanted him. And not the other way around.

I turned to face Panther. Those puppy-licious eyes pulled me towards him and summoned me to take a seat. But only cause I wanted them to.

Panther stroked the tips of my wrap with one hand. I loved for him to play in my hair. The other hand he placed over mine and said, "Listen. I need you to do something for me, Sandy."

Panther never looked so serious. I was hoping for a proposal, but why play the fool? I was only kidding myself. I said, "Whatever you need, baby."

"Good," Panther said, "because I'm being framed for killing this rich, white man by the name of Patrick Alden.

I felt my heart drop. It couldn't be, I told myself. I didn't hear what I thought I just heard. Panther was wanted for murder. For actually killing another human being. "Patrick Alden is that wealthy banker and real estate developer. He's a client with my firm. He's been murdered, and their blaming you for it. Baby, how? Why?"

"I don't know" Panther said, "but I have to find out. I was at his house yesterday and he was alive when I left. We had an argument but that was all. I never touched the man. They're saying that I'm only a suspect but the media is going to spin this against me. That's why I'm going to need your help, baby."

But what could I do, I thought. I couldn't even think straight. Confused and afraid all at once. But Panther needed my help. That meant I had to get it together. I had to be strong and do all that I could for my man. He had been there for me, and in the darkest time in his life, he was going to need me to do the same. I was too frightened to think about what was going to happen, but I couldn't run away from it either.

I said, "I'll get on the phone and call my boss. He should know who'll be best to help us through this."

Panther said, "No, baby. I don't need that kind of help from you."

"What do you mean you don't need that kind of help, Panther? This thing could get ugly. You need a good lawyer. A rich, white man possibly killed by a black man, and they're calling your name. If you don't need me to call my friends then what do you need?"

"I need you to be my alibi."

Like a tourist in the hood, I was more lost than ever. I didn't like the way this was going, but I also needed to know more.

Panther read my mind. He said, "I just need you to trust me, Sandy. I'm going to need your word to beat this. The murder took place some time yesterday evening. Where were you between six and eight last night?"

The pressure mounted up like a pile of rocks stacked onto my head. I had to pull myself from out of the rubble of fear. "I-I—I … was here," I said. "Here the whole night. Around six, I was cooking. Stayed in and watched a movie. "Love Jones."

Panther nodded. "Did you speak to anyone last night?"

"Just the hospital to check on my aunt."

"Good," he said. "Then that's the way it went down. If they come to you, Sandy, can you run with this and stay cool?"

"Yes baby," I said. "Of course. You should know that I will do whatever it—

"Exactly like that, Sandy. And nothing more."

Panther's stare focused on the pupils of my eyes, showing that he meant business. I needed to secure his trust in me.

But I also needed to somehow summon up a sense of trust in myself. I wasn't sure what I was getting myself into. I knew that Panther dealt in all kinds of business, yet I never examined what the consequences would mean someday. I grew comfortable with us being on top of the world, even though I feared that one day that world would crumble beneath us.

We had been together for a year now. A beautiful year, and I wanted Panther to give up that life so we could settle together quietly, make our money in West Palm Beach or Atlanta. I wanted what was best for us. Our future. Once this ugly murder thing was settled, then I'd tell him what I had in mind. I just wanted him to know that I was there for him, 100%.

Panther clicked to the news, and sure enough, there was his face and a report of them saying they needed to know of his whereabouts. They said that Mr. Alden was a prominent businessman for over twenty years, and that he and Panther had dealings in the past. They claimed that he was the biggest investor in Panther's plans for a T.V. station, but at the last minute Mr. Alden backed out, and harsh words between him and Panther were exchanged. They ended the report by saying that "Parish Coles, a man with a criminal lifestyle, was betrayed, and probably felt like Patrick Alden was his worst enemy."

I turned to Panther, whose face was as rigid as stone.

"Fuckers," he cursed under his breath. He flipped through channels as his face screwed up in anger and disgust.

Assholes. They didn't know my Panther. Nobody knew him. And I understood why he was here. Why he came to me. The world was against him and I was the only person that he could trust. I was his woman, his confidant. I would have to take care of him in a way that no one else could. We had to put our energies together to be strong. But I could only imagine how Panther was feeling right now. It was him against the world, but at least he was not alone. He had a good woman at his side that would do whatever it took and fight with him to the end.

❧ 3 ☙

Rachel

I was tired, but I had to keep going. Staring for hours at a computer screen could really fuck with your head, but I wanted to get this project done. Especially for Ace. He reminded me so much of Panther. Black and strong, he approached the world like he owed no one anything. It was unusual to see that in a thirteen year-old boy. But one thing I was sure of, like Panther, Ace would have people that either understood him, or couldn't stand him. Either they would've loved him, or hated him.

It was 8:30, over two hours since I had been working on this project. My goal was to create an activity where my boys could channel their anger towards a positive outcome. That was easier said than done when you have been surrounded by anger and hostility throughout your life. The correctional officers treated them like animals, and that just made the boys' situation even harder. It was difficult for all of us, but I would often tell my boys that no matter where you were in life, we all have a purpose, and we should all strive to achieve it.

A familiar knock at the door broke my concentration. I was grateful because I needed a break anyway. And Panther had a way of pulling me out of my crazed world. I loved how we would talk for hours about nothing and everything. His words were like poetry; strong, sensuous, rhythmic, always taking me on a high. He often recounted his childhood to me, and I assumed that those stories would've been difficult for him to speak about, yet it proved to be the magnet that brought us closer. Our bond was strong because I understood things about him that other people couldn't relate to.

I checked the peephole just in case. Panther looked divine. The outside hall light made his beautiful, black skin shine like gold. I didn't know what got me all giddy to see him, but I was like a little girl that had won first place in a beauty contest. Before I opened the door, I checked myself, brushed my ponytail back with a hand, and cooled my hot ass down. I still had to play the sweet girl role because we had only been kicking it for nine months.

I opened the door slow. Panther smiled that smile of a million granted wishes and kissed me on the neck. I was ready to jump on him, but I played it cool, gave him a shy thank you, and invited him in. He took long, strong, smooth steps over to my black and gold couch. I was checking how his calf muscles tightened from when his feet planted to the ground. I doubt I was going to get much work done tonight.

I eased the door closed, glad that I had thrown off that boring, two-piece business suit, and had slid into a cute, pajama short set. It emphasized my petite figure and plump ass. My slim, brown sugar-toned legs were my best asset. And the fact that I had no bra on underneath my top offered Panther a double-dose of what I had to give.

Panther sat down on my leather loveseat and I sat close to him, crossed my legs so they would brush against his, but Panther barely looked my way. His attention was elsewhere, on the abstract, African paintings on the walls, the sculpture of a black dancer, and my small, two-shelf bookcase with books from Malcolm X to Toni Morrison.

I tried to catch his eye.

"Are you okay," I asked Panther.

He shook his head.

I was worried. I said, "You feel like talking about it?"

He didn't answer.

I rose from my seat and stood before him, tried stroking away the stress on his head with my fingertips. "I'll go and get you something to drink. Try and make yourself comfortable."

In the kitchen I put some water to boil for tea. Panther always liked the flavors that I bought. I chose the peppermint herbal tea, his favorite. If he wasn't feeling well, I hoped that the tea would help.

I went back out to the front and found Panther holding and studying a photo from inside my picture case. There was a lot on his mind, I could tell. I was going back into the kitchen when he called.

He asked, "Are these the boys from the group that you council?"

I told him yes. Walked over, stood next to him, and recounted the stories of how each of one of them ended up in the hall.

"This one here is Ace. He was selling rocks, but actually got locked up for killing a man. One man owed him money, but Ace says he didn't kill him. Just happened to be in the wrong place at the wrong time. He's awaiting trial now. His father is nowhere around and his mother is addicted to heroine. He's only thirteen years old. Another one of our young, black men caught up in the system without much help.

"Poncho is up on grand theft larceny. He is some character. He used to steal rims then turn around and sell them right back to the person he stole them from. He got greedy and messed up big. He stole a set of rims that belonged to a cop. This cop loved cars and he went in search around the neighborhood for his rims. Poncho swore to the cop that he bought them, but the cop had receipts for all four serial numbers. It was probably the only time that Poncho ever found himself lost for words.

"Larry and Jamal are another case altogether. They were cursed with bad luck from the time they were born. Their mother died giving birth to them as twins. Father was an abusive alcoholic, and their relatives never really cared about their well-being. They bounced around from house-to-house, sleeping in the basements and bathroom tubs of family and friends. It's almost like they couldn't help what trouble they got into. They stole from people because it was their only way to help their father pay rent at times. It became a lifestyle. And that's what placed them in the detention center. They are up on ten counts of burglary, including a breaking and entering that took the life of an elderly man when the man reached for Jamal's gun. I don't know where they'll go from here, but I can only hope for the best. They're only fourteen."

Panther said, "Funny how they all look happy for some cats that's locked up."

I smiled as the memory of that day filled my mind. "Yeah, they were at the time. Poncho told us a joke about how he planted dogshit in his mother's ex-boyfriend's car. Said his mother kept asking what the hell was that smell and her boyfriend said it was coming from outside. His mother said no it's not, told him to look at his shoes, and sure enough, it was shit all over her boyfriend's K-Swiss', all over the pedal and brake, on his carpet, and the worst part, there was more shit right underneath his seat that he couldn't get to. He was so embarrassed he didn't come around for days. We couldn't stop laughing at that one."

Panther barely smiled at my story. His eyes were still distant.

"What's wrong?" I asked. "You're not acting like yourself, Panther."

He laughed. "Yeah. That's because I have to deal with a bunch of hypocrites and wannabe gangsters. They play the game so much that when they lose, they do whatever it takes to win."

For a moment I was lost. But like always, Panther considered my thoughts before I even uttered one word.

"Rachel, baby," he said, "something has come up, and I need your help."

I folded my arms, nerved about what I was going to hear. With my stomach knotting up in dread, I asked, "What is it?"

Panther placed the picture back inside the photo case and took my hands from my chest, held them like his life depended on it. He said, "I'm a suspect in a murder case."

The whistling heat from the teapot echoed the sound in my mind.

I pulled my hands away from his and folded my arms again.

Panther said, "I was at this man's house yesterday on business, Rachel, but I didn't do it. We had a disagreement but someone else killed him after I left. Now the police are after me. This doesn't look good for me because I don't have any witnesses to my claim. So I need you to be my alibi for when this all took place."

"Rachel," Panther called, under the signal of the boiling water.

I had already turned away, taken aback from what I heard. I hoped that Panther was joking as he always did, but that was the fantasy side of my mind talking. I was faced with reality everyday from boys who spoke, and breathe, and bled innocence, yet in the eyes of the world, they were animals and criminals. They all had good hearts. Panther was the sweetest, strongest man I knew. He was alive with spirit and rich with soul. I felt free and protected with him. But now I was facing him being treated like an animal the way they did my boys. I couldn't picture my man being weak and brought down. I was so used to it being our world, and had just really started to understand what it felt like to be free and alive with a man. But now all I could imagine was that world being torn down, and separated by rows of steel bars.

Panther came up behind me and wrapped his massive arms around my waist. I caressed his forearms, whispered, "Come closer", and he placed his cheek against mine.

He asked, "Were you home around eight last night?"

I nodded.

"Did you go anywhere or talk to anyone?"

I shook my head.

"Perfect," he said. "Then this will be where I spent the night. I didn't eat anything and I didn't talk much. You were working on the computer, and I went to bed early. Are you okay with that if someone were to ask?"

I cleared my throat. "Before we go any further," I said, "I need to know why you need me as an alibi. Are you able to tell me where you were last night?"

I trusted Panther, but instead of just counting on the words from his mouth, I turned to him so I could also read the truth from his eyes.

He said, "To be completely honest, I was with some family. They were doing things that I can't talk about. I'm trying to help them get out of that lifestyle but if anybody, you can understand that it's not that simple. But I'm not out killing people, Rachel. I may not be a saint, but I'm doing my best to make things right for everybody."

Panther's eyes were showing truth. I didn't know what I was getting myself into, yet I didn't want to make a decision that I would regret later.

When Panther and I first started kicking it, he helped me to make a decision that changed my life forever. I was an administrative assistant at R.F.K. Middle School straight out of college. In my first year there, it felt as if the days grew longer, and my patience grew shorter. All I did was file papers about disruptive students and drew up paperwork to suspend students for fighting. Most of these students were in the At Risk Program. I knew what this program was all about but I doubt that any parents did. I started going to P.T.A meetings to find out. About five parents showed up at every meeting, and it was the same five people, and none of them had students in the At Risk Program. The next school year I decided to get more involved. For each student chosen to the At Risk program, I called their parents and told them it was mandatory that they come to the first P.T.A. meeting before their children was selected to the program. Sure, I lied, but I got forty parents to come out. When I asked them if they knew what the At Risk program was, I got no response.

I said, "The At Risk program is designed to help certain struggling students pass on to the next grade, but I doubt that it helps your children at all."

"I don't see why not," one parent yelled out. "Some children need more help than others. Why shouldn't they get it?"

"You're absolutely right, ma'am. Some students may need more attention than others, but they're not learning anything from the At Risk program. Its designed to push your children out of the schools quickly, but they miss out on their education."

"Do you have any children?" The same lady asked.

"No, ma'am, I don't."

"I have two children," she said. "My son has been through the At Risk program, and my daughter will be going through it this year. My son is a junior, eighteen years old. If it wasn't for the At Risk program he probably would've been a twenty-year-old junior. And no parent in here wants their children left behind their class."

"Of course not, ma'am, but your children still deserve the best. Do you even know why your children were chosen for this program?"

"No, but I'm glad they were chosen. The school system is looking out for their best interests."

"No, they're not, ma'am. The school chose your children because they are trouble students. It has nothing to do with their grades. You think your children are the only ones failing? If your children fight, or maybe, so-called disruptive, or have some kind of psychological temperament that displays something that may be abnormal, then the school doesn't want to deal with them. The school would rather put them in a daycare type of class, get them to the next grade, so your children can be servers at McDonald's."

"You don't know anything," the lady yelled as she stood. "I'm coming to the school tomorrow and I'm reporting your ass. Ain't gonna tell me how to raise my children."

The lady stormed out and slowly the rest of the students followed.

When I came in to work the next day, that same lady was leaving, and a few minutes later I was fired. That night I told Panther about what occurred. He agreed with me for standing up against the At Risk program, but also pointed out that I was not following my heart working as a school administrator. He recommended I try working as a counselor with juveniles. Before that day I never thought of working within the juvenile system, but it was exactly what I needed to hear. And within a week, I realized that it was my dream job.

While we walked to the kitchen I held onto Panther, asked him to stay for the night and he agreed. It was one of the reasons why I was so in love with Parish Coles. There was nothing that he refused me, and after he helped me find to my dreams I was determined to do the same for him. I didn't want to lose him to the streets, like I lost my brother. I knew exactly what I needed to do. I went ahead and made the tea. I needed both Panther and some of that tea to help me get through the night. I might have a whole lot to face tomorrow.

∞ 4 ∞

Deidra

I was already running late for school and a knock at the door had me wanting to run my foot up someone's ass. It was probably one of my silly ass, couldn't pick up a curling iron to save their life, clients. Like Shakita, these females never listened. They only did what they wanted, popping up whenever they felt like it.

I was dragging my books when I went to the door and checked the peephole.

Oh shit. It was the police.

I crouched down quick, hoping that they didn't spot me, let my bag go and chilled for a moment. I had to get myself right. This could be it. The big test. But I had no reason to sweat. I had been through this type of shit before. Plus this was for my man. These ho-lice officers didn't know who they were fucking with.

"Who is it?" I yelled.

"Police," one of the officers said. "Ms. Deidra Williams, we have some questions we want to ask about a friend of yours by the name of Parish Coles."

Since they were fucking with me and my man early in the morning, I decided to fuck with them back. "How do I know that you're police?"

He put his badge to the peephole.

"Let's make this easy," the officer said. "Ms. Williams, my name is Detective Shorter. All we want is to ask a few questions. If we have to come back, we will, with a warrant. I promise that this won't take long."

Too short, the rapper wouldn't have been short enough. I didn't want to go through this at all. I didn't want Panther going through this. Still, this was the time to be soldiers. I knew the plan, and I would stick to it and hope that these assholes would find something better to do with their time.

When I opened the door, the three cops were standing still like the dicks they were. They eyed me like I was a Playboy centerfold.

The one named Shorter finally said something. "Is Mr. Coles in there?

I shook my head.

Detective Shorter laughed, looked for some company from his other two officers who were Black and Hispanic, and they grinned on cue like a couple of trained robots. Detective Shorter was the best looking of the three. One of those tall, pretty, redskinned niggas, but still, he looked good. He was kinda young looking too, trimmed goatee with a low-cut and deep waves. His body frame looked thick and muscular beneath his suit. Either his body was just that nice, or his suit was too damn small. The Spanish cop resembled Shorter, while the other black one was a skinny, scary looking fucker.

Detective Shorter chuckled. "Of course he isn't here. But I bet you know where he is."

I threw them a fake smile. "Surely don't."

"Well do you know where he was the night of October 9, the night before last?"

I could feel all six eyeballs of the three stooges on me. They were studying me to see if I would stutter or slip. But I knew the game too well to get caught up.

"That afternoon he was with me."

"Around what time?"

"I said afternoon. Do you want to know what time I took a shit too?"

Detective Shorter laughed under his breath, tugged at his tie. It felt good making his ass sweat. Even the Hispanic one concealed a smile by clearing his throat.

"Ms. Williams," the ugly black cop spoke up, "we need to establish a timeline because that is how we follow the leads we have. It would be in your best interest if you just answer the question."

I blew out a breath to let them know they were getting on my nerves. They looked like a couple of rookie cops that probably couldn't shake a meow out of a cat. I was even bored, so I toyed with them a little by standing in the doorway with my leg twisted into a bowlegged stance just to see if they were some typical men. I caught Detective Shorter peeping between my legs.

This was too easy.

I grew tired of entertaining these perverts. "Four o'clock, all right. He was here between four and six o'clock. We had some Haitian food, watched Rap City, and he bounced around six. And that's all I know. Now can I get on with my life?"

Detective Shorter shrugged. "Sure. I suppose that will be all."

"Good. Thank you for not taking up any more of my time."

Detective Shorter smiled. "You bet."

The three blind rats walked off my porch.

Then Detective Shorter turned back around. "Oh, by the way," he said, "Ms. Williams, what was Mr. Coles wearing when he left?"

I held still, but my head and heart were racing for an answer. I didn't have a clue. I didn't see Panther at all the day before. These dudes were slick. They almost had me.

I said, "I really don't remember, officer."

Detective Shorter flashed a dirty grin. "You don't remember. He looked to his partners again as he laughed at whatever his smartass was thinking.

I was about to have a fit. Stay cool, I told myself. It was just a scare tactic.

"You know what's funny?" he said.

I crossed my arms. "Other than that cheap ass suit?"

Detective Shorter shook his head as he stepped back up onto my porch. "No, not that. I'm talking about how you were able to remember the time Mr. Coles was here, the food you ate, even remembered what you watched on T.V. for two hours. Yet, you can't remember what he wore. Can you at least tell us if he had on jeans, slacks, shorts, a miniskirt?"

I was about to smack the shit out of his silly ass smirk.

Cool, Dee. Stay cool.

Think.

"He had on shorts," I finally blurted.

Detective Shorter smiled, turned to his partners as they smiled with him.

He turned back to me. "Are you sure?"

I told him yes. If I reneged on my first response, they would have surely brought me in for more questioning.

"We have witnesses that say otherwise," Detective Shorter said with his chest puffed out. "Like Mr. Coles fleeing the scene at approximately 6:30 wearing a pair of black, baggy jeans. Are you sure there isn't something you want to tell me?"

I felt stuck, but still, I wasn't stupid. Games like these were played everyday.

"I said he had on shorts. And how do you know what he had on? Where's your proof that he had on black jeans?" I asked.

With another dirty grin, Detective Shorter turned to his partners. The Hispanic cop stepped up on the porch.

"Right here in the morning papers," he said.

I sucked my teeth when I snatched the paper away, but I was scared of what it may have read. And there it was, plain as day, a report of what witnesses confessed to what they saw at the dead man's home. They also claimed they spotted a gray S.U.V. fleeing the scene. Panther's main ride was a gray Cadillac truck.

Detective Shorter angled his head around the paper. He was lucky I didn't poke him in the eye with it.

He said, "Anything else you have to say?"

I hated feeling helpless. I thought I might go crazy. The officers kept staring me down, studying my face, tapping the ground, testing my patience.

I could feel my heartbeat quicken. Perspiration started building up all over my body. I felt like screaming. I was going to lose it.

But out of nowhere, Panther came from behind the house. He terrified the shit out of me when I saw his figure from the corner of my eyes.

"Relax, baby," he said.

I was about to scream at him, but my frustration faded away when Panther took me into his arms and gave me his shoulder for comfort.

*   *   *

I couldn't help but cry. I had never been so scared in my life. And I never thought that I would find myself fighting for a man like this. It was hard enough to find a man, and I had been taken further than I possibly thought just to be able to keep him.

Panther wiped away my tears. "It's okay, Sandy," he said. "These guys work for me. I had to do this because this is what might happen. And the best way to be prepared is through experience."

He was studying my eyes. I knew he was trying to see if I was shaken. If I could be trusted. But hadn't I proved myself? Yes, I was afraid, but that was normal. I was still a woman of my word. Panther should've known that I was trustworthy.

"I am prepared," I told him.

I could've sworn he saw straight through my lie. He continued to hold my waist. I played with his suede shirt collar, rubbing it up and down, then gripped his chiseled arms. I wanted to please him one last time if possible, both of us getting lost in the beauty of love making, and forget all the crap that was going on.

But Panther saw through that too. "I have to go," he said.

His cop friends had already left and gave us some privacy. "But what if I don't see you again?" I said. I jumped onto the kitchen table with my legs slightly apart. Maybe I was delusional in my thinking, but I wished we could just make love the whole day. I didn't want to think about cops, or murders, or my man going to jail. None of those things made me feel good. I wanted to be happy, free, and leave my troubles someplace where I never had to see them.

Panther gave me the most beautiful smile ever. Then he kissed my forehead. He said "You don't have to do that. As long you hold on to what you want, it'll come to you."

*   *   *

And I melted in his arms.

Why was this happening when I was growing so close to Panther? It was as if I found my soul mate. He came in my life at a time that I needed him. Now he was leaving earlier than I planned.

"When will I see you again," I asked.

He said, "When destiny decides to work with us."

I could feel myself floating in the comfort of his words. I asked him for a picture and he agreed. I had him take it alone, standing next to my fish tank. I wanted to remember him in a peaceful setting, despite the ugliness that the world cast over him with a dark cloud.

We embraced for a long time before he left, and I wish it could've been longer. When I studied the picture I took of him, his face was distant, as if he didn't know who he was taking the picture for. I didn't like it. I wanted a picture that made him seem closer to me, like the picture from the boys in my group. Maybe I should've taken the picture with him. I ran to the door, adamant about not allowing Panther to leave just yet, but he had disappeared. The picture was the last memory I had of him, and I was afraid that it might have been the last thing I'd ever get. But then I thought how silly it was of me to think like this. I always told my boys that they could do more than people ever gave them a chance to do. I believed in them. And I believed in Panther the same way.

ഇ 5 ഇ

Deidra

I f it wasn't for my little sister, I swore I would've never gone around my old hood. Dope fiends roamed the streets looking for their next fix, and dope boys constantly hugged the walls, hoping that the quick money could fix their problems. I often worried over my brothers, Luke and Joe, but they maintained the only way they knew how. At fourteen and sixteen, they had already chosen their way of life. And without a father around, those ways weren't going to change overnight. I told mama dozens of times that I would take Luke, Joe, and Tracy in to live with me, but she always argued about her having to be a mother to her kids. Funny how she was worried about being a mother now, and not when I lived under her roof. The truth was she wanted to be a mother that received all the government aid the she could get. Mo' shorties, mo' money.

As usual, coming through the hood, I had to pass old friends, some that became haters since I was pushing a brand new Infiniti, and fake, wannabe D-boys that had less money than me. And I didn't even have a full time job.

A couple long time residents of the hater-hood, Raheem and Toya, came up and swarmed around me like some buzzards. As if I was the mail lady holding their checks.

Broke ass Toya was all in my face. "Damn, girl," she said. "Every time you come around here, you're in a new car. What size feet on that Infiniti, thirty-fours?"

I tried ignoring her silly ass. Faked a laugh to make her feel like she was important. "Girl, you too crazy."

Didn't take long for the bitch to get on my nerves. She was checking me out harder than Raheem, acting as if they never seen a girl with nice shit on. I played it cool, though. When you're in the hood, a lot of people don't like your ass, and when you leave the hood, there's a whole lot more people that can't stand you. But I was here to see Tracy, and not get into any unnecessary beef with a jealous bitch. Oh yeah, Panther had definitely humbled me.

"Damn, baby." That was Raheem

"Damn what?" I threw him some attitude just to see what his scary ass would say.

"You're looking too good to be by yourself. Got on your little Apple Bottom shorts and heels. You need a body guard. Make sure they watch that body real close."

I laughed right in his face. What an el lame-o.

"You're right," I said. "And the first thing I'm going to do is have him make sure that your body is nowhere near mine. Bye-bye."

I strolled off, my tight, Apple Bottom ass switching away from them. The friendlier I acted, the friendlier they would try to be. And I was already certain of who my real friends were.

One thing I never missed about this place was going up the pissy stairwell. It made me appreciate more what I had in my home with Panther. I just hoped that he was okay.

The door to my people's apartment was wide open. Kids that my mama babysat for others had turned the house out. And there was my mother, lying up on the couch with some nigga, and not the same one I saw her kissing about two months ago. And one that I didn't care to know either.

"Hey, Dee," mama said. "How's the new homeowner? You get married to that fine ass man yet?"

I looked away from her. My eyes settled to the T.V. with Monique doing stand-up comedy.

"No," I said, blowing out an irritated breath. "Is Tracy here?"

"She's in her room," mama said. "Did you bring the weave like I asked?"

I told her yes.

She rose from her position on the couch. With all of the children around, she had on no bra. Her little boyfriend's hand was in between her ass the whole time. I handed her the bag and started to walk to the back.

"Hold up," mama said. "You know I'm still your mama. You can speak to me."

"I didn't come here to talk. I came here to see Tracy. You already have your company to entertain."

"You can still be nice to people."

"What for?"

"Because I'm your mother. You're running around here with a man that done murdered somebody. You think I don't know about that. You need to watch yourself before you end up like your brother. Don't forget about the people that raised you. Your man may not be around to help you no more."

With my temper, I had to laugh to keep from going off on her ass. She knew how to get to me, but I wasn't going to let her.

I said, "You should be the last person to tell me what man I'm supposed to be with. You can't even decide that after you wake up in the morning."

And I left her standing there, her man lying on the couch with a stupefied look. Mama wasn't worried about me anyway. There was a man waiting to get his hands back in between that ass.

I knocked on Tracy's door and was invited in. I found her on the bed concentrating on homework. She made me proud. I wished that I could've taken her home with me. Even though I knew Tracy was a good kid, the things that mama did around her were not the type of things that a twelve year-old girl should be seeing.

"Wuz up, girl?" I felt like I was her mother, happy as I was to see her.

"Hey, Dee." Tracy jumped off the bed and hugged me like she hadn't seen me in umpteen years. "What you doing here?"

"I came to check on my main girl. Is that all right?"

She let out a sweet giggle. "Yes."

"Good," I said. "I also came to give you this."

I handed her the plastic bag in my hand.

"Ooh, my favorite movie, *Stomp the Yard*. How did you know I wanted this?"

I rubbed her head. "Probably because I know it's your favorite movie."

She let out another soft giggle.

I asked her "How are your brothers?"

"They're fine," she said.

"You know where they are?"

"No. You know they don't tell me nothing."

"And how about your mama?"

Tracy rolled her eyes. "Being mama. Either she ain't here, or she's here with some kids, or one of her boyfriends."

I was worried like always. "Nobody's been bothering you, right?"

"No. But Luke and Joe always look out for me anyway. They make sure I eat when mama don't have nothing. Joe even took me shopping on the weekend. I got some nice stuff, too. Wanna see."

"Yeah," I told her. "Let me see what kind of styles my baby sister got."

"You know I got styles, right."

"Well, stop talking and let me see what you got."

Tracy guided me towards her closet. We went through her clothes and I was impressed. She had some cute Baby Phat outfits, couple of things from Ecko Red and Rocawear. My brothers were definitely taking care of things. Like always I gave her some money too. Told her not to go on a shopping spree even though I knew she knew better.

After that, I fixed up her ponytails, feeling halfway jealous over all of that long, pretty, Indian-type hair. Tracy's dad was Cuban, a good-looking, dark-skin man that came and left Tracy with nothing but that beautiful hair. We were all a part of that same curse, and I wanted to make sure that Tracy knew that she deserved better.

I asked her, "What do we do when a man asks us for something?"

Tracy threw her hands on her hips. "Don't give him nothing."

"Right," I said. "And when he gives you something, what do we do?"

"Don't give him nothing."

I gave her five. "That's my girl."

We hugged once more before I left. I hated to leave her in this house alone with no real adult supervision. If I tried to leave with her, mama would only start up another argument, which I couldn't win because Tracy was her daughter. I just hoped for the best and prayed for her like I did every night. I was sure that God would take care of her. And she'd be with me when the time was right.

On the way out I walked right by mama and her company and didn't say shit. Slammed the door on any smart remark that she might've wanted to get out. I was ready to get my ass back home anyway.

The side of the building that mama lived on had no lights, and I was speed-walking to my car. Everything around looked crazy. Even the trees were looking like gangbangers. I held on to my Coach bag tight.

Then I slowed up because I swore I heard footsteps behind me. When I turned, there was nobody there, but I knew I heard someone. Or something. Worried, I picked up the pace. The car was near and I snatched the keys out of my bag. I hit the alarm, jogged the last couple of feet, keys jingling as I searched for the one to the ignition. When I got to the door, I flung it open, tossed my bag to the passenger side and—

Wham.

I was knocked on my ass. Couldn't scream because someone held me in a choke hold, my lungs begging for a pinch of air. He had a good grip on one of my arms as his legs wrestled with mine. I was petrified, shaking uncontrollably. All I could think was 'Lord, please don't let this man rape me. I was kicking with everything I had, but it wasn't helping. When I tried reaching around, his hold on my throat grew tighter. I didn't know what was going to happen. I began crying, praying to God in my head, wanted whatever was happening to be over with. But that's when he tried unbuttoning my pants. I pushed my body against the ground, but he kept pulling me up to get his hand back in position. He popped me in the back of the head, told me to shut up, and zipped down his pants. When I pushed down he pulled me up. I fought back and he choked harder. His hot breath went across my face and I cried. I was losing it. I was scared. I—"

I could breathe again.

The man was knocked off of me.

Somebody, another man, was tossing furious blows and kicking the shit out of the rapist. The asshole then had my hero off balance and threw him down to the ground, but then my hero caught him with a kick to the chest. When my hero was back on his feet, the guy fled. The man began to give chase, but then stopped. It was dark as hell and the asshole must've been a crackhead because he caught wind like he weighed about thirty pounds. As I struggled back on to my feet, my hero ran over and gave me his hand. My head was spinning, heart beating a thousand miles a minute.

"You all right?" the man asked.

"Yes," I told him. "Thank you."

As I brushed myself clean and tried to get my head together, the man opened my car door.

"Have a seat," he said. "Anything you want me to do?"

"No, thank you. You've done a whole lot already. I don't know what to say. I don't even know how to thank you."

"You don't need to thank me," he said. "I'm supposed to be here for you."

The voice sounded familiar. I sat down in the car, and when he brought his face closer, I saw that it was Panther's friend, Detective Shorter. I was pleasantly surprised.

"What are you doing here?" I asked. "How did you know I used to live here?"

"Just doing what I was asked to do," Detective Shorter said. "Panther wanted me to check on you from time to time."

I said, "I'm thankful that you were here at the right time."

"I am too," Detective Shorter said.

I tried wiping my face dry but the tears kept falling. I couldn't believe that I was almost raped. I asked Detective Shorter "Do you know where Panther is?"

"Running, of course. Have you talked to him since yesterday?"

I shook my head. I was grateful that Detective Shorter was here right now, but I still felt alone without Panther. What almost occurred was not Panther's fault, but then I thought, what if I never saw Panther again. What if something crazy had already happened? What if they knew of his whereabouts and were close to catching him. I couldn't deal with the thoughts of any of this, grabbed some tissue out of my purse and wiped my eyes and nose dry.

"Hey, don't sweat it," Detective Shorter said. "You know Panther's gonna holla back soon. It's obvious that he cares for you a lot. Got me out here rumbling with crackheads."

I smiled. "Yeah, detective. You're right."

He was laughing as he picked up my keys and handed them to me. "And I'm not a real detective," he said. "My name is Dalvin. I'm just one of Panther's homeboys. Not five-o."

I was feeling real stupid right about now.

Dalvin said, "Do you feel like you need to go to the hospital?"

"I'm okay," I told him.

"All right. Then I'll just make sure you get home safe. I'll be right behind you."

I told Dalvin thank you as he helped me get situated in my car and followed me out. On the way home, I kept looking through the rearview to make sure he was still there. I was spooked as hell. And what made matters worse was I still had to sleep alone in a big ass empty house. But I planned to pray 'til my heart grew tired. I had a lot to thank God for. And more help to ask of him. And after what almost happened to me, I needed to get my sister away from my old hood immediately.

Dalvin was right at the driveway as I entered my home. I waved him goodbye. Of course he had other things to do, but I didn't want him to leave. He had been a guardian angel, and may have been the only one I had until Panther came back. I put all the chains on the door, tore out of my dingy clothes, got on my knees, and I prayed. I cried and prayed, shaking as I confessed all of my worries to the man above. I let all of my pain out to God, and in the end thanked him for helping me, and for always listening.

❧ 6 ☙

Sandra

PrimeTime was interested in everything at our meeting place, except me. But maybe it wasn't me at all. Some niggas today were just ungrateful. Here I was, telling him that I was going to put in all this hard work, yet his eyes were on every hoochie that passed by. Our meeting was over anyway. And I wasn't trying to sweat him. Hell, why should I? I was the one who had their own management company. He needed me. Talented rappers were like dogs; they were either stray or owned, but once you had them, you could command them to do whatever you wanted.

"Did you like the food, PrimeTime?" I asked.

"Oh, the grub was butter, ma. Straight Butter. Man, this whole joint is phat. I appreciate the love, ma."

"Don't mention it," I said. And I really didn't want him to. I mean, could PrimeTime use some regular, English words, like yes and thank you? We were on a business meeting, and he was talking to me like I was a groupie. Did I have to give the nigga a lap dance to get some respect? I was determined to establish myself as a real business woman in this rap game. Maybe if I wore something that hugged my curves, instead of a loose-fitted business suit, he would've jumped all over my deal.

"So give me a call, PrimeTime," I said. I was ready to leave.

For the first time tonight, he wiped his mouth with a napkin then mumbled, "No doubt."

We stood and hugged. I held him tight so he could feel my breasts pressed up against his chest. The hoochies weren't the only fine women in the spot. Primetime's hands settled on my waist, and if I was taller than 5'2, they would've been all over my luscious ass, which I caught him staring at when I bent over to pick up my purse. Oh, I was definitely getting him interested in my deal now.

"I'll have the contract ready for you next week," I told him. I was making the decision for him. "You can read it over for another week before you have to sign it. In the meantime, I want to work on your image more. You're a handsome young man, and that's going to work for you. Girls are gonna go crazy over you. So we want more songs geared to what the girls like. That way we can get radio play and get you into this industry like the big Pimp that you are, right?"

"For sho', ma. For sho'."

"Because PrimeTime is a pimp, right?"

"No doubt, baby."

"So you call me whenever you need me, but we are having a meeting next week so you can get this contract, all right."

"It's all butter if you got the bread, ma."

So we gave our hollas, our peace signs, and our keep your head ups before we hopped in our fly rides to do some big pimpin'.

But after all of that, I was pimped out. I loved my career, but at times, it was too demanding. And now I was on my way to another serious part of my life. Aunt Mabel was in the hospital, and had been expecting me an hour ago. I was sure that she would've boiling over like lava because I hadn't seen her in three days. It wasn't what I intended, but I wanted to be home if Panther were to pop up.

On the way to the hospital, I figured I'd better try being more at ease, for Aunt Mabel's sake. Her doctor said the calmer she was the better. Yet calm wasn't a word in Aunt Mabel's vocabulary.

When I got to her room, Aunt Mabel was giving the nurse a verbal ass whipping. I was sure that the nurse was trying to be patient, bless her heart, but I bet it was hard as hell trying to stay professional while wiping someone's ass, and get cussed out by them at the same time. Relief ran over the nurse's face when I came in. It meant that she could escape while all the cussing got thrown my way.

"Sandra, baby," Aunt Mabel said. "I need you to come here." She was talking with a voice flooded with pain, but knowing Aunt Mabel was, it probably just a dry ass lie. "Come help an old lady out, baby. These hospital people don't do nothing for you. They stick you in a cold room, do all kinds of tests, fill you up with every which o' medicine they could find, then expect you do to everything on your own, as if people ain't sick. I'm here because I am sick. Not because I want to watch T.V. and have a bunch o' strangers look at my ass all day. Lord knows, they about to make me sicker. Wooh, child. Grab that water, baby, and make your auntie some tea. Lord, child, I'm so glad to see you. Where you been all this time anyway?"

It had started already and I hadn't said a word. If I didn't answer her, she would've just kept going until I did. And it didn't matter what my excuse was. There was no reason not to see my dying auntie.

Aunt Mabel said, "It ain't no reason not to see your dying auntie. What done happened to you?"

"I have my own management company now, auntie. A lot's been going on."

"Too much to come and see if I was alive?"

There was no stopping her.

I said, "I knew you were alive, Aunt Mabel. I speak to you everyday."

"Child, just because you speak to me on the phone don't mean you know if I'm all right. You could've been speaking to an imposter. 'Guisin' they voice to sound like me. People do things like that all the time, girl. You see Martin Luther King got killed. You don't think people was playing on his phone. And what's this mess about your new company? You still ain't got no man to take care o' you, girl."

I contemplated finding a nurse and asking her if she had anything to help Aunt Mabel sleep. All that talking, I knew she had to be tired. I just got there and was already tired of listening.

"Aunt Mabel, I'm a grown, independent woman. I don't need a man to take care of me. I have the ability to do things for myself."

"You can do whatever you want to do, child. But don't say you don't need a man. Because when you're on disability, you're gonna need a man. You ain't supposed to be doing all the work. You're supposed to make a man help you. You seen what your Uncle used to do to me, right?"

"I know, Aunt Mabel."

"God rest his soul, but you know that lazy man had me doing everything, running crazy. He's the reason I'm sick today. That's why if you let 'em, a man will run you into the ground. So you don't let 'em. You make that man provide for you. You can't work and take care of the house. Your uncle always used to complain about how sick he was. Yet, he was healthy enough to cuss me out when he didn't have his food waiting. He was healthy enough to go out drinking. You don't ever make a man think he ain't able to do for you. Because if he think he ain't supposed to be a man, then he won't act like one. Don't think twice about turning your man into a real man. Throughout time, many of us had to do it."

I nodded humbly while Aunt Mabel sipped her tea. I knew she was referring to Panther indirectly. She never liked him. He was too mysterious for her. She claimed if you could never figure a man out, or what he did for a living, he wasn't the right type of man. That thinking was drilled into me. But since I met Panther, I never had a reason to think that he wasn't the right one. All I had to do was listen to him talk and I knew that he was my type. The reason I began my own company was because of him. He told me that my ambition and assertiveness were undeniable, and they would propel me to greater things. I mean, I always knew that I had the gift to gab, but he took it to another level when he showed me that being in control was kinda like being a mother. I could only be a guide if I got you to listen, and I only got you to listen if I showed that I cared for your needs. But I wasn't sure if Aunt Mabel understood all of that.

"I'll be fine, auntie," I told her just to kill all of the complaining.

"Well, I hope so."

She began nodding off, thank God. That was my chance to run before she got started again.

I plopped up Aunt Mabel's pillows and straightened out her sheets. It looked like the nurse really didn't do much while she was there. I fixed Aunt Mabel's gown, put everything in its place, and emptied out the trash. By the time I was done tidying up the place, Aunt Mabel was out like a light.

I tuned into the news, and after they confirmed that Panther was still on the run and still a suspect, I turned it off. I didn't care to see anymore. I kept the telephone close to Aunt Mabel just in case she needed me. And if it so happened, just in case I needed her.

As I was walking out, Aunt Mabel called to me.

She said, "Baby, a man can't do nothing for a woman if he's in jail."

Her eyes were closed when she said it, and right after, her mouth fell open with a loud snore. Deep in sleep, but I was sure that Aunt Mabel knew exactly what she was saying. And it was one of the few things she said recently that I could agree with.

ಬ 7 ೞ

Rachel

I was excited about this project because it was going to answer a lot of the questions about the boys in my group. I had all four of them, Ace, Poncho, Larry, and Jamal, act out the words and actions of an important person in their life, and tell what made that person important to them.

Poncho acted out his brother Bruno, who Poncho said would make people think he was cool with them by telling a joke, and then would beat the shit out of them afterwards. I asked Poncho what made Bruno important to him and he said because everybody respected him for his fighting tactics. People never knew what he was going to do.

Larry and Jamal were into sports, and so were the important people in their lives. They threw a couple imaginary passes to each other and acted as if they were a mini Jordan and Magic, shooting hoops inside the trash can.

Right before I called on Ace, a new group member came in. He was a tall and quiet young man. I asked him to introduce himself but he ignored me. I remained patient and asked him again.

"Do I have to be here?" the boy asked as he grabbed the seat next to Poncho.

"Yes," I said. "Now can you introduce yourself to the group for us?"

He rolled his eyes while his hands sat cupped over his midsection. "My name's Sam."

It was normal for a new group member to act this way. Even though I didn't like it, I understood and tried to show our new member that he was welcomed.

"Sam," I said, "would you like to share anything about yourself with the group?"

He shook his head. Kept his stare glued to the ground.

"No problem," I said. "You don't have to."

I asked Ace to stand up and act out an important person in his life. To my surprise, he rose and strolled to the center of our circle without hesitation. This was the first time he participated in one of my activities. We were finally making some progress.

What Ace acted out in front of us almost brought me to tears. He sat on the floor Indian-style and acted as if he was his little sister playing with her baby doll. As he pretended to stroke the doll's hair, he said, "We're going to eat soon, Ashley. Mommy's going to come home with a pile of food, like chicken, and biscuits and candy, and we're going to be fine. Mommy's just a little sick from the shots that she takes in the bathroom, but when she gets better, she's going to bring lots of food. Mommy won't let us be hungry for long. I know your stomach hurts. Mine does too. We'll just get some sleep and that way, the pain will go away. Then tomorrow, everything will be all right."

Tension clouded the room as all of the boys' faces looked as disturbed as I felt. I had to suck up that feeling and be professional. If I broke down, then word might get out that I wasn't fit for the job. I loved what I did. And I would do whatever it took to keep it and do it right. Whatever was best for my boys.

Ace returned to his seat with the same calm movements that he had when took the floor.

He made an impression on me. I asked, "Why did you choose your sister to be the important person in your life?"

He said, "Because she showed me how important I was to her."

Now I knew why I loved my job so much. It gave me a chance to be with boys like Ace, and to show them that they were important to everybody, including their selves.

After thanking Ace for his participation, I asked Sam to join us in the activity. Sam shot me a look like I was crazy. I almost threw one back, but he surprised me as he rose from his seat and faced everyone.

He balled his face up in a sickening grimace, doubled over holding his stomach, and cried out in pain, saying, "I need to get high. I need some rocks. I need my pipe. I don't want to take care of my daughter and her baby doll. I'm not bringing home any chicken and candy. I'm a crackhead. I don't know—"

Ace rushed to his feet and jumped on Sam. They tossed each other back and forth, wrestled each other down, and threw vicious blows at one another. The smaller Ace took the majority of the beating, yet continued going in for more. He was lashing out like a wild man, crying as he threw blind punches.

I begged them both to stop, but my pleading was shut out by their fury. The guards finally burst through the doors and wrestled them down. Took them back to their holding cells where once again, as time has proven, nothing gets solved that way. It only built up their anger. I felt as if I had failed the whole group. One of my first, big projects, and I fudged it up.

What would my superiors think?

Would they see that the fight wasn't because of my project, and that I was trying to help, but it just got out of hand?

And since I had only been on the job for three months, would they give me a chance to show that I can do the job, even when things got crazy?

A few minutes later, I went in to see Andrea, my supervisor. I was afraid to sit down. Andrea's face was tight with anger. She had Ace's and Sam's files spread over her desk, marking things down in each file like she was taking notes about what happened before I uttered one word about it.

"You can sit," Andrea said. "I heard you had an incident in your session today. Is this something I should fear will happen frequently in your groups?"

Andrea continued taking notes into Sam's and Ace's files. She hadn't looked up at me since I entered the office. I doubted if she cared at all about anything that I had to say.

I took my seat, leaned in close, hoping to sneak a peak at Andrea's notes. She finally glanced up at me over her thick-rimmed glasses.

"No, Andrea," I said. "This is not something that will occur frequently. Sam is new to the facility and may just have wanted to get respect. I can assure that I have it under control, Andrea."

Andrea removed her glasses. Her dark fingers tapped the desk. "And how can you assure me of this?"

"Give me some time to talk them, each of them alone. I can understand what Sam is going through, being the new kid and all, and Ace is starting to open up. Right now they need that comfort to know that they will be safe here, and that they can trust me. Please, Andrea. Let me try."

Andrea kept tapping the desk. She then put her glasses back on and clasped her hands together. "I know it's not your fault what happened, Rachel. These things happen all the time. I'm just glad that you are smart enough to know why it happened, and you also show great intelligence by wanting to communicate after the incident occurred. Just be careful. There is such a thing as too much trust, and that can hurt you too."

I told Andrea I understood. I left her office and after lunch I arranged a meeting for Sam and Ace at separate times.

Ace was quiet when he came to my office. He had fallen back into his shell. I understood that he was embarrassed, but that shyness sometimes disturbed me because I didn't know what he was thinking. I got nowhere with the questions I asked either. So I finally asked if there was something that I could do to help him. He shook his head. Said he wanted some time to himself and I agreed. He left without saying anything.

A month of working on change, it seemed, had been washed away. But I wasn't giving up. Not as long as I had the chance to try. Both Sam and Ace would see how they could've earned their respect without having to kill each other for it.

A few minutes later, Sam strolled into my office with a laid back, relaxed air about himself. Floated like he was on top of the world, and everybody else had to look up to him. He was a nice-looking young brother with cut, muscular arms, and a tattooed tear next to his left eye. Seventeen years-old, he had been in and out of trouble since the age of twelve. I also saw in his file that he was prone to using violence. His last time in the hall, he busted a guard's nose. Maybe I should've been worried, but I wasn't. I didn't want any guards in the office interfering with my boys' feelings of comfort. And I never had to scare my boys into talking.

"It's been a whole two days. How do you like your stay so far?" I asked Sam.

He shrugged with an all-mighty look printed over his mug.

I wanted to slap it off of him. He had really set me back with my work. But I had to think professionally. Situations like these were just an ugly part of the job.

"Why did you make fun of Ace's family?"

Sam shrugged again. "Just felt like it."

"Why? What were you trying to accomplish?"

"Nothing. It was just funny."

I was blown away. This wasn't about respect at all.

I said. "So you did it to get a laugh?"

"Yep," he said. And those arrogant eyes curled up at me.

I began to feel sorry for this boy. He was more lost than I imagined.

I decided to use his game against him. "So how would you like it if I laughed at your situation? Wouldn't you feel hurt?"

"Don't try that with me, Ms. Baxter," he said. "For one, I'm human. I could laugh at whatever I want. And two, look where I'm at? How can you judge me as if I'm the only one with a problem in this joint? So don't talk like I'm nine years old. If you really care about me then try being cool with me first."

Sam was a veteran at this all right. And he got me good. I felt silly, having a seventeen year-old tell me what I was supposed to be doing in my own field. But he was right. I had slipped and forgotten my first rule: Don't take anything personal because their anger was not geared toward me.

"That's true, Sam. But why would I want to be your friend when you're picking on people and starting fights? Who would want to be your friend?"

"Because you get paid to at least act like it. And I notice something in you that I hardly see in other counselors. It's not about the money. I can see that it's not an act at all. And I respect that. You're a young girl that believes in hope for me. I've never seen anybody in this place that looks the way you do. You have a look that can motivate others. You're special."

Was this boy trying to run game on me? I couldn't believe him. Underneath the bad boy image, he was extremely intelligent, and somewhat charming. He had some very likable traits, but that wasn't getting him off the hook.

I said, "So why don't you let me help you? Since you know so much, and feel motivated, let's see what we can do together."

"How do you know that I even want help?"

The arrogance was gone from him now. He started reminding me of Ace. I told him, "Because I can see it in your eyes."

He sucked his teeth, and began rubbing his eye. "That's probably just some crust."

I laughed so loud I had to cover my mouth to quiet the noise. Sam looked like he could be a lot of fun.

I said, "Smart and funny. Why don't you tell me a little bit more about yourself, Sam?"

"Naw, naw, naw," he said with a growing blush. "You're the one trying to be my friend. Why don't you tell me something about you?"

"Like what?"

"Like, do you have a boyfriend?"

This kid was crazy.

"Excuse me," I said. "I don't think that is appropriate in this place. And also, that's not really your business."

"What's the problem? Ain't like I can take you away from him in here."

There it was. I knew it wouldn't take long for that cockiness to spill through.

"A mack daddy," I said.

"Nothing like that, Ms. Baxter. I just like seeing that pretty-ass smile. If we would've met under different circumstances, I would've had you smiling like the joker."

Okay. That was enough of the playing around. Sam's tongue was getting a little too loose for my juice. I said, "I'm glad that you're a confident young man, Sam. But I don't think that my boyfriend would appreciate you talking to me like that. And like I said earlier, I don't think that type of conversation is appropriate in here."

He laughed. Shook his head. "I can respect that."

"Good."

"I can respect you respecting your man," he said. "And I don't think talking about relationships can be bad, especially if it's probably a relationship that hurt you. It's still a way to communicate. So who's the lucky man stopping you from being with me?"

I laughed. Sam couldn't help that he was such a huge flirt.

I said, "Fine. I will tell you about my relationship only if you promise to tell me about yourself."

"That's cool. You're in charge. Motivator."

I shook my head. Sam was too crazy.

"His name is Parish Coles," I said. "A very nice man that I am in love with, so don't try to holler at me anymore."

"All right. I feel— wait a minute. Parish Coles. I heard that name before. I'm trying to think of—"

"I don't know," I said, trying to throw Sam off. I didn't realize that Panther's name may have been out there and already all over the nation. "You might be thinking about Parish from EPMD."

"That's where I know it from," Sam said, smoothing down his low cut hair. "That's the man that's been all over the news for killing that white man, right? Is that your man? Your hubby is a murderer?"

"He is not a murderer. I mean—I don't know. Listen, he's only a suspect and—"

I paused. What was I thinking? I was careless with my actions. I didn't know what type of person Sam was. If it got out that I talked about my personal life at work, and how my personal life included Parish Coles, I might lose my job, and even find the police questioning me about Panther's whereabouts. I had to fix this fast.

"None of that matters," I told Sam, my voice hard and cold as the pen gripped in between my fingers. "The only thing that matters is everything that we've discussed in this office is confidential. Everything. Is that understood, Sam?"

With his hands up in surrender, Sam prompted me to relax. He gave me a look like I was freaking out. "Ms. Baxter, it's cool," he said. "Don't forget where I'm from. And plus, it's like even if I did talk, I don't have any friends in here to say anything to. Me and you are just talking as far as I'm concerned."

I said, "On a confidential level."

He raised his right hand and placed his left over his heart. "On a confidential level," he said. "Now do I have to break out a bible and start speaking in tongues for you to believe me? Mama-say-mama-sa-ma-ma-kuu-sa."

I burst out laughing and felt at ease again. Sam reassured me that everything was cool with the joke and crossing his heart. I still wasn't sure if I could trust him. I guessed that only time would tell. But maybe now I could get what I wanted out of him. He had promised to open up the lines of communication, which also meant that he would open his heart to me. As I waived goodbye to him, I thought that maybe I could've been someone to make a difference in this boy's life. I wasn't sure how it was going to happen, or what I had to do, but I was up to the challenge. And I always kept my word. I just hoped that Sam did too.

ଞ 8 ଓ

Deidra

O w, girl," Tina screamed. "What the hell, Dee? You trying to kill me?"

"Ooh, I'm sorry, Tina," I said. "Are you all right?"

"Hell no. My head hurt like a motherfucker. Is it bleeding?"

I checked her head because I really wasn't sure. "Girl, you all right," I asked. I thought I had given my client a concussion.

"Long as I'm not bleeding, I'm fine," she said. "But I think you need to hurry up because you got a lot on your mind."

And I did. I was taking out my frustrations on poor Tina's head while washing her hair. That crackhead that tried to rape me last night really had me bugged out. I couldn't think straight. Had Tina's head all twisted up in the sink, banged it against the faucet. Tina was one of my best customers. I couldn't afford to scare her away, especially when I didn't know when I would see Panther. It had been three days, but man, was I missing that nigga.

I finally had Tina's hair all rinsed out.

"There we go, girl," I said. "We're done."

"Praise the lord," she wailed. "I thought I was going to be the first person on earth to drown from getting her hair washed."

I gave her the crooked eye. "Keep talking shit."

Just as we were walking from the back, a knock was at the door.

"Go ahead and get under the dryer," I told Tina.

I went to the door and checked the peephole. I was shocked, but happy to see the face behind the door.

My guardian angel from last night.

When I opened the door, Tina damn near damn near busted her ass running up to see Dalvin. That was bitches for you. Always checking for some dick.

Dalvin walked in and asked, "How you ladies doing?"

"Fine, thank you," I said.

Tina said, "Hi." And sat down all calm and sophisticated, yet, just a second ago, she did a Gail Deavers to the door. Phony ass.

I offered Dalvin a seat, and when he moved, I could see Tina clocking him the whole time. You couldn't blame her, though. He was kinda fine. Had on an all white, Miami Heat short set, crisp, white sneakers, and thick gold links dangling from his neck and wrist. But that's how it was with men. The fine ones always hung together.

He introduced himself to Tina, and she was basically throwing the pussy at him. Telling him about her personal life and how her last boyfriend did her wrong, and all kinds of things that you wished she shut the fuck up about already.

Tina was thirty-five, but barely looked it. She had a petite figure, short with a caramel complexion, and kept herself together. Had a good paying, bus driving job with the county, but I guess when you didn't have a man, or kids, you're likely to get lonelier than most women.

I watched Dalvin's reactions. How he was respectful and let her talk, but I knew he was as tired of her ass as I was.

"Tina, go ahead and get under the dryer, baby," I told her. "Knowing you, we'll be sitting here all day listening to your life story."

She waved me down and got under the dryer.

Dalvin said, "It's all right. If you and your friend want to talk, I'll just come back. Y'all should be done talking by tomorrow."

I liked that he made me laugh too. "Stop it," I told him. "What you gotta talk to me about?"

He turned his head to Tina and I looked too. The dryer was on, but her head was nowhere near it.

"Let's go in one of the back rooms," I said.

We went to an empty room that I had reserved for Tracy. I offered him the desk chair, but I was offered it back while he stood.

He said, "You haven't heard from Panther?"

I told him no.

"Shit's been crazy around the way," Dalvin said. "5-0 keeps coming through the hood, trying to shake niggas down and find out how they could get to Panther. You still don't know when that nigga's gonna be around."

"I wish I did because I need to see him. That is my man. It ain't like this shit happens to me everyday."

"I know, Dee," he said. "Everything's gonna be all right. You know Panther ain't no joke."

"Yeah, I know that, but on the real, I'm almost scared to go to sleep at night. I been praying so much that I think God is tired of hearing from me. I'm not used to having this feeling so I'm just trying to deal with it the best way I can."

"Well, I would say just keep doing what you're doing. Everything will work out fine. I also got my boys around looking for that nigga from last night, too. He was probably a junkie and you know they can't keep their mouth shut. So as soon as I got some info, I'll let you know."

"That's good looking out, Dalvin. Last thing I need is my little sister living around someone like that. His ass needs to be in prison."

"I almost forgot something," Dalvin said as he reached into his pocket and came out with a wad of money.

"What's that?" I asked.

"It's five grand."

"For what?"

He put his hand down and laughed. He knew exactly what I was saying. When a man offers a woman some money, he either wants you to give him something, or owe him something. And I wasn't trying to do either one.

"It ain't even like that," Dalvin said. "This is some of the money that Panther gave me to watch you. I was kind of insulted when he gave it to me, but you know how he is. And now I'm giving it to you because I think it's best that you have it."

It was so crazy to me how people thought just because a man had a criminal record that he had a problem. There were a lot of good men, like my older brother, who wanted to do more for themselves and their families, yet their lives were turned in another direction. I saw Panther and his friend as being some of those good men. And sometimes I hated being a part of a society that continued to discredit that fact.

"I thank you so much, Dalvin. I know you mean well, but I can't take that. My man gave it to you because he felt he was supposed to, and I can't go against that."

Dalvin put his hands up in surrender. "I won't argue with that," he said, and slid the money back in his pocket. "But," he continued, "I'm still gonna make sure that you're okay."

I nodded. "That's a good idea."

We went back out to the front. Dalvin waved bye to Tina. She banged her head on the dryer trying to get out of it.

Dalvin said, "As soon as you hear from your boy, tell him to holla at me. We could use a word from him."

I said that I would.

Tina held on to Dalvin's arm as they walked out the door.

"That's a good woman," I yelled out to Dalvin. "I don't know many women that'll hold up a hair appointment for a man."

I caught Tina's middle finger at the door. I didn't care, though. I was happy for her. At least she had somebody to holler at. My man was missing and I didn't know if or when I would see him again. Even though I had my business and school to keep me busy, it still wouldn't have been enough to keep my mind off Panther. I felt like the lonely bitch that I took Tina to be. Seemed like God had a lot more listening to do tonight.

‪‬ಬ 9 ‪ಉ

Sandra

I was just about to enjoy a dinner of baked salmon and vegetables, and watch Jeopardy, but the phone killed it.

I had a long day and didn't want to talk to another soul if it wasn't my man. Or somebody with some money for me.

It was Dennis, my boss.

"Hope I'm not catching you at a bad time," he said, "but it's important."

What could be so important when I wasn't in your office, I thought. Did he misplace some files or something and need help finding them? How did that man ever become a lawyer anyway? He was lost if he didn't have assistants around.

I said, "What do you need, Dennis?" letting him know that his timing was as bad as a man who hadn't noticed the condom was broke until after he came.

He said, "I'm done with your contract. Just thought you wanted to know."

Aside from being my boss, Dennis was also my lawyer. He was convenient. And cheap.

"Already," I said. "I didn't expect it for another week."

"Yeah, but it was nothing to it. I just made the time for you because I figured you were ready to start making some money."

"Oh, I'm always ready for that."

"I like that attitude," he said.

And I liked his. His was always business. Always about how to make more money.

He said, "Any new acts?"

"Not yet," I told him. "But I'm going to a talent contest tomorrow night at Dreamers."

"And how is it going with PrimeTime?"

"It's going good. I told him that we need to work on his image."

"And you're right. I noticed that the thuggish type is not in nowadays. MTV plays the party jams. The kinda of jams that I like. At least some of them."

Dennis could be a rich, arrogant asshole too.

"Hip-hop is not just about parties and thugs," I told him.

"Sandy, you don't have to tell me that. I know something about hip-hop. I know that there is Talib Kweli and Common out there. But I just don't think PrimeTime should be the rapper that wants to save the world."

"He's an artist, Dennis. He can be whatever he wants."

"So let him make some money first, which in turn is going to make you some money. After you've made your money, then he can be an artist. Any and every business should be about making money, and if you're not then you should get out of business. Let real men do the job."

And that's what Dennis supposedly was. A real man. Only thing real about him was his money. He talked about it constantly. I didn't bash him because every man should want to make money. And lots of it. But if the term, 'stick up your ass' wasn't taken, Dennis would've tried to make money off that too.

I told him, "Real women can do the job, too, Dennis."

"And right you are, my lady. I get the impression that you can honestly do whatever you want in any arena. And if there's anything you need, I'll be more than happy to provide it for you."

I was a little thrown off because I didn't know if Dennis was trying to hit on me, or if he was willing to do whatever I asked.

Either way, he was a sucker, because I would've had him running around like an errand boy. So I didn't mind the offer. In a crazy business like the music industry, I may need all the help from all the suckers that I could get.

"It's good to hear that," I said.

"My pleasure."

"I'm already comfortable for the night, so I'll get the contract tomorrow."

"Sounds good."

We said our good nights and I went back to my favorite spot on the couch. I flipped through the channels because I wanted to get into something more fun than Jeopardy. I wasn't in the mood to be intellectual. I wanted Panther here with me like never before. Things were so different since he left. I couldn't just call his cell phone and expect to hear from him. This murder case has made it hard for him to do anything, even just to come by and make love. It had been a whole week without me getting any. So I was backed the hell up.

I clicked to videos on B.E.T. just to get a different type of mood in my head. I got tired of seeing the same video for the nineteenth time. I put my head back and pictured Panther undressing me. Then I pictured him sucking on my breasts, holding me by the waist while I straddled him. I loved to ride him too. What could I say? I liked to be in control.

The T.V. was disturbing my fantasy with Panther, so I placed it on mute, dropped the remote down, and ran my hand over my knee, down between my thighs, and over my pubic hairs. It was kinda fun playing with them, pulling each silky strand with my fingertips while my other fingers brushed the other parts. I shaved it just right; not too short, but enough for each hair to curl.

When I put my leg over the couch, I imagined seeing Panther's nakedness kneeling in between me, the muscles in his arms and stomach dark and glistening. His manhood was strong, circumcised and black. He slid it down both my thighs, the veins in his hardness pulsating against my skin.

Then I put a finger to my clit and worked it slow and easy, wishing that I could replace the feeling with Panther, but the most I got was fake thugs on video sets that could probably never mount up to my man. I turned from the T.V., frustrated and worked the finger a bit faster as my pussy grew wetter.

Panther worked me well. Had my knees pressed up to my breasts. While I had one hand gripping on to his thick arm and bicep, the other rubbed over his smooth, clean-shaven head.

He slid in deeper.

I put a finger inside.

He worked me faster.

I took my index finger out, replaced it with my ring finger, and dug inside as deep as I could.

Panther picked up my legs, threw them over my head, and pounded me. Strong. Long. Deep. Hard. His pecks were damp with sweat that trickled down to his pulsating six pack. I was gone in the moment. Lost in beautiful pain. Then he stopped abruptly, pulled out, flipped me over and raised my ass high in the air.

I turned over too, anxious to keep up with what I envisioned Panther doing. I missed him so. But I dealt with what I had. Slid my arm underneath me and placed two fingers back into my throbbing pussy.

Panther's hands were huge. He had both ass cheeks in the palms of his hands as he stroked me. I couldn't move, but then again, I didn't want to. I was in heaven. Panther's strokes grew longer as he grew himself. He hit that certain spot, and a tingle shot through me, all the way down to my toes. If I could, I would've ripped his dick off and kept it there.

So I found that spot with my two long fingers. And I kept pressing at it. I was so gone I could barely breathe right. Each stroke made my whole body shudder. It felt good. Real good. Too fucking good.

And so did Panther. I turned back just to see how he looked while making me feel this way. And my face must've gotten him excited because his strokes turned to pounding. And I invited it. I heard myself calling his name and telling him I loved it. Give me more. So he went stronger, longer, harder, and deeper. I gripped the edge of the couch while my ass rammed into Panther's midsection. Then he grabbed me by the shoulders. My body was trapped between his dick and hands. And his pounding didn't let up. Moving faster as each stroke grew longer.

My fingers also went faster, my pussy, soaked and soar. Ahh, I heard myself say. I couldn't stop. My fingers felt so damn good.

In my mind, Panther was feeling so damn good. With one hand on my shoulder, he pulled me in, and the other hand held a good grip of my hair. I placed both arms on the sofa for leverage. Panther kept pulling while he pounded. I heard myself moan, trapped in agony and ecstasy. Yes, fuck me, I told Panther. And he listened. I told him again, and he fucked me harder. I tried telling him again, but he had gone deeper than I ever imagined he could. My mouth was stuck wide open.

"Ahh," I screamed. My fingers were magic as they got deeper. They were setting me on fire. I couldn't escape.

Panther hit that spot again. And again. I was tingling all over. I told him that was the spot I wanted him to hit. Don't stop, I said. And he kept going. Harder. I told him yes. He kept going harder. I told him yes. I told him yes. I told him—

"Ahhhhh. Ooh. Ooh, shit."

I shook as adrenaline and ecstasy ran through me like a shot of liquor. I couldn't catch my breath. My body collapsed over the couch. Air left my body fast. I was drained, soaked everywhere, exhausted but relieved. Oh my God, it had definitely been a while. Too long. My body finally started to cool down as the air conditioner blew over my exposed, drenched ass. Then my breathing relaxed. Slowly I sat up. I wiped the sweat from underneath my eyes and brushed my hair back. Man, what a trip.

The dinner I made was cold. I was upset that I even took the time out to make it, but some things were worth letting go. I got up and put the food in the microwave. Hopefully I'll get up to eat it later, I thought. Instead I went to bed and served myself up a much needed rest.

ಬ 10 ಚಿ

Rachel

I was awakened by a loud knock at the door, crashed out with my face up against the spacebar on my pc? How late was it? I looked at the computer screen and didn't have one word typed. So much for creativity. I never said my job was easy.

11:30.

As I went to the door, I figured it could only have been Panther coming around this late. And it was. His darkskin face was gorgeous as I stared for a second through the peephole. I unlocked the door in a rush, excited to see him, hoping that no one else did. He gave that smile that I had been waiting like forever to see.

I closed the door and we embraced passionately, kissing as though we were reaching for each other's souls. I hadn't felt this good in days and I didn't want to let go. We finally came up for some air. Soaked in Panther's presence, I inhaled the scent of his hypnotizing cologne that I adored, ran my hands up and down his arms and back, and rested my cheek against his chest.

I said, "I miss you."

He stroked my hair while I did the same to his face. He had grown a full, sexy beard. I never saw him that way and it made him that more appealing. Natural and rebellious. I was sure he had grown it to use as a disguise, but still, I was digging the flava.

"Let's go sit," he said.

Panther took me by the hand and led me to the dining table. A pot of tea and two cups were sitting there that I didn't remember taking out, but it was conveniently perfect.

Panther offered me a chair and poured us both a cup of tea. Strange it was still hot. I figured I must've made it to stay awake before I fell asleep. I watched Panther sip his slowly.

"Is everything all right?" I asked.

He said, "You know everything's fine. But I want to know about you. Look's like you have a lot on your mind."

"Of course, I'm stressed," I told him. "I've been worried about if I would ever see you again."

"I'm not going anywhere," he said. "I'm always with you."

I knew he was trying to make me feel better, but I was afraid.

"It's not that easy," I said.

Panther touched my hand. "It's not easy for anybody. All you can do is hold on to what you have and what you know."

I wanted to take Panther at his word, but it was hard. I wished this never would've happened. Maybe I was selfish for not looking at it his way. He was the one that had it hard, not me. And my paranoia wasn't making things better.

We finished our tea. Panther stood up, took me by the hand and led me to the bedroom. I ran hot with excitement, wondering what I was in for, but didn't bother to question Panther's motives. I was a slave to the moment.

Panther picked me up and laid me down on the bed gently. I missed him so. I was ready to hold him for as long as I could.

But instead of lying next to me, or on top of me, he knelt down at the edge of the bed.

Was something wrong with Panther? Why was he holding back? Had I made him feel as if now wasn't the right time? I hoped I hadn't because I was ready. Just in case this was the last time, I was open for him. And God knew how my mind needed the break. If only for a little while, I was sure it would've been enough to release some of my tension.

I pulled him.

"Not right now," Panther said.

"But I want to."

He grabbed my hand and caressed my fingers. "It's okay," he said. "We'll have time."

I took in a deep breath and tried like hell to clear my head. Had to calm myself down. I hoped this was a dream because it was fucking with my reality. Frustrated, I just threw a pillow over my face.

I felt the edge of the bed move as Panther took a place there. Is this it, I thought? He moved the pillow from my face. I gazed at him innocently, yet my body was burning for hot sex on a platter. I mean, why couldn't he have just tried. He should've known that it was okay to have me. What was he waiting for?

He said, "When you want something, you don't always get it. That means you have to go in deeper to figure out how to get it."

Exactly. Go deeper. That was what I planned to tell him as soon as his body entered mine.

But what was Panther talking about? Was he saying that he didn't want me and I needed to figure out why? I already knew. He didn't know how to be comfortable with all that was going on. But it would've been okay if he decided on just a quickie. I wouldn't mind.

He stroked my hair gently. "You play the game," Panther said, "but you don't show your cards. You hold on to what you have and what you know. In other words, you can win a battle with the weapons that you choose, and not the ones that somebody tells you to use. And even if you don't get it when you want, that's all right. If it's that important, it'll come."

"But I don't mind showing my cards," I told him. "I want you. You are important to me, and I don't know if I'll get this chance again. I don't have to play a game when I know what I want."

He said, "I understand. But what if what you want doesn't come to you."

"Then I'll make it come to me."

"And how would you do that if the person already knows what you want."

"Then I'll just keep making things up until I get him."

Panther kissed me on the forehead. He said, "Exactly."

He got up and left the room.

I called to him. He didn't answer as he continued off. As I rose from the bed to follow him, I heard the front door unlocking.

"Panther?"

I raced to the front, but before I reached, Panther slammed the door as if he didn't hear me calling. What was he going through? And why was he putting me through this too? I opened the door. He was nowhere in sight. I listened close for the sound of heavy footsteps, car keys jingling, or an engine starting, for a sound other than crickets chirping, but nothing ever came.

I turned around and stared at the emptiness of my place, the dry, suffocating silence. It was eerie. My apartment had never seemed so scary. And I never felt so alone. The cups and the teapot that Panther and I left on the table had disappeared. That couldn't be, I told myself. Panther didn't have the time to move them. So who did? I took careful steps toward the table. I sensed that I wasn't alone. Somebody had been in my house. Was Panther playing a joke on me? I hoped so. Everything else in the living room was in its place. The computer was still on an empty screen. But could somebody have been in the kitchen?

I inched up in easy steps. Slow and cautious. Was somebody in there, watching us? If there were, I would've screamed. Screamed at the top my lungs until a neighbor came running. So there had better not have been anybody in there. Nobody. As I touched the kitchen door, I thought—nobody. Warmed up my vocal cords and said to myself—nobody. I pushed the door open and—

Wham.

The front door slammed shut.

I awakened with my head resting on the keyboard, staring at a blank computer screen. Scared like shit, I stood and looked around. My living room appeared to be in the order that I remembered. This time I ran to the kitchen. It was the way I remembered leaving it. No water boiling, and no tea cups lying around. It was just a dream. I left the kitchen and switched on every light in the house, checked the bathroom and bedroom while I was at it. I went back out to the front, turned off my computer, and made a mental note to try putting some extra effort into getting some work done tomorrow.

Something told me to check the front door and when I did, I found it unlocked. I grew shook all over again. I always locked my door when I got home. I didn't bother to entertain why it wasn't, just locked it and dashed straight to my bedroom.

First thing I did was grab the phone and call mama. I had to talk to somebody.

"Why are you calling so late," she asked. "What's wrong?

I could feel myself shaking. Calmed myself because I didn't want that to come through in my voice. I told her, "Just have a lot on my mind, like work and everything."

"Hmph," mama said, as if to say she knew I was lying. "Everything meaning your boyfriend that's on the run."

That's why she was my mama.

I said, "I had a dream about him mama, and it seemed so real. I could still feel his touch, still remember his words. It's like it wasn't a dream at all."

"Chile, chile, chile," mama said. "I think you need to lay off that computer screen. That thing is messing with your head, girl."

"Mama, I'm serious."

"I know, baby. I just don't want you to take things too serious. I mean, how do you feel about this man? Do you want to keep on going with just seeing this man in your dreams?"

Now it was starting. I knew it would come sooner or later. "Mama, I didn't call you for that. I wanted a friend to talk to. Not somebody to criticize who I choose to be with."

"I'm not criticizing at all, baby. Just asking. You've told me that Parish is a good man, and I believe you. With all the losers you've been with in the past, I can believe that you have found someone that's worth holding on to. But I'm asking because I honestly want to know. Are you willing to go to bat for this man?"

I let out a frustrated breath. One thing I didn't expect was for mama to second-guess me. I said, "You know I'm with him all the way."

She paused for a moment. "You're a strong girl, Rachel," she said. "Stubborn, but strong. But that's good, though. Because you're gonna need it."

"What do you mean by that?"

"I mean how important is your man to you? Because people are going to come after him. And in fact, they may come after you. Now, I'm glad that you're strong in your stance. But when things start coming down, will you be strong enough to keep standing there? I know you will because you're stubborn. But how much are you willing to take for one man. If he isn't worth a lot to you, then I would say leave him in your dreams. But if you think he's a great man, and not just a good man, have your back prepared. Because you're going to need it to withstand the blows.

Mama never talked to me that way about a man before. It was obvious that she was worried about me. And I was grateful. As a matter of fact, I was inspired. She let me know that I could go through anything. And if I had to, I could help my man with whatever he had to confront, too. That was what I promised Panther.

I thanked mama.

"Well, goodnight, chile," she said. "Sweet dreams."

"Yeah, you too, mama. Sweet dreams."

ಇಾ 11 ೞ

Deidra

It seemed as if my wish for some rest was never going to be granted. I hadn't sat down a good four minutes and already had someone pounding at my door. Ignoring it was useless. To everyone that knew Dee, and not Deidra, my car sitting in the driveway meant that my black ass was sitting inside the house. And because I was a hustler, I was prone to make time for my clients, even if they had to bang on every window on the house. But sometimes I needed that rest without any kind of interruptions. I needed moments to myself, away from everybody, just to keep my sanity. Just to make some time for Dee, too.

I went to the peephole anyway and wanted to kick my own ass for at least not trying to hide. Dalvin's overconfident mug was staring dead at me from the other side. What did this nigga want now? Even Panther knew when it was time for us to give each other space. Seeing too much of anybody could piss you off. Yes, I was grateful for all that Dalvin had done, but it wasn't like I wanted him to be my little, personal Captain Save-a-bitch either.

"Give me a minute," I told him. I had to straighten up a bit first, place the dishes in the kitchen, pick up all the loose weave hanging around, and burn a stick of incense to air the place out. The last thing I wanted was a man to think that I was living like a pig, especially if whenever I stepped out the door, my shit was on point.

I thought I was being courteous as I let Dalvin in, but his cologne busted through the door before he did and damn near tackled me. That shit was so strong it drowned out the incense. I almost took off running as I went to the kitchen to light another stick.

Other than his cologne that damn near knocked me down on my ass, Dalvin's look took it easy on me. He kept his shit together; jean shorts, crisp Akademiks shirt, and clean, white sneakers. I wondered if he and Tina had gotten together. She hadn't called me with any details, and I damn sure wasn't about to ask him. Men had a tendency to think you wanted to fuck them if you asked about their personal life. I offered him a seat and something to drink.

"No, thank you," he said.

I was glad. That meant he didn't plan on staying. I lit the incense anyway.

I asked "What's up?"

"Maybe we should sit down," he said.

I tensed up at that instant. My hands shook as I held a lit match. Sit down for what? Usually when somebody recommended you take a seat, the news was bad. Like if the news shocked you, they wanted you seated so you wouldn't pass out. I had never passed out in my twenty-four years of life, but I took a seat anyway. Dalvin also sat down. Oh God. Something better not have happened to my man. I wasn't ready for this shit. Not right now.

Dalvin looked me square in the eye. "Everything's cool," he said, as if he read my mind. "Just had to tell you that we got that nigga that was fucking with you from the other night."

The tight feeling in my chest dropped. I was in shock now.

"What do you mean you got him? Got him how? Y'all body-bagged him?"

"Not yet," Dalvin said. "He's on stand-by at one of our spots, waiting on your call."

"Call for what?"

"For what you want us to do with him. He came across the wrong woman, and we're going to handle this the right way. The way you want. I know Panther would've made the decision by now. But since he's not here, you've got the call."

I was shocked, all right, but not on the verge of falling out. I was speechless. Dalvin and his boys put in the work, like some real gangsters. And made it seem so easy.

I asked, "Who was it?"

"A nigga named Henry Jones," Dalvin said. "He just did ten years for molesting little girls back in '97. But now we got his ass, and we hope he doesn't touch or see anything ever again. All we need is your word."

I didn't have any words to give. I was dizzy with confusion. This was moving all too fast for me. A motherfucking child molester was around my little sister, and if he didn't come after me first, he might have gotten to her. He should've been dead already, I thought. Shouldn't have had the freedom to breathe, let alone be released from prison. And I wanted to see exactly when that nasty motherfucker took his last breath. I wanted to be the one to strap his ass in the chair and hit the switch. Lights out, motherfucker. Have a good time frying.

Dalvin stood up. "So, what's up, Deidra. You want us to send that nigga to God?"

My hands were shaking. Heart pounding in my ears. I had never been so heated. Angry and afraid at the same time. All of my emotions were screaming, 'do it'. Put a toe tag on that nigga. But my heart was holding back, telling me calm down and think. But I couldn't. I didn't know what to do. And I couldn't just blindly trust Dalvin like that. Yes, he was Panther's homeboy, but I didn't know him. I wanted Panther to help me. Not some trigger-happy brother that was paid to do this every day.

I told Dalvin, "Just hold him down for right now. Too many things is going on with me. I need to cool out a minute and just wait."

Dalvin screwed up his face. "Wait on what?

I crossed my arms, rubbed away at the bumps popping up on my skin. I said, "I don't know. Panther, I guess. With this murder thing going on, I think I should wait on a word from him."

"Deidra, you don't know when that nigga's gonna be back. It's not like my people can sit around babysitting this nigga like they don't have shit to do. This needs to be handled ASAP. You want this nigga out there loose? Next time ain't no telling what he—"

"Just wait, okay. I'll hear from Panther soon. I know it. And he'll make the call. I can't think straight right now. Just wait."

My message was clear as my tone raised up a few decibels.

Dalvin offered no more words. He threw his hands up in surrender. "All right," he said. "You gotta do what you gotta. But just understand that we do, too. When you're ready, give me a call."

Dalvin wrote his number down and rushed out the house. I was glad because he was pulling on my third nerve. I didn't bother saying anything when he left. Just locked the door and went straight to the back.

I ran myself a hot bubble bath. My head had been worked and I needed time to chill for a minute. Calm my nerves. I couldn't see straight if I was under pressure. And Dalvin damn near blinded me.

I couldn't wait to sit my ass in the tub. Once I stripped, I dipped my feet in the steaming, hot water, sat down, and laid down all of the burdens that had stacked over my shoulders. It felt like heaven. In here, I had no worries, no dead bodies, no nappy heads to do, and no drama. The only person I wanted around me at this moment was Panther. His strong hands wrapped around me, massaging my shoulders, caressing my arms and back. Then I'd turn the other way and face him so he could perform the same magic on my legs and feet. That man could work wonders in many ways.

Panther had me tripping like this from day one. Meeting him was so crazy. There I was in the dopehole with Eric. I was only there because this was a new connect, and Eric didn't trust anybody else to go with him. We knocked on the door, and a gorgeous dark skin brother in a black suit was walking out. After making way for us to go in, he smiled at me, and even though I threw attitude at fools that sweat me, I couldn't resist smiling back. He was like whoa. I was hoping he'd come back. But that was the end of my flirtations, and now I was face to face with a fat, Pillsbury doughboy-looking mother, called Monster. He had on thick, link chains over a blue sweatsuit. I remembered thinking he must've worn it to sweat the fat off his chunky ass. He introduced himself. My brother and him were eyeing each other closely, and I wanted to get the hell out of there. Even though Eric said Monster was cool, this type of thing was always scary.

It had just turned evening and all the lights in the house were on. The blinds closed. We were standing at the dining room table and could smell the strong scent of jerk seasoning flow from the kitchen. Posters of Haile Selassie, Bob Marley, and a notty dread lock boy, covered the off-white, smudgy walls, while Buju Banton chanted low from a radio in the bedroom.

Monster took a puff from a blunt then set it in an ashtray. He said, "Ya get da money?"

Eric said, "Man, don't even waste my time like that."

Monster flashed a big grin, blew out a cloud of smoke. "Soljah, get da stuff," he called to his partner who stood at the door.

But before Soljah moved, a knock came at the door. "Who is it?" Soljah asked.

The person responded, "Panther".

Soljah let him in and Panther stood at the door. He looked our way and said, "Is that your ride with the dubs on it?"

I told him yes.

"Can you come here for a minute," he asked. "I need to show you something on your car. Looks like it's about to have a problem."

I looked at Eric and Eric looked at Panther.

"Can it wait until we finish?" Eric said.

"Homeboy, I have business to tend to myself. If you don't trust it, we could leave the door open."

I knew Eric was skeptical of Panther's motives, but I was curious about what Panther had to show me on the car. Plus I didn't mind stepping away to talk to his fine ass. "It's all right," I said to Eric. "Go ahead and handle your business."

"What you doing, Panther?" Monster asked. "Me take care of me tings right now."

"Chill out, fatboy," Panther said. "Grab yourself some jerk chicken. You can eat and talk at the same time, right? Good."

I couldn't help but crack a smile as I walked towards Panther. He was talking to big time dope dealers as if they weren't about shit. And acted as though he was the shit. It was sexy. I tried to hide how much I was digging him.

As we walked out, I asked "What's wrong with my car?"

Panther bent down. "Come check out this tire."

I came closer but I chose to stand and watch him.

He said, "I want you to come right here and grab this piece behind the tire."

I looked at him like he was trying to jack my purse. "What's going on?" I said.

He said, "Do it like you're checking the tire cause they're watching you too. They plan on killing the both of you when you go back inside the house."

I couldn't believe what I was hearing. I searched Panther's face for bullshit, but I saw none.

Panther urged, "Do it quick, or else they're going to think something's going on. Just grab it and tuck it in your waist. But do it smooth."

This whole thing felt crazy. A stranger was giving me a gun and warning me that I was about to be killed. Who did he think I was? One thing I had never been was a fool, so I didn't look back or hesitate. I grabbed the nine from behind the tire. As I placed it at my waist side, I asked "How do you know?"

He ran his hand over the rim, still acting out his innocent role.

"Fatboy never talks to me like that," Panther said. "I supply him. I heard he knocked off a couple of d-boys recently. Fatboy's getting greedy. I can't have nobody like that working for me. Besides, I didn't want you leaving earth without me first getting a chance to know you."

That time I blushed and didn't care if he saw. I was with him and didn't even know his real name.

"As I was walking out," he continued, "I saw one of them standing behind the door with a sawed-off."

I said, "I have to get my brother out of there."

"I'm right behind you," Panther said.

Instincts told me this wasn't the way. Yeah, Panther may have been telling the truth. But they worked for him, and he could've been in on it. Then again, I thought, why did he give me the gun? I wasn't sure how to handle this and decided to be cautious.

I said, "I think it's best that you go in first. I'm not sure I can handle this."

Panther said, "You can handle anything as long you trust yourself. But if you're not sure, then I'll take it. You ready?"

I wasn't. But if we waited much longer, something might happen to my brother. Or both of us. I told Panther to lead the way.

He rose to his feet and strolled to the door. I followed with timid steps. Panther's posture was strong and confident, while I could barely move my legs.

Soljah closed the door behind us when we walked in.

We stopped right at the front. I kept one eye on Soljah. Couldn't turn my back on his intentions.

Monster asked, "Everyting crisp, my yout."

Panther answered, "For sho."

It happened in a flash, but I could see everything as clear as a film in slow motion. Panther turned to me, grabbed the gun from my waist and shot Soljah in the chest three times. At the same time, from a gun in his waist, Panther blasted on the man behind the door. That was two people that Panther took out in about two seconds. And I still couldn't move.

Panther walked up on Monster and Eric.

They froze up like ice water.

"There's no need for me to explain," Panther said to Monster. He put two bullets in Monster's head, and two more in his gut.

I had never witnessed a man killed at close range before. Monster's head rested limp over his shoulder, his eyes and mouth wide open.

Panther said, "We got to get out of here."

And I was slapped back into reality. We hauled ass out of there. Eric and I jumped in my car after Panther told us to follow him. Everything else was a blur, but since then, I had been feeling Parish Coles like a sunny day. Felt safe knowing that he was with me. As tense as I was, his presence loosened me. Had me believing that I was going to survive that crazy day. And that I could survive anything.

But soaking under the mist of vanilla scented candles and soap, I wasn't so sure now. The thought of that sick rapist breathing over my neck ran through my mind, and I couldn't help but to think, *what if.* Tears tried soaking my eyelids, but I wished them away. I wasn't going to break down over something that didn't even happen. Instead I wiped my eyes dry with my shoulders and bathed myself with my soft scrubber. Got my attention fascinated with the small and large bubbles forming and dissolving from my arms. Told myself to be cool. I still had someone to confide in even if Panther wasn't around. And it was almost visiting day. I would take that long trip down south to see my brother. Eric Thomas.

❀ 12 ❀

Sandra

It was Saturday night and Dreamers was crunk like the trunk of an amped-up ride with twenty-inch speakers. I should've expected it since it was one of the biggest talent shows in Miami for the year. And the place was packed with potentials, producers, ballers, and top executives from all over the industry. So I had my shit on tight when I crept up on the scene. Nisha and Tati were right behind me looking just as good. They had been begging me at work for the longest to hang out, but I never had the time because I had a man. There was no reason for me to run the streets. But being in the music business forced me to make time. You had to go out there and find the talent, and they weren't always out on the block freestyling.

All eyes were on us when my girls and I stepped up to the front of the line. Niggas was clocking and bitches were hating, as always. But it wasn't like they could've talked shit about it. Whenever I strolled into Dreamers I was practically a star. Everybody knew me. It was like Panther had access to everything, and v.i.p. in Dreamers was one of them.

Barry, the bouncer, took my hand and escorted me and the girls right through the front door.

"Damn you look good, baby," Barry yelled. "Y'all about to run all these other females outta here."

I laughed and playfully touched his arm to make sure we had our bottle reserved.

"Who are your girls?" Barry asked.

I told him that Nisha and Tati worked at the law firm with me and he almost had a heart attack.

"Ooh." He scoped the girls out and turned back to my ear. "Think you can hook me up with the red one?"

He was talking about Tati. I had expected that eyes would be all over her. She sported a tight-fitting black dress, with the convenient, attention-grabbing slit in the front. Her wrap was done beautifully, and she reminded me of Alliyah whenever she rocked it that way. She was a shorty like me, with a slim waist and silky shape. But while I had the nice titties and fat ass, Tati had a cute, young face and a smooth, light skin tone that was flawless. I looked back to see if she knew that Barry was sweating her, but her and Nisha were busy peeping the environment.

"Don't say nothing right now," Barry said. "Wait until y'all get to the table and then later on, you tell me what she said."

I nodded, but there was no way in hell I was about to try my girl like that. Barry was all wrong. He was a nice guy, and that alone killed it for him. If he had a prayer of a chance with Tati, she would've eaten his ass up for everything he had, including what was on his plate. And something like that wasn't easy because Barry was a pudgy motherfucker. Half the time he'd be sweating from running back and forth, and his breath smelled like shit. It was burning me up to stand so close, but I had to find a way to stay cool with my hook up.

He escorted us to our table upstairs so we wouldn't have to fight off the touchy perverts trying to get a feel off of everything on the sly. We were seated just over the stage. Perfect view to see who was worth scouting. Our bottle was even waiting on us. After a long day of work we were ready to do it up big.

"Holla back," Barry yelled in my ear before he walked off. "Don't forget me."

I wanted to tell that nigga don't forget the breathmints. He needed them two days ago.

"Girl, you are the shit," Nisha said, her slender shoulders bouncing to the d.j.'s skillful mixing. "I didn't know you had connects like this. You're running things in here. You don't mind if I do the honors?"

"Help yourself," I said as I passed the chilled bottle of Grey Goose. Nisha was my girl. She was straight up with you about how she felt, took no shit from anybody, and still was down to earth.

I looked over at Tati, and of course she was sitting there trying to be cute. Let her tell it, every man in the world wanted her. She was good peoples and all, but was still young in the mind. And since I was going to have fun tonight, I decided to start with her prissy ass.

I tapped her out of her Barbie dreamland state. "Tati, you know that bouncer, Barry is checking for you."

"Who?" she said with a face that said even his name was stink. "You mean that nigga that brought us up here?"

I nodded. "Yeah, girl. That's my nigga. He good peoples. Got a lot of lovin."

Tati sucked her teeth, rolled her eyes and switched her body away from my comment. I knew I had her. Nisha laughed sipping on her drink. I burned inside waiting on a response.

Tati said, "Only love he can give me is from his pockets."

I couldn't stop though. I said, "Yeah, I'm sure he has something long in his pants that he doesn't mind sharing."

Tati took a sip from her drink. "Well, if it ain't green I don't want it."

Nisha put her drink down and turned to Tati. "Eeww, green dicks. Girl, what the hell you fucking, aliens?"

The whole table busted out laughing.

Nisha continued, "What color is the cum, neon green? How many balls them niggas got? I knew you came to work walking kinda funny. Is that nigga still in your ass? Girl, go in the bathroom and fart that nigga out. Lord, you about to burn that little green motherfucker up."

I swore we hurt from laughing so hard. We hardly had a buzz yet, but the liquor had begun talking for us. I calmed the giggles and dried my eyes while Nisha was pouring her second glass of champagne. Tati pulled her mirror out and checked her *perfect* face.

Then some old brother strolled pass us rocking a suit as old as he was. Oh God, I said to myself. If Nisha saw what I saw, it was about to be on again.

Oh no," Nisha said. "Oh, hell no. Is that George Jefferson's old ass over there? No, that can't be George Jefferson. Is that him? Cause that nigga look like he jumped straight out the T.V. set and into the club. As a matter of fact, I should call him over here. Deacon!" Nisha was fucking with this man right in the club and we couldn't stop her. "Deacon Fryer. This don't look like the church to me. You need to stop laying your hands on these young girls before I tell on your old ass."

The show was starting and I was glad. Messing around with Nisha, I would be laughing and drinking all night. I grabbed my glass and told the girls to stand at the balcony with me. We drank and laughed some more, watched the ballers pass by, but played it off like we didn't see a soul. At least I was playing it off. I didn't like any man thinking that I wanted him unless he was my man. And since Panther wasn't there, I didn't see anybody else. Tati played it cool because she *knew* her shit didn't stink. And Nisha didn't give a fuck. If a nigga was fine, she peeped him out, but not so much to have him thinking she was desperate or something. Like I said, my girls were good peoples and down to earth. Not stupid.

And besides, I was out on business. If I got too caught up in the moment, I might miss out on a prospect. I had to go after my opportunities. And sitting on my ass wouldn't cause them to jump up in my lap. Working as a paralegal for the rest of my life, I couldn't see it. I had dreams to do my own thing, making dough like a baker. I was ready for this world. Ready to get away from my nine-to-five. And ready to have more out of the life I was living.

By the time the show kicked off, I was nice and buzzed. Another drink would have me leaning. And I needed to work. The artists that had already taken the stage were decent, just enough to get my ass and shoulders moving. But in the middle of the show, there was one M.C. named Streetwise that caught my eye. I liked his flow. His ruggedness was hypnotizing. Even Tati commented on the nigga's style; the way he dressed and the lyrics he was spitting. I saw potential, and I had to have him. Like *The Matrix,* he was the one.

When Streetwise's performance was over, the crowd gave him an overwhelming show of love and props. Mainly from the niggas because he rhymed about the street life, shady niggas and trifling females. That type of flow along with talking about the club scene and things that women liked was a sure way to make some bread in this business. So he was workable. Hell, anybody was workable as long as they listened to me. Especially a man.

I needed to go down and meet with Streetwise, but I had to wait for the groupies to climb down off of his nuts first. In an environment like this, everybody was a hound. Everybody wanted something from somebody. It was a way for all of us to eat off of each other, and if you didn't represent for what you could bring, then you stayed broke and never ate.

Some bitch finally undid herself from Streetwise's sack and I jumped after my chance. I would've been surprised if he wasn't already being represented, but I wanted him to at least know who Sandra Reese and Right-One Management was. I told the girls that I'd be back, went downstairs and made my way through a crowd of sweaty niggas and cheap perfume. My take-no-shit face was on high beam to let them know that I wasn't the one. When I reached Streetwise, I turned into the sweet lady of the south. I touched his arm and smiled.

"Hey, what's up Streetwise? That was a nice performance. I was feeling it."

He looked down and gave me a nonchalant smirk. "Thank you, baby" he said, and returned his focus to the stage. I knew he was thinking that I was another groupie whore, hungry for a nigga with potential, but it was cool because he just didn't know me yet.

I said, "My name's Sandy Reese. I own Right One Management, and I was wondering if you were being represented by anybody yet?"

He looked down again and shot an easy smile. He was even sexier up close. Had his braids freshly done, was about six feet tall, build was thick and wide, and best of all, he smelled good. And even though he had on a thick chain with the shining diamond-studded cross over a white UM football jersey, it didn't mean that he was paid. But I liked that he took pride in presenting that image.

He said, "Right now, Ms. Reese, I'm representing myself."

"Oh," I said, "you have your own company?"

He took a sip from his beer. "No. It's just where I choose to be until things change."

I nodded, thinking he knew about the business and was putting up his guards. But it wasn't a game when it came to the skills that I possessed.

I asked, "You don't have a problem with managers, do you?"

"Not at all."

"So it is possible for someone to help you get signed and become a big star?"

He studied me as if he was examining my words.

He said, "It's possible for someone to help me get what I want."

He was being cautious again. I guess his name was Streetwise for a reason. I respected a man that knew what he wanted and didn't just jump at every offer that smelled sweet.

I offered to buy him a drink and he agreed. Told his homeboys that he'd be back and allowed me to lead the way to the bar. I liked that because it made it look like he was with me and not the other way around. We grabbed a seat on the stools and I bought him another beer. Wasn't about to play the fool and buy an expensive drink for a brother that I didn't even know.

I faced him and said, "So what do you want?"

He said, "What do you mean?"

Now he was playing stupid when he knew exactly what I meant. I was a business woman and this was about business. This was about the cream.

But I had the gift of gab. I said, "You told me that it's possible for someone to help you get what you want, and I want to know what that is."

Our drinks came, but instead of grabbing his like I did, he just studied me. I knew he liked what he saw. He didn't have to say it. It was printed all over his face from the time that I introduced myself. And even though he was the artist, I was in charge. He could've fantasized about fucking me all night, but the reality was we were only going to talk. And talk business.

He said, "I want everything."

I sipped my beer. "A whole lot of money, right?"

He laughed. "Yeah, that too."

"Yeah, that too? Of course that, too. I see it in you, Streetwise. I see that talent that needs to be out there. That voice that wants to be heard. We can do our thing in this industry and get paid. That's all I'm about. And if you're not about money then there's no need to be in this business. Am I right?"

He nodded. "Yeah, you're right. But there's also something else I want other than money."

I was baffled. "What's that?"

"To be myself."

"Fair enough," I said. "Why don't you take my card so we can talk on it some more, because I honestly do believe in you and your talent."

"How can you believe in me when you don't know me?"

"But that's what I'm saying, Streetwise. I want to know you. I want to represent for you and everything you need. You just give me a call whenever you can and we'll talk, okay. You're in this game for a reason, and I want to represent you the best way I can for that reason. So just give me a call and we can talk."

He nodded and took the card. We shook hands and Streetwise walked off. I was glad that was over. He killed my buzz by acting all paranoid. I understood his concern, but damn. Either you're down to make money or you're not. And I wasn't about to sit around convincing Streetwise what he wanted to do. There was too much talent to make money off of to sit around playing Oprah to a paranoid thug. He was still fine though. If he decided to work with me, I'd put everything into making Streetwise the biggest name in the game. So big that he'd slap himself for being worried in the first place.

Before going back upstairs to my girls, I checked my voicemail. Just like I figured, Aunt Mabel left like thirty-five messages. It was too late to call so I went back upstairs to get back to my work and play.

After the show was over, I dropped the girls off. We still had work in the morning and decided to make it an early night. But I wasn't ready to go home yet. I was only going to be alone and wasn't too thrilled about it. But then I thought about Aunt Mabel and how she was always alone. It wasn't the greatest feeling to have. I could see why she called me so much. Both of our men were gone and it was hard for either of us to get through our days. For her it was worse because she was ill and had no one to care for her at all. Thinking of the way her voice sounded on the messages, I had to see her just to know that everything was all right. And when I arrived at her room, she was sleeping peacefully with the television on, the telephone close to her ear. I almost felt guilty about even going out and leaving her by herself, but I had no choice. I needed to take care of myself. And not having Panther around made me work even harder. Soon Aunt Mabel would understand. I was a business woman. I was supposed to take care of myself. When things got better for me and my man, then maybe I'd consider slowing down. But until then, Aunt Mabel would just have to deal with the late night visits.

ಐ 13 ಜ

Rachel

Because of the drama that went down on Friday, Monday started off tense. We sat facing each other within our little circle inside the big room. The boys were quiet and I had no clue of what to say. I hadn't come up with any new projects between the night before and this morning. I knew I had to think of something quick because the boys were getting restless. And if I didn't have anything to direct their mind to, they usually said and did whatever came to mind, a lot of violence and more time to serve than what any of us really wanted.

Think, I told myself. *Think*. I was losing a grip on my greatest talent. I couldn't even pin it down to one single issue that was messing with my head. Just figured it was stress. All the stress that sat on my back for the last few days had taken me for a ride. But I couldn't allow it to keep controlling me. I had to be a professional. All personal problems had to be put aside so I could be focused on the real problems. My boys. So think, I told myself again. Lose the stress. That was it. In the dream I had, Panther said that I needed to let go of the stress. So that was what I would do. Try to be happy. And make my boys happy too.

I put my clipboard down. Crossed my legs in my favorite gray business skirt. I said, "Why don't you all tell me about a fun or happy experience that you've had."

I smiled, waiting for a response, but nobody smiled or spoke back. Poncho didn't even blurt out a funny story, and he was the mouth of the group.

"Any volunteers?" I asked.

Rocking legs and stares glued to the floor was all I received. This was not like my boys. Ace was usually the only one that had a hard time opening up, but now the whole room gave me the silent treatment. I hadn't seen mugs like this since the day we first met. There was something deeper here than what I was seeing. Each boy had his own individual personality. They never all looked and acted the same way at the same time. What was going on? What had I done?

I picked on Poncho because he was the easiest target. His tongue was too active to stay quiet for long. I stared him down good. Didn't say a word, just caught his eyes and spoke to him with mine until his mouth couldn't take anymore and threw up the white flag. It worked. His eyes danced around, a sly grin sprang over his face as his head turned in Ace's direction.

So that's what it was. It had to do with Sam and Ace's fight. I should've known. Sam's silly antics made all the boys uncomfortable. And I couldn't blame them. The boys had learned how to channel their anger, but with Sam prone to act out whenever he felt like it, he could've provoked any one of them to just snap. The last thing I needed were fights to break out in back-to-back sessions.

"How about I start," I said. "When I was thirteen years old, I went to my first concert. It was Bobby Brown, TLC, and my girl, Mary J. Blige. I was so hyped. I was sweating through the whole thing, especially when Mary J. came on. I didn't even sit down. But the craziest moment came when my mother took me back stage. I didn't know she had backstage passes, and you should've seen me. Tears were tumbling down my face, my legs shook like jell-o, and my heart was moving like a jackhammer in my chest. Man, I was on my mother's arm like skin. And then I saw my mother introducing herself to Mary. *The* Mary J. Blige said, 'Hey Rachel,' and I fell out cold. I mean completely out. When I came to, my mother was pulling me out of the backseat and into the house. I couldn't believe that I passed out when Mary J. Blige spoke to me. I felt like crap."

I paused and all the boys were staring at me and smiling. One thing I knew for certain was that my boys were human, and at some time in their lives, they too have had at least one exciting moment.

"The next morning when I woke up," I continued, "my T-shirt of Mary J. had some writing on it, and it read, 'I'll never forget that I met you, Rachel. Love, Mary.' And I still have that t-shirt to this day. It's never been washed."

Poncho clapped for my story. Then the other boys joined in. I was embarrassed, but glad that I had gotten some type of response. A good response. And from everybody at the same time.

Bravo! Bravo! The boys were yelling and screaming and embarrassing me.

"All right, guys," I said. "Thank you, but we do have to keep it down. We're not at a Mary J. Blige concert right now. But now that I see that everyone's in a better mood, can we have a volunteer to share one of their crazy, exciting moments."

For a second, the room was still. All of a sudden, Sam shot his arm up. I was skeptical of what he had to say, and even hesitated before acknowledging him, which I shouldn't have done. I didn't want to give the impression that I had favorites. But Sam leaned over, smiled, and prepared to speak as if he hadn't even noticed.

"My most exciting moment, Ms. Baxter," Sam said, "was when I met you and spoke with you yesterday."

I picked my clipboard up off the ground, brushed my hand back over my ponytail. I wasn't in the mood to play this game with Sam. I wanted to say shut up, and just move on to the next person. But I was too irritated to find a way to say shut up professionally, so I had to swallow the irritation.

"Thank you," I said. "That's sweet. Sam, but we would like to hear about some exciting moments in your life. I know you have at least one. And it could be anything."

"And it was yesterday," he said with eyes that lit up like bright stars. "I told you I never had anybody talk to me the way you did. You showed that you cared about me, laughed with me, told me what you liked about me, and was even able to share some of your personal life with me. And you said that you don't do that with nobody. So yes, when I spoke to you yesterday, I knew we had a bond that was more special than anything I've ever had. And I know it was special to you too, right?"

What the hell did I get myself into? This boy Sam had lost his mind. He used the conversation we had yesterday to make it seem as if it was personal. But it wasn't. This was my job. It's what I was supposed to do. And nothing more.

"Of course it was special," I said, "but—

"And you shared your personal business because we have a special bond that you only have with me, right?"

I could feel the eyes of the room center in on me. My boys were confused. They wanted an answer.

I never had any boy from one of my groups speak about me that way. Something was definitely up with Sam. Something psychological. And it had him confused.

"Now wait a minute," I said. "I shared my personal business with you in confidence, Sam. That doesn't mean that—"

"And that's another thing you told me. That you liked my confidence."

"Whoa now, Sam. Hold up. I think you have things mixed up. So why don't—"

"No, I don't. You said you like my confidence, you told me your personal business that you would never tell any one else. I even made you laugh. You were mad before we spoke, right after you finished speaking to this other boy over here, and I made you feel better. Nobody else did that. He couldn't do it. It was all about us. It was all about—"

Wham.

Ace jumped on Sam and knocked him to the ground, wrestling, punching, and kicking the shit out of him. They were going at it like some wild bulldogs. The other boys crowded around and boosted them on. I called for the guards in a hurry. I stood back, trembling, eyes teary and head weary, allowed the guards to clean up the mess that I couldn't stop.

But now I was going to have a bigger problem. Two fights in two days. I had a lot of explaining to do. This was all Sam's doing. That's what I tried telling myself, but I knew where to put the blame. I had slipped. But I wasn't sure if Sam really was confused, or just fucking with me. What he managed to do was fuck with Ace, which probably fucked up the little trust and respect that Ace maintained for me. The progression that we made was falling away, and I wasn't sure if I'd ever gain it back. A lot of what I knew about my boys came from late night conversations with Panther. But now that he was no longer around to give me advice on how to handle certain situations, I was afraid that I would lose a whole lot more than Ace's trust.

Sam and Ace were handcuffed and dragged out of the room. Sam wore his arrogant smirk, and Ace looked more lost and alone than ever. The rest of my boys were standing around like what to do next. I didn't know what to tell them, because I was asking myself the same thing.

I was called into Andrea's office for the second day in a row. When I walked in, Andrea was more agitated than the last time I was called in. Her hands were busy, frantic with writing notes into Ace's file. And for the first time since I began working at this facility, I noticed that my file was sitting on Andrea's desk, too.

I said, "Andrea, I'm sorry that this occurred, and I can assure you—"

With her free hand, Andrea signaled me to stop, and continued writing in Ace's file with the other hand. Where was Sam's file? Why weren't Sam's actions in question and logged down? He instigated the whole thing.

I said, "I'm not trying to undermine you in any way, Andrea, but you should know that Ace was innocent in all of this. It was the new boy, Sam, again. He craves attention and manipulated Ace into coming after him. I can tell how this whole thing started."

"I already know how it started," Andrea said. She finally put her pen down and looked at me. "From what these young men have told me it seems as though it started with you."

I was in shock. "Hold on, Andrea. I can explain all of this."

"I'm sure you can, Ms. Baxter. And you probably can assure me that this won't happen again, right?"

My head shook in frustration. I was speechless. I couldn't believe what was happening. It had been three months since I began working at this facility, but Andrea made me feel as though I didn't even have the job yet.

She removed her glasses. Her eyes had softened some. "Listen, Rachel, I know your heart is in the right place. But I'm not sure that you can handle this place. This job may not be right for you."

"Andrea, can I at least have an opportunity to explain?"

"You will," Andrea said. "Darnell has requested to speak with you."

"I smiled. "You mean I can go up and talk to Darnell?"

Andrea opened up my file and began writing. She said, "Just make sure I have that report on my desk by the end of the day."

I didn't stay behind to see what bullshit Andrea was about to write in my file. If it was up to her, I probably would've been clearing out my desk by now. Thank God there was at least one other person I could show why I should stay.

Darnell was the warden of our facility. He used to work in the men's prison but said he felt he had a better impact in the juvenile system. Hopefully I could convince him of the impact I was making with my group.

For a gentleman over fifty years old, Darnell was better looking than most men in here. He had a salt and pepper low cut and trimmed goatee. His build was strong, and you could see the definition in his thick biceps through a long sleeve shirt. His light brown skin was smooth, and his smile was angelic. A lot of people in the facility looked up to him.

When I stepped into Darnell's office, he was busy at work, but dropped his pen and gave me his full attention.

"Rachel," Darnell greeted me smiling. "Good to see you. Come in."

I was surprised. Darnell gave me a look as though I did something good.

"Thank you, Darnell." I sat down. "It's good to see you, too. I'm glad we have this opportunity to talk."

"So am I," Darnell said. "You are the best counselor I have. I should've told you that sooner."

I smiled, even though inside I was questioning what the hell was going on. "Yes, you should have told me sooner," I joked.

"It's only been three months, though. And like any game, you don't show your cards right away."

I said, "So this means you're not going to fire me."

Darnell clasped his hands together as he leaned back in chair. "There are a few people who feel that you cannot handle this job. I don't share these feelings. I think you're doing an excellent job. You just had a couple of rough days. Everybody around here has them.

What do we expect? It's not like we're running a day care. Just be careful."

I let out a soft sigh or relief. "Thank you. I will."

"As a matter of fact. Take the rest of the day off. I'm sure you need it after what just occurred."

Today was getting stranger, yet better by the moment. "Are you sure, Darnell? I still have to give a report of what happened today."

"You can do it tomorrow. Go home. Spend some time alone with your boyfriend."

I laughed. "I'll be spending time alone, and it won't be with a boyfriend."

Darnell sat up in his chair. "Now that's kinda hard to believe. What sort of young men do we have out there that will pass on an intelligent, beautiful woman like yourself? I need to teach these young men a thing or two about game. They are losing their minds out there."

I laughed. I didn't know how else to respond. Darnell was nice looking man, but I always looked at him as someone that could be my father.

"Thank you," I finally said. "That's sweet of you. But I will be fine."

"I'm sure you will. You have everything an intelligent man would want. Let just hope that whoever he is, he will open eyes and see it, too."

I smiled like a shy, little girl when I told him thank you. As I was leaving Darnell's office, Andrea was coming my way. I was still smiling when we passed each other. She stopped and I could feel her eyes burning my back with those magnifying glasses of hers. She could stare all she wanted. There were other eyes in here that was watching my back.

ಹ 14 ೞ

Deidra

I couldn't stand coming up in this place. I couldn't understand how some women did it every week. It was cold as hell, smelled like Cheeto's, and the guards always scanned my body like my tits and ass were weapons. But I dealt with it. Made the hour long trip down south like I did every month. At one time, it was twice a month with my brothers and Tracy riding shotgun. But after about six months, Eric grew frustrated, claiming he couldn't deal with seeing a family that he wasn't able to be a part of. I told my brothers the truth and they understood. Tracy had to settle for a lie about Eric moving upstate. But I kept at least one of my visits because Eric was never going to deny me.

I got to the window and saw Eric sitting there confident and strong as always. He resembled a black superhero, growing in mass and muscle in his shoulders and arms every time I saw him. It was an inspiration to me just to see him alive. After my eyes told him how much I missed him, we picked up our receivers.

"What up, baby doll?" he greeted me half smiling. "You don't look too happy to see me. Everything all right?"

After forcing a smile, I nodded. I asked, "What about you?"

With a calm face Eric let out a hard sigh. "I'm still here. Guess I'm doing as fine as I could. How are the young ones?"

"All of them are good."

"Your mama still trippin'?"

"Yes," I said. "Your mama is still trippin'."

He nodded with his head down, studying the cuts and bruises in his brown hands.

He said, "I heard about your boy. All they do is talk about him in here. Dumb motherfuckers betting cartons of cigarettes that he's already dead, or out of the country. And the look on your face says that you believe one of those theories yourself."

I responded with a, "Hmph." Eric knew me just as well as Panther did. I said, "So many theories and crazy thoughts about Panther and everything else running through my mind that I don't know what I'm supposed to do."

"Why don't you tell me what's up with you? What crazy thoughts are you talking about?"

I let out a frustrated breath of my own. "I don't know, E. It just seems like things are getting worse, and I don't know if they're ever going to stop."

I couldn't look up at Eric. I felt the fear printed over my face and it forced me to look away. In this place Eric had no choice but to be strong. It would've been hard to deal with his reality in there if he had my problems stacked over of his shoulders too.

"It's all right," he said. "You need me just as much as I needed to see you."

I relaxed and smiled inside. My brother really did know me.

I said, "E, if you had an opportunity to take away something in your life that's hurting you, but was afraid of the consequences, would you take it? Or would you let God take it away himself."

Eric's face read confusion. But I knew that soon he'd get the idea.

He said, "I think you already have the answer. Hell, you know what I'm living, Dee. And some of the same shit you go through out there, I face in here, too. Do I believe in God, yes. And I believe in prayer, too. But there are times that shit needs to get done like right away. And when he doesn't answer, I use everything I can think of to help myself."

I nodded. My eyes began to water. I said, "I kinda figured that. Just wanted to know if I was right for feeling that way."

"Only God can judge you, baby doll. And since he knows why you do what you do, I'm sure he'll understand."

I thanked Eric for setting things straight. We talked some more, laughed about the old times. I told him the haps on the dizzy females that came and got their hair done and everything else going on around the way. He already knew about Luke and Joe and was hot about it. Felt like it was his fault. Said that a man couldn't do shit for another man when he was locked down. He was excited to hear how good Tracy was doing in school. But if he knew exactly how mama was acting around her, he wouldn't have been able to act right. And Eric didn't need any more time in there than what he already had.

I always felt worse on the ride back and wished that Eric was right beside me when I exited those gates. I was sure that he felt the same way. He just never bothered to say the words that were attached to the tone in his voice.

After a long trip, I made it home and crashed on the sofa. My body was relieved and I concentrated on getting my mind there too. I reached over the side of the sofa and played the answering machine. First I received a couple of dial tones from some no-life having motherfuckers. Then Shakita called about her weekly. I was happy because I needed the bread. Without Panther around, I had to step up the hustle. But that was all the messages I had. Still no word from Panther. I called Shakita and let her know that she could come through. Even though I wasn't into doing hair at that exact minute, I could use the company.

But before I got a chance to dial her number, I heard a car pull up outside. I rolled off the couch and went to the peephole and saw that it was Dalvin.

This nigga had to have radar on me. He was by himself again and I always took that as a show of respect for my home. In my neighborhood, too many niggas hanging around usually alerted the whole police department. He knocked softly, but loud enough to let me know that someone was at the door.

I buttoned my jeans and pulled my shirt down. Brushed my bangs neatly over my eye before opening the door.

"Hey, Dalvin," I greeted him with the door opened wide enough for him to pass.

He said, "What's up, Dee? Good to see you."

"Same here," I lied as I took a seat on the edge of the sofa. I didn't know how to tell Dalvin that I still hadn't made a decision about that nasty rapist yet.

He said, "Guess what? I got something for you."

I was bubbling with excitement. Was Panther about to walk through the door and surprise me again?

"Come with me," Dalvin Said. "We gotta ride out."

"Where we going?"

" Don't worry" Dalvin said. "Trust me. You're gonna like this. Come on."

Dalvin grabbed my hand and guided me to the door.

"Hold on," I said as I pulled away and snatched my keys. "I want to drive myself. Got some errands to run later."

Dalvin shrugged his shoulders. "That's cool. Let's roll then. We ain't got much time."

I could've rode with Dalvin, but I worked hard for my own ride so I didn't have to depend on others. Besides, Dalvin was one of Panther's soldiers. In the eyes of the law I was still clean, and there no was no telling what kind of dirt Dalvin had on him.

We had a forty-five minute ride all the way down by the Port of Miami. The sidewalks were lined with warehouses and Cuban delis that stayed open twenty-four hours where you could buy breakfast for $2.50, and still ate like a king. Homeless people roamed the streets in search of ways to survive. And dark skin Cubans and old school Haitian men played dominoes in front of deserted buildings. Funny how they argued with each other and couldn't understand a lick of what the other was saying.

Dalvin pulled up to an abandoned warehouse. On the way down here I could not help but wonder, was I going to see Panther. Was he in there waiting on me? And if he was, would this truly be the last time we saw each other face to face without being separated by a thick sheet of glass.

I followed Dalvin inside. Some baby faced looking thug that was no older than sixteen allowed us in. In the first few seconds I realized that I should not have been here. Panther was nowhere in sight. The place stunk with dead fish guts that were lying all over the ground. Flies buzzed in and out and around our faces. And Dalvin and his boys had some man in there half-beaten to death, tied up to a chair in the middle of the room.

The man yelled out. "Y'all couldn't do the job yourself, huh. Weak motherfuckers. Had to go and get a bitch to help. Pus-ass niggas. Let me out of this motherfucker."

The flies amplified the irritation I was feeling right now. I slapped some away from my face then grabbed Dalvin and pulled him to the side. "Is that who I think it is, Dalvin?" I whispered. "If Panther ain't here, why the fuck did you bring me here?"

"Wait a minute," the man said smiling. "I know that ass. Yeah, I remember. That's a nice, soft ass right there. I was just on it the other night. Felt good, too. Let me guess. You here so I can finish the job, baby."

I walked up on the sick, old man, reached into my purse and sprayed his ass with the mace. "Finish this, motherfucker."

The man started choking as though he couldn't catch his breath. His eyes twisted in the back of his head. And his body jerked back and forth as if he couldn't control himself.

What the fuck. I stepped back.

Dalvin grabbed me and pulled me back even farther. He said, "Finish that motherfucker, big Rick."

Big Rick wasted no time as he pulled a gun from his waste and put three in the man's chest.

I was used to the sound of guns going off, but today they shook me. My eyes were shut tight. I felt out of place. Outside of my element. This lifestyle was not for me anymore. I walked out and headed for my car, refusing to say anything about what just happened. I was through with Dalvin. And just like that rapist, I never wanted to see Dalvin again.

‍ഌ 15 ‍ങ

Sandra

T hank you for lunch," I told Dennis.

"My pleasure, my lady," he said with a stuck up posture.

I said, "The contract looks good. Now I just need some acts to sign it."

"They'll come in time. You don't get rich in one night. But the night you do start earning money, every night after that starts to look much better."

He laughed at his own corny analogy, and I pretended to be amused by tossing him a fake hee-hee. I wasn't about to fuck up. Everything was already going smooth. Outside our window, skies were clear. I was hoping that it was sign of something good would happen. I mean, I had my contract printed, and now, I was sipping on some Chardonnay after eating my favorite Chicken pasta from the Cheesecake Factory. Of course, Dennis was paying so that made it even better.

He said, "How did it go Saturday night? Heard you girls had a blast. Did you find the talent you were looking for?"

"Not really. I hooked up with a few producers and djs. But there was one rapper that I liked by the name of Streetwise."

Dennis was sipping on a glass of Chardonnay, and pulled it from his face like it had a bug in it. "Streetwise," he said. "And how many years has he done?"

I shook my head. "That's not nice, Dennis."

"I'm sorry. I'm just having a little fun. Anyway, is he willing to sign with you?"

"I don't know. He took my card. Just have to wait and see."

"And if he doesn't, oh well. There are a lot of gansters who wouldn't mind you making some money off of them."

I took a sip of my wine. "Stop it, Dennis."

"All right, all right. But speaking of gangsters, I have to tell you, I spoke with David Greene of the D.A.'s office, and he said that they're going after your boyfriend pretty hard."

I had to put my glass down because I almost choked on my drink. "What?"

Dennis wiped his hands and mouth after he placed his food off to the side. He leaned in close to me.

The waiter broke between us and asked if we needed anything. Dennis told him only the check. After the waiter walked off, I stared Denis down with an impatient glare. He knew I wanted an explanation to what the fuck was going on.

He said, "The maid and a few workers were there when the argument took place between Panther and Mr. Alden. Multi-million-dollar deal falls, the state says it's enough of a motive."

My eyes were buried into the contents of the leftover food on my plate. I was broken up inside. "So why are you just now telling me this? Why didn't you tell me this morning?"

"Because, you were so excited about the contract and everything, and I didn't want to you to lose focus on the relevant issue."

My chest tightened, and I could feel myself getting ready to let loose on Dennis. I only kept cool because we were in public, took a deep breath before I unleashed on him. "What the hell do you mean, relevant issue? Panther is very relevant to my life, Dennis. You just don't know how relevant he is."

Dennis leaned back in his chair, gazed at me with suspicion. "I hope it's not too much. The way things are looking, he may not be able to help you with anything ever again. And that may not be the thing that you want to hear, but the probability of something like this happening is always greater when you live the lifestyle. You work in law. You know how it is. I'm just sorry that it had to be your boyfriend on the losing end. We all make life decisions. This is the life I've chosen, and evidently, he has chosen his. You see where mine has gotten me, and where his is about to take him."

I nervously tapped on the table with my fork. It seemed as if everything was at the edge of falling on my head and I had no way to escape it. I never thought that it could get this serious. I never saw Panther's life, our lives, taking this kind of blow.

"You don't know Panther," I told Dennis. "He'll be fine. I truly believe that. And I believe in him, too."

"Maybe so," Dennis said. "But life doesn't always turn out the way you believe it should."

I picked up my glass and hoped that the alcohol would numb the irritation. The waiter came back with the check. Dennis spoke to him with the usual snobbish demeanor. As if the situation with my man was an afterthought that hardly phased him. And I could barely look up from my plate.

"I'm ready to go," I said. I grabbed my purse and walked off, not caring to wait for, or hear Dennis' response.

Inside the car, we were both quiet. I had nothing to say, and could've cared less for Dennis to say anything to me. He'd said too much. There wasn't a lot of remorse in his tone either. Talking about he chose his life and Panther chose his. Who was he kidding? The way I saw it, Dennis and almost every lawyer on earth were paid criminals.

I could still remember how crazy it was when I first met Panther. My car had broken down on the turnpike in the middle of the day and nobody would stop. I called Dennis to let him know that I would be late coming back. He made a stink about it and I hung up. I wasn't about to deal with his shit when I had my own to deal with. Then a black BMW pulled up behind me and out jumped Parish Coles, one of finest men I had ever laid eyes on. He was clean from head to toe, had on a sharp, tailor-cut suit and snakeskin shoes. In my mind, all I could think was this had to be an athlete, a Miami Dolphin or something. He moved with confidence.

"You okay?" Panther asked. "Are you hurt?"

"No", I said. "Just my baby."

He went under the hood and started checking all of those wires and engine parts. I was kind of shocked because he was so clean, yet didn't mind getting his hands dirty. Definitely my kind of man. Not a pretty boy that spent more time getting manicures than he did fixing things.

But then again, I thought Panther was acting like any man in this situation. When it came to pretty woman, men would roll around in dirt to get a crack at the pussy.

"Excuse me," Panther said, and reached for his cell phone. Within five minutes he had a tow truck there. His mechanic, who was also a tow truck owner, named Big Joe, told me what the problem was and how long it would take to fix it.

"Wait a minute," I said. "How much is this going to cost?"

Big Joe turned to Panther then Panther turned to me. Panther said, "Some company for lunch."

I knew that I was dealing with a baller. Maybe even a player, which I usually didn't waste my time with, but I figured I had nothing to lose. I was going to have lunch with a fine man while my car got worked on at no cost to me. What else could I ask for? I agreed and we were on our way.

Panther took me to a spot where live jazz music was played while we ate. The restaurant was immaculate, the food divine. I was feeling this man and I had only known him for forty-five minutes. I wanted to get to know more of him. Panther asked what my favorite song was, and I told him it was 'You're just too good to be true' by Lauren Hill. Two minutes later, Panther spoke to our waiter and the featured saxophonist came to our table and serenaded me with my favorite song. I almost melted. He grabbed my hand and a tingle ran up and down my spine. I couldn't remember the last time I felt this way about a man.

When we were done with lunch, the car was waiting on us, and it started up like it was brand new. Panther gave me Big Joe's card if I had any future problems, then gave me his number so we could have future conversations. I was sure I was going to use it, but I didn't tell him that.

"But why place such a good time on hold," Panther said. "How about we go jet skiing."

Where did this man come from, I thought? Cupid must've broken my car down so he could shoot me in the ass. Panther was like a lover's dream.

"I got to work," I said. "I called my boss and he didn't sound too happy. But I let him know that I wasn't happy with his tone by clicking on him. I'll be lucky to have a job once I get back."

Panther said, "I'll follow you back to work."

"Why?"

"Because I want to make sure that you'll be all right."

I agreed and Panther was right behind me. When we got there, Panther walked me inside. Every female's head in the building did a double-take. I pretended not to see them as Panther walked a step behind me.

"Where's your boss?" Panther said.

I pointed to Dennis' door and Panther walked in without knocking. Back then, I didn't even pull shit like that. Panther walked out as calm as he went in. He came to me and planted a kiss on my forehead. He said, "I'm sure everything will be fine. Enjoy your day."

I watched his fine ass strut out like he owned the firm. I knew I was going to give him a call.

Then Dennis came storming out his office and straight to my desk. Oh God, I thought. What had Panther said to him?

"Are you all right?" Dennis asked like he worked for the Fire-Rescue or something. "I heard your car just gave out on you. You're not hurt, are you?"

I shook my head baffled. "No, Dennis. Everything is fine."

"Okay," he said. "Let me know if you need anything."

I nodded and Dennis hurried back to his office. I didn't know what happened between Panther and Dennis in that room. But I knew who I was calling later on that night.

"Did you hear me?"

"Huh."

"I said let me know if you need anything," Dennis said.

I had snapped out of my daydream and saw that Dennis and I were a few blocks away from the firm. "Yeah, yeah," I told him, just so he could shut the hell up. Ever since that day, and that meeting Panther had with him, Dennis never fucked with me on a jackass level again. For all the money and power he had, I was the one that got all the respect. I owned him.

"You know who Keith Grimes is?" Dennis asked.

I looked at him like he was stupid, then turned back to the front. "Of course I know who Keith Grimes is."

Dennis said, "Do you know him personally?"

I laughed. "I wish. I probably wouldn't be scrounging for artists like I do now. Keith Grimes is the man. I can only hope I get on his level some day."

"Well, maybe I can set up something between you two."

I almost didn't believe what I heard. I said, "Excuse me."

Dennis said, "Keith Grimes is a client of ours now, and I met up with him last week. Maybe I can set up a meeting."

"What do you mean maybe, Dennis? Set up the meeting."

Dennis smiled proudly. "I'll see what I can do."

"Ooh, please," I begged. "Dennis, I'll be so grateful to you. It would mean a whole lot to me."

"No problem," Dennis said as he chuckled. "I just want you to be happy. I want you to understand that I can still be of help to you, even though you think that I'm not."

"No, you were right," I said. "You have to do your job. I understand. And I'm glad that you understand things can be a little hard for me right now. But now I know where your heart is, and I can't be mad at you for that."

Dennis threw up his hand and I gave him five with his corny ass. He was hooking me up when there weren't too may people around that I could count on for that. And not having Panther there, I could use whoever was worth using. Besides, Panther was a winner. He'd be back, and when he was, I'd be strong as ever.

ಹ 16 ಆ

Rachel

A ndrea, my supervisor, gave me a look like I punched her in the nose and she couldn't get me back. This was nothing new to me because we clashed often. Her personality was as dull as a brick building. Today she had on an all black, grandma-style outfit, with shoulder pads in her blouse, ruffles at the cuff, and a long, black skirt that grazed her ashy ankles. Her glasses sat at the edge of her nose while she read my report about yesterday. I pretended to be engrossed in the pictures of her adopted niece and nephew just so she wouldn't notice that I was pissed about sitting there for thirty minutes. The plaques and accolades that covered the walls became annoying. Made her forty-five-year-old, boring ass, seem as if she was a saint instead of the old hag that I knew she was.

"Is this all you had to say?" Andrea said after she set down the report.

"Yes," I told her, "everything's right there."

"Good," she said, "because they've decided to try Ace as an adult."

"What?" I couldn't believe what I was hearing.

Andrea took off her glasses. "From your report the other day, we sent that to the D.A., and they've decided that A.J. is, and always has been a problem."

"But, but...I mean, he's young. He didn't know what he was doing. He was provoked. What do you expect? His mother was on crack. He had no way to eat. Didn't you also read that in my report?"

"Yes, but—"

"So why isn't he being given the benefit of the doubt? Why haven't you or Darnell intervened to help him?"

"Darnell has gone up to Tallahassee. And it's not my decision to make."

"But you make recommendations. Why didn't you recommend him to stay to undergo more evaluation?"

"It wouldn't have made a difference."

"Why not?"

"Because the D.A. had already made his decision. The report only stopped him from getting criticized by the protesters. I'm sorry, Rachel. I understand that you wanted to help Ace, but the reality is you can't save everybody."

Too irritated to continue arguing, I just shook my head. It was like nobody cared about the work I had done or the improvements that my boys had shown. Sometimes, I wondered if Andrea really cared for these kids at all, like she claimed to have cared for her adopted kids, or was it all a show to cover up what was inside her rigid, cold heart.

I said, "But Andrea, you didn't have to show him that report."

She laughed. Clamped her dark, wrinkled hands together. "Rachel, just because another individual didn't do things like they were supposed to doesn't mean that I have to follow. Like I said, you can't save the world. Some people have to learn to save themselves."

Yeah, like your selfish ass is doing, I thought. I said, "Is that all?"

And like an old grandma, Andrea nodded with her eyes closed.

As I was walking out, Andrea called to me and said, "I know you're going to meet with Sam now."

I said, "Yeah. And..."

"And I don't want to lose your head."

"Oh, I'll be fine, Andrea. I'm not the one who's lost my head."

I slammed the door before Andrea could comment, and on the way to my office, I asked a guard to bring Sam in. I wasn't wasting any time.

After a few minutes Sam knocked on my door and I called him in. Knowing how I worked, the guard stood outside the door. Sam didn't bother waiting for me to offer him a seat. He strolled to the chair like a broke ass pimp, licked his lips like I was the sloppy joe he had at lunch.

"Mrs. Baxter," he said, "I was hoping I'd get to see you again."

"Sam." I paused before I cussed him out. I said, "I'll get right to the point. Your antics in the past couple of days in my classroom cannot be tolerated."

He threw up his hands in innocence, his face drowning in guilt. "What are you talking about?"

"You know exactly what I'm talking about. Don't try to play me, and don't try to deny it. All I want to know is why."

A smile emerged over Sam's face as if he was dying to get it out. "I'm sorry about fighting, Mrs. Baxter, but what was I supposed to do? He jumped on me."

"Bullshit, Sam. You started with him. Taunting and provoking him, what did you expect?"

My blood was pumping with anger. I calmed myself when I noticed Sam throw up a surprised look. If anyone else were to spot how I acted, I might've been the one handcuffed and thrown into a cell.

"My apologies," I said. "I didn't mean to curse—"

"No, it's okay," Sam said. "I should be the one apologizing. I didn't mean to upset you. I was trying to make you smile."

Sam's tone was serious enough. His expressions seemed genuine. Either that or he was a great actor, which probably wasn't too far from the truth since he was addicted to drama. But I didn't get a laugh, or a wannabe LL Cool J, lip smacking routine from him. Hell, even the arrogance was gone, and some humbleness had settled in. Maybe I was wrong about Sam. I felt stupid about thinking the worst. I almost forgot that he was just a child himself.

I told him, "I can believe that you didn't mean it, Sam. But you can't keep doing things like this. If you don't respect people you could get hurt. And you might also end up getting transferred to somewhere you don't want to be. So I suggest you stay away from trouble, or else the trouble will just stay with you."

"I know". Sam's eyes saddened. "Just don't be mad at me. Like I said, I was only trying to make you smile. You're a beautiful person, and I like seeing your smile."

Sam's vulnerability opened me up, and tears were on the edge of breaking free from my eyes.

"You do make me smile, Sam. And I'm not mad at you."

The corners of Sam's lips curled up as his face lit up with joy. "Really. You're not mad at me?"

I smiled. "Really. I'm not mad."

"Good, because I plan on making you laugh and smile whenever I can."

"And I want you to. Laughing is good for all of us."

"And speaking of laughs," Sam said as he inched up closer to the desk, "what happened to that scrawny, little boy that was trying to fight me?"

I wasn't amused by Sam's ridiculing of Ace. Sam still had a lot of growing up to do. I said, "That scrawny, little boy's name is A.J. and he has one of the biggest hearts in the world. Unfortunately, I was told that he is being transferred upstate, where he will be tried as an adult."

Sam leaned back in his chair, his face bottled up with tension. "Damn, I feel sorry for him". A smile widened over Sam's cheeks. "Now he's really going to get his ass whipped."

I let out a frustrated breath. "Goodbye, Sam."

I called for the guard.

"But—but wait," Sam pleaded. "I was only playing."

"I know. That's why it's time for you to leave."

When the guard snapped on the cuffs, Sam's face sunk in despair. "It's okay, Ms. Baxter. I understand. And I understand something that you just won't get."

I crossed my arms. "Oh, yeah. What's that?"

The guard pulled Sam through the door, and just as Sam's face fell from my sight, he yelled, "The same thing make you laugh, Ms. Baxter, also make you cry."

What did Sam mean by that? 'The same thing that makes you laugh can also make you cry.' Before I could ask the door slammed shut.

ஐ 17 ©

Deidra

D amn, girl," Shakita complained when I pushed her through the house and straight to the back. "What's your problem?"

"Girl, I've been doing nappy heads all day," I said.

"Well, you haven't done mine." Shakita put her head down in the sink.

"You're right," I said. "I haven't touched your nappy head yet."

"Ha-ha. Whatever. Anyway, girl, you haven't chilled with your girl in a while. I'm your best friend. Why are you rushing me?"

"Because I'm tired."

She raised her head out the sink and gazed at my reflection through the mirror. She said, "Too tired to talk about that rapist man."

I didn't bother to respond. Shakita followed me as I walked back to the front.

She said, "Girl, the whole hood knows about it. Why didn't you tell me?"

"Because I didn't want the whole hood to know."

"Hee-hee," Shakita teased. We plopped down on the couch while I waited for her mouth to start flapping. "You know I'm so happy that you're my homegirl. Everybody's saying that you are straight thugged out. You got the hoes and niggas over there shook."

"Shook for what?"

"Because of how you chose to do that nigga. They say that nigga is at the bottom of the Okeechobee River with a broom stuck in his ass. Girl, that shit is gangsta."

"Who told you that?"

"Girl, everybody was talking about it."

"Motherfuckers," I yelled. I was hot. What kind of dummies was I dealing with?

"Girl, why are you stressing?" Shakita looked at me like I was the crazy one. I was thinking that I should fuck her hair up just for being stupid.

I said, "Why do you think I'm stressing? I got the hood talking about I had somebody killed and my sister lives there, my brothers and my mama. You don't think I should be stressing?"

"Dee, ain't nothing gonna happen to you. Like I said, that nigga's at the bottom of the river. Ain't nobody thinking about his nasty, raping ass."

Sometimes Shakita could be real ignorant, and I questioned what made *her* my best friend. But now I had another problem to deal with. I had to find a way to straighten out this mess before it turned into a disaster. It was crazy. Trying to save my life had only made things worse. Now my name was being used. The only way to stop it was to let it be known that I wasn't having it. I picked up the phone.

Shakita said, "What are you doing?"

"Calling Panther's homeboy so I can get an explanation and get this handled."

"And how are you going to do that?"

"By cussing his ass out."

Dalvin's phone rang. And rang.

"Just don't be all night," Shakita said. "I need my do done."

I was about to curse at Shakita, but I tried to stay cool for when Dalvin picked up. But his phone kept ringing. And finally, I got his voicemail.

I said, "Dalvin, please give me a call. This is Deidra. You have the number. Bye."

I put the phone down and Shakita studied me.

"Ooh," she said. "You probably hurt his feelings with all that cussing."

"Shut up," I said, "before I hurt more than your feelings."

She threw her hands up in surrender. "Touchy."

I was antsy and couldn't calm myself. Had to get this heat on me to cool down. But waiting on Dalvin was killing me. It was amazing how in the last couple days Dalvin had been on my ass like a pantyliner, yet when I really wanted to see him, he couldn't be found fast enough like a bottle of painkillers. And the more I thought about it, the more stressed I became. So I went and started on Shakita's hair. Turned on some videos while waiting for the phone to ring. Two hours passed and Shakita's do was done. She shot me a bigger tip than usual and I was thankful for it. I knew exactly why she was my best friend. She was one of the few people in the world that understood me, like Panther. It's almost been a week since I last saw him and I was missing him like crazy. He was who I needed to see.

Dalvin still hadn't called but I didn't sweat it. I already had a plan in mind. Threw on some sneakers, a short set, and drove down to my old hood with Shakita. This was going to be handled tonight.

When we got around my mama's, the police were crawling all over the place. That was a regular thing, so there was no reason to sweat. But I went and checked on what was the haps. Shakita and I had to fight through a crowd. I spotted Toya in the front and she looked at me like I was about to cap her.

"Girl, what's wrong with you?" I said.

She looked over in the direction of the police car. When I saw Luke's dreads and Joe's nappy fro sticking up from the back of the police car I almost lost it. I was about to scream. I tried desperately to keep my cool when I stepped up to the police. They were on the sidewalk laughing like a couple of drinking buddies at happy hour. I stepped in and broke up the party.

"Excuse me, officer," I said.

They threw me some annoyed looks. "Can I help you?" a short, fat cop with red hair said.

"Yes, officer, those are my brothers in the backseat. What's the problem?"

The cop said, "There is no problem, ma'am. Your brothers here beat up on this gentleman, and they are now being charged with assault."

They were talking about Raheem. He was standing off to the side with his mother at his arm. His white t-shirt was covered with blood as he held an icepack to the side of his face.

"But officer," I said, "How do you know that gentleman didn't assault them first. Why isn't he being arrested?"

"Look, lady we responded to a call from his mother. She said they assaulted her son for no reason and your brothers will be taken into custody. You can come down to the station if you like and have them bailed out, but you better believe that we are taking them in."

The cop turned from me and back to his partner, as if I wasn't even there. I wasn't going to get anywhere with them, so I strolled over to Raheem and his mother, Audrey.

I said, "How are you, Audrey?"

At first she acted if she hadn't seen me, then looked at me and rolled her eyes. "God is good," she said. "All the time, God is good."

I had a feeling that her hypocrite ass was going to act smart. "Listen, Audrey, you've known us for a long time. And boys get into things. But you know they don't mean to."

"Well," Audrey said, still staring off into the streetlights, "they should've thought about that before they beat up my boy."

"And I'm sure that they're sorry about it. But we don't really have to let the law get—"

"They ain't sorry about nothing. You see my boy. They tried to kill him. Now they'll feel sorry for it."

Audrey was that loudmouth on the block that no one could stand, and yet now, she didn't want to talk at all. Raheem was shook out of his sneakers. I could see the tears well up in his eyes whenever he took a sneak look at me.

"Hold on," I said. "What happened out here, Raheem?"

"Don't say nothing," Audrey told her son. "You know anything you say can be used against you in a court o' law."

What a nasty bitch. Audrey knew her son caused just as much shit around there as anybody else. Now because she wanted to play hard, I had to scrap up every bit of change that I didn't have to bail my brothers out. I should've blackened her eye to match her son's own.

I said, "Audrey, are you going to try to talk about this?"

She kept her gaze away from me as if I had never spoken. The old Dee would've stomped a pothole in her ass. This was one of the reasons why I had to move, and why I wanted my brothers and sisters with me. Shit like this was what ended up happening.

"All right," I said. "Fine, Audrey. I thought we could handle this like some civilized adults, but you're too nasty to be civilized. But I'm not even worried about you. That stank ass attitude of yours will get you one day."

I walked away. Just before I stepped back through the crowd, in the slightest sound, I heard a voice say, "She can't be calling me nasty. That man should've raped her".

I wasn't sure how it happened, but I saw myself slapping the shit out of Audrey's head and face. She screamed, and I swung. She was running and I was kicking. My arms were held back and I almost dragged the people with me as I lunged my foot at Audrey's ass. She ran off and hid behind the crowd, everybody hollering and going crazy, talking shit. Steamed beyond belief, I could barely keep my composure. I told her that I would beat the hell out of her and I said it loud enough for my whole hood to hear. At that moment, I was slammed to the ground and handcuffed. And knocked back into reality. I realized the mess I made for myself. The crowd was with me, cussing at the police and chanting "Leave Dee alone". But none of that mattered. I was shoved into one of the cop cars. The crowd continued shouting and pumped their fists at the sky. "Leave Dee alone". I was already in over my head. I didn't have bail money, and if I did, there was no one to help collect it. Panther was gone. When I scanned the crowd, I spotted my mother with Tracy standing at her side, my mother shaking her head while tears flowed down Tracy's face. I whispered I'm sorry to Tracy, but I wasn't sure if she noticed. The car started to peel away as we made eye contact. Then the chants of the crowd peeled away, too. I had no one near when I needed them the most. Even my heart deserted me and sank down into my gut. The tears that I was trying to hold back eventually ran off too as they slowly rolled away from my eyes.

ಬ 18 ಚ

Sandra

I t was feeling like one of those days. My period was on, I hadn't had
dick in like forever, Nisha called in sick, and I was swamped in
work. If Dennis didn't have the hook up with Keith Grimes, I would've
ditched work, too. But I had to stay on his good side until I got what I
wanted. I even went to the mall last night, picked up some cute outfits,
which showed off all of my good sides. Had on a baby-blue Donna
Karen suit that was made to turn heads, thanks to its pronouncement of
my sugar brown legs and plump ass. Dennis stopped by my desk a few
times to "check some documents", and I was sure that he read more
than what was on a piece of paper. I had ways of getting what I wanted.
And just before I went to lunch, Dennis called me into the conference
room.

"Sandy, you've heard of Keith Grimes, haven't you?" Dennis said
as he introduced me to Keith Grimes.

I almost couldn't keep my mouth shut and my temperature cool.
Something a woman should never do is lose her cool in front of a man.
But this wasn't just any man. Shit, I didn't know if he was even a man.
He was like—like—like Superman. Just picture the finest man you've
ever seen in your life. Now picture him with a lot of money. That was
Keith Grimes.

I snapped back to my cool, calm self before I fainted. All I had to
do was picture myself on his level and he was a regular man to me.

And a regular man I had always been able to conquer. I said, "Pleased to meet you, Mr. Grimes."

"The pleasure is mine," Keith said in a voice that wrapped me up in the power of his presence.

"And in more ways than one," Keith continued. "Dennis told me you were talented, but he failed to comment on how fine you were. I ought to cut him off for being so blind."

I blushed like a freshman being asked to the Prom by the captain of the football team. I offered my thanks, tried looking away before Keith noticed I was trapped in his gravitational pull, and my eyes falling to his crotch for a brief moment. And it was only brief because I felt his eyes still on me. What had this man done? I couldn't break the fascination of being face-to-face with him.

"Oh, she's a very beautiful woman," Dennis jumped in and saved me. "Her talent by far outreaches any man's expectations."

"Is that so?" Keith said. He was studying every facet of my frame.

Thank God for women's instincts. The new outfit was on point. I scored without saying a word. But still, this was about business. I had to prove that I was worth Keith's investment.

I said, "That is so, Mr. Grimes. I have only been in business for a few months but already have a few promising artists that can basically change the game. And bring in some large sums of profit while they're at it."

Keith shot a smile that lit up my insides. He turned to Dennis and said, "The longer I'm around this young lady, the more I grow to dig her style. She has that something all right." He turned back to me and his stare seemed to grab hold of my soul. "And I want to see some more of that something. Here's my card. Give me a call on Saturday and we'll hook up."

"Looks like we're hooked up," I said as I took the card. "Would you like to meet with my artists too? His flow is nasty, kinda like the late, great Biggie Smalls. I even have an up and coming artist that has that Tupac vibe. He's—"

"Not necessary," Keith said. "We'll be talking business, so you should come on your own."

"Oh, okay. Well, I'll just bring his demo so you can—"

"Sounds good." Keith cut me off again. "Listen," he said, "I don't mean to be rude, but I do have an engagement that I gotta make in about a half, so it's goodbye for now, but I'll be looking to hear from you on Saturday."

"Uh… no problem. Thank you for your time." I gave him my hand again.

Keith kissed me softly on the cheek. His lips were sweeter than chocolate. He said, "The pleasure was all mine."

I turned to the door and Dennis started bragging to Keith about a big investment that he cashed in on. My presence wasn't needed when I couldn't speak on terms of money like they could. But I didn't mind. The best thing that could ever happen had just happened. I was about to do business with one of the biggest names in the music industry. My life was about to be redone, and I had to put all my priorities in order. The first thing I had to do was call my artist. The one responsible for initiating this change.

"PrimeTime, what's up? This is Sandy."

He yawned over the phone like it was twelve midnight instead of noon. "Hey… Sandy… What's up?"

I laughed. "I hope you are."

Yawn. "Yeah, yeah. I'm up. What's poppin?"

I said, "Tell me you have a new demo of the songs you just did."

"You know I do."

"Good, because I need it like two hours ago. I'm meeting with Keith Grimes on Saturday."

The phone rattled on the other end. I must've had PrimeTime wide awake by now. He said, "Keith Grimes who?"

Obviously the excitement had swirled around in his stomach too. I said, "Keith Grimes Hussein." I had to laugh at his silly behind. "What other Keith Grimes do you know?"

"You—you mean Keith Grimes—Keith Grimes?"

"Yes, PrimeTime. Keith Grimes, Keith Grimes. I need your demo, and we have to go over a few things. Did you sign your contract yet?"

"No, but I'm going to."

"Good, because this might mean some big things for us. I'm arranging a meeting tomorrow night before I meet with Keith. I need your demo done and ready, and the contract signed. If you have any questions about the contract, you need to ask now."

PrimeTime said no. I was relieved. Everything was going smooth. Now all I had to do was convince Keith that my artist and I were worth his time and money. It would be the biggest test that I ever faced in my life, but I was ready for it. My status was about to change. My future was happening right now, staring me in the face, and I wasn't about to back down. I've never believed in the word can't. Aunt Mabel had done too much in her life for me to think that I wasn't capable. If only she understood just how much this meant to me. She's only thought in terms of a man providing for a woman because a woman does so much already. But hopefully she would see. Hopefully everybody, including Panther, would be a witness to a young, black woman doing it. And doing it all on her own.

ഏ 19 ഓ

Rachel

After lunch, I was back in Andrea's office for the second day. All this private meeting stuff grew on my nerves because I could've spent this time being productive with the boys. I had a new agenda for them. Since the last few days in the class were stressful, I decided to bring in a few board games, Chess, Life, and Monopoly. This way the boys didn't have to concentrate on any painful memories they didn't want to talk about, and still have a good time with learning how to function in society.

But Andrea had other plans. I could do without any more bad news, like another transfer, or even worse, one of my boys had hurt someone else. I mean I knew the boys did wrong at times, but how else were the boys supposed to learn to do right if there weren't examples and role models to show them how. That was a part of my job. I once thought it was Andrea's too, but now it seemed as if she no longer believed in second chances.

She said, "Rachel, I don't know how to say this, but something has come up and I have to make a decision."

I blew out a frustrated breath. "Which one of the boys is it this time?"

Andrea fiddled with some papers on her desk. She said, "It's not one of the boys this time. It's you."

I was confused. "What about me?"

Andrea grabbed the papers on her desk and stacked them neatly as if they weren't already straight. "You're suspended for two weeks with pay. During that time I want you to relax, go away if you can, and get your mind off the boys. It's been causing you a lot of stress and—"

"What stress? What are you talking about? I'm fine. I don't need to get away."

"I think you do."

"And can you tell me why you think this?"

Andrea grabbed the papers, turned them my way, and clasped her hands together. She said, "Sam came into my office today, said he didn't feel comfortable with you, told me that you cursed at him, that you made threatening remarks while he was in your office—

"Oh my God, Andrea. Are you going to believe that?"

Andrea snatched up Sam's statement. I stayed quiet, boiling over with anger as I waited on her response. With her glasses sitting at the bridge of her nose, Andrea read through the statement. She turned it to me and ran her finger over a specific part.

"Mrs. Baxter told me if didn't respect people I could get hurt and be transferred."

"That's the truth, Andrea. He needs to respect people."

"Mrs. Baxter threatened me," Andrea continued as she turned the report back around. "She said that my trouble would get me in trouble. I felt as if she didn't like me and was favoring the other boy. Her tone was hostile and threatening. She even cursed at me. I don't feel comfortable around Mrs. Baxter. I believe she brings her personal problems to work and does not act in a professional manner. I am not sure how she acts with the other boys, but if it is possible I would like to be changed to another counselor."

Andrea set the statement down and clasped her hands. "What do you have to say to defend yourself?"

Speaking of tones, I thought, Andrea's sounded as if I was guilty and there was no reason for me to defend myself. I said, "It's not true."

"Which part?"

"All of it."

"But you stated that it was true that you told him that he could get transferred."

I blew out a breath in disbelief. That little bastard, he was fucking with me, playing another stupid game, but now I was a victim of its outcome. And my only defense was my word. I couldn't believe all of this was happening, but now I knew, I had to be a professional, no matter what. Never again could I treat any of the boys like a family member or friend. But that also went against my purpose for being a counselor. How could I say I wanted to get to know my boys and help them, but could never befriend them? How would they trust me if I wasn't a friend? And how would they trust me if to them I was just another person who got paid off of their misery?

I put my emotions in check before speaking. I said, "Listen, Andrea. I admit I said those things, but not in the way that Sam described them. I know that sounds crazy, but Sam...Sam has some issues that need to be psychoanalyzed. My comments were not threatening in any kind of way. I apologize if it seemed that way to him, but I assure you that I have always been and continue to act in the most professional manner."

Andrea nodded, "So you admit that you said these things to him."

"Yes, but not in the way that he says."

"What about bringing your personal problems to work?"

"I don't know what he meant by that. I think he is a disturbed, confused young man. He may have played it off as if he had no problems, but with these allegations, it's obvious that the boy needs some help."

Andrea poked her lips out, weighing her thoughts. She said, "Maybe so. Maybe Sam does need some help, and I commend you for recognizing this. I've heard your side of the story and his, and I still believe that it is best that you take this time off—"

"But Andrea—"

"I believe you have been doing a good job since you have been here, but if Sam has a problem, I believe it should've been detected before he came to me with these allegations. That is why the state hired you, to sniff out these problems amongst our youth so they can try to stay on the right path. I need you take some time off, and when you get back, I recommend that you take some classes that will enhance your faculties so that we can give our children the best assistance that we can give provide. Are we clear, Rachel?"

I couldn't believe what I was hearing. I must have been talking to myself. Despite what I told Andrea, I was still being tossed to the curb. I could feel the tears drown my eyelids, but I didn't care. I wanted

Andrea to know what this felt like. To pour your heart out in innocence and still get rejected, tossed aside like a torn candy wrapper. I lost all respect for her. And I doubt if she cared. The reality was that after two weeks, I would come back unemployed. In this profession, that was how it usually worked. There were thousands of psychology and sociology graduates clawing at a chance for this job. Andrea wouldn't even get a paper cut giving me my walking papers.

I said, "Yes, Mrs. Anderson. We're clear. When does it start?"

She clasped her dark, wrinkled fingers together, looked straight through my tears and said, "Immediately."

The tears streamed down just as fast as I raced out of that place.

ೲ 20 ೮ಃ

Deidra

It is funny that with all the drama surrounding my life, I had never been locked up. It was an accomplishment that I could say I was proud of. Sitting in a dirty ass cell with only one toilet, I could understand why. The air condition was set to ice cold. My master bedroom was bigger than the whole cell. It took every drop of patience that I could build up to keep from screaming or letting another tear loose. I had grown use to being in control of my situations. I felt as out of place as a rapper doing country music. All of the other girls, my cellmates, seemed right at home. They gaggled and gossiped about seeing this and that person once they got sent upstate. And I prayed that I would never get the chance to be that friendly with any of them to want the same.

There were six of us in the cell and only four beds. I didn't care because I didn't plan on sleeping. I still felt this was a bad nightmare that I would soon wake from.

"Hey, new booty," one of the girls called out. I didn't think she was talking to me, so I acted like I didn't hear. Then she stepped away from her flock of chickens and stood a few feet in front of me.

"Hey," she said. "Are you deaf, honey? Do you un-der-stand sign lan-guage?" She screwed up her hands and face as if she were retarded. The bunch behind her laughed.

I gave her one good 'don't fuck with me' look before I rolled my eyes off.

"Hmm," the girl said. "Hoe must think she's too good to talk to anybody."

"Well, maybe she don't want to talk to you, Jeannie," said another inmate that was about three times the size of the girl named Jeannie. "I mean look at her. She is kinda cute. Got a nice, thick body and a fat ass. If she can get all the attention in the world, why the hell would she want to talk to you?"

The bunch busted out laughing and Jeannie spun back around toward them. "What you trying to say, Tiny? I ain't cute?"

"Girl, sit your crack epidemic ass down," Tiny yelled. "Hell no, you ain't cute."

While scratching her ass, Jeannie strolled back over to the rest of the cackling chickens. I kept my stare glued to the bars, acting as if I hadn't noticed them or their conversation.

"Yeah, new booty is very cute," Tiny said. She stepped away from the bunch slowly. "I bet she's used to getting that pussy beat in."

Underneath my calm exterior, I was burning inside. I swore that if the bitch got any closer, I was going to stomp the stretch marks out of that ass.

"Ain't no dick around here," Tiny said as she stepped in just a few feet away from my face. "But we won't have a problem taming that fat ass."

"Bitch, I'll fuck you up," I screamed, jumped up and tightened my fists as hard as I could. My heart and breath were running about one hundred miles an hour. Tiny stood stout and King Kong-like, her fists also tight and ready. We stared each other down, itching for the other person to scratch.

"Tiny, you know better than that," a woman that looked about my mother's age called out. "That young lady hasn't disrespected you, so don't you do it to her."

"Shut up, Ms. Eleanor," Tiny shot back. "You always getting into stuff that don't concern you."

"Woman, I am not your child. You know you can't talk to me that way."

Tiny waved Ms. Eleanor off and strolled back to her bunch.

Ms. Eleanor stepped away from the card game that she was playing with another middle aged inmate. She took up the seat next to me.

"You all right," she asked.

"I don't care to make friends," I said. "Thank you for assistance and all, but I can take care of myself."

"I know you can," she said. "You made that obvious when you stood up to Tiny. But there isn't anything wrong with being human. That's all I'm doing. You can't let nobody in here take that away from you."

"Well, I won't. And I'm also not going to take you from your card game, so you can go ahead and get back to it."

She laughed as if I was joking. She asked, "What's your name, young sister?"

I turned to her, allowing my eyes to help her understand. "Like I said, I don't want any friends, so there's no need to have my name, right?"

I rolled my eyes to let her know that I didn't care for her response either. She let out another laugh. I guess I embarrassed her and that was her way of blowing it off. Good for her. She had her way of controlling her situations, and I had mine.

"I don't need your name, sister," Ms. Eleanor said. "And I don't have to be your friend. But for now, thanks to these bars, we are in the same world. All I want to tell you is in the world, inside or outside of these bars, you don't always have to use your hands to win a battle. It's always your choice."

And as fast she came to my bench, she left and returned to her card game. I appreciated the fact that she was a woman of few words. And those words clung to me. I didn't feel like I was beneath her, like my mother used to make me feel. Maybe that was the reason Tiny hadn't confronted her. Maybe Ms. Eleanor could so easily command respect from others because she gave it so freely.

"Deidra Williams," a guard called. "Let's go. You made bail."

I looked around to see if there was another Deidra Williams with us, but no one moved. Then everyone stared at me, figuring that I was Deidra Williams since everybody else's name was known.

The guard stood at the bars dangling her keys off one finger. "You do understand English, don't you?"

I jumped up, didn't care about looking cool and patient, and moved to the world on the outside of the bars.

"Who posted my bail?" I asked the guard as we walked to the booking area.

"I don't know," she said, "but your bondsman is waiting for you out front. Sounds like you've never gone through this before."

"Sure haven't. And don't plan on going through it again. Would you happen to know about my brothers?"

"Can't say I do. I've been on this side for most of the day."

I nodded. Felt thankful enough to whomever for at least getting me out. I'd just have to find out about my brothers later. But it was bugging me to find out who bailed me out. I thought I was alone in the world. At least from having someone I knew that could provide bail money. Eventually I knew that God would take care of me, but I had to see who this angel was in person.

The bondsman was a bald, middle-aged, white man. "I'm Ronnie, from Smiley's Bail Bondsmen," he said as he smiled and extended his hand. "You ready to go?"

I shook his hand and nodded. I rubbed the goosebump from my arms, and followed Ronnie's duck walk out to the front of the Police Station. His penguin-like legs had me almost running to keep up. The sound of the streets and Miami's warm, night air put me at ease.

"You can hop in the front," Ronnie said, as we came up on his four-door Chevrolet.

"No, I'll take the back. I don't mind."

When we pulled off, I wasted no time. "Who posted bail my bail, Ronnie?"

He laughed. "You don't want me to turn on your favorite radio station first?"

When he turned to me smiling, I gave him a look that said I was ready to go back to jail if he didn't answer. He nodded and turned back to the front.

"Panther did."

I couldn't believe what I had heard. "Ronnie, don't play with me."

He said, "The fact that I even know who Panther is should tell you that I'm not."

"Well, I don't know. You could be F.B.I."

"Yeah, right. Fat, bald idiots."

I laughed at the joke but waited on him to respond. I didn't know if I could trust him.

"Your brothers are home," he said. "Panther got word of what was going on. Your brothers jumped on Raheem Townsend because he was trying to be the funny man about you almost getting raped. Next thing I know, I get a phone call to bail you out."

"You spoke to Panther?"

"No, I spoke to Shorty, one of his associates."

"So you don't know if Panther's okay."

Ronnie laughed. "Trust me, Deidra. Panther's fine. You're the one I'm worried about. Sounds like those few hours in jail shook you up a bit."

It was true. I could feel the tension in my voice. But it had nothing to do with my time in the cell. Someone had contacted Panther and I had to find out how.

I asked Ronnie, "Do you know where he is?"

"Nope."

"What about that guy, Shorty?"

Ronnie shook his head as he laughed. "Come on, Deidra. We both know that Panther is fine because Shorty doesn't even know you. But for Panther to have himself exposed by bailing you out means that he really cares about you. Either that or you're valuable to him in some other way. Regardless, it's obvious that he's still alive. Just be thankful for that."

Ronnie was right, and I was very thankful, but still afraid. "I know," I told Ronnie. "I just wish I knew more."

ౠ 21 ఆ

Sandra

I couldn't move fast enough once I received the news. Ducking and dodging through the evening traffic, I was sure that a few drivers tossed me the bird. Fuck them too. I had to go. The hospital called and said that Aunt Mabel had a serious stroke. There was no need to wait for another word. I was out the door. Good thing I finished up the meeting with PrimeTime. It was one less worry on my head. But until I was positive that Aunt Mabel was fine, everything else was placed on hold.

When I arrived at her side, she had breathing tubes stuck up in her nose, and another one under her ass to drain her piss. Aunt Mabel looked hopeless, void of life and texture in her darkskin face. The gray edges of her hair were bushy from the new growth, which I was to blame for since I was in charge of the hygiene duties that the nurses failed to provide. Still, it wasn't their fault that I hadn't seen Mabel in days.

Once when I was sixteen, I planned a trip to Busch Gardens with my dance group. We were set to leave on a Thursday night because there was no school on Friday. When I told Aunt Mabel she was happy that I wouldn't be around and she also planned a trip for her and Uncle Warren to Key West. But the night of my trip, I found Aunt Mabel in a robe and her hair in curlers, ironing her work uniform with tears used for steam when they fell onto her skirt.

I threw my books on the couch. "Aunt Mabel, what happened? I thought you were going out of town."

She gave me a sympathy smile. "Girl, what's wrong with you? I can't be worried over no stupid trip. I have to work. Ain't nobody else in this house to take care of us."

"But I thought you said you had some extra money saved up for a vacation?"

She laughed and kept on ironing. "Child, I don't have any extra money. Your uncle used that on some medical bills for his daddy. Said his daddy got too much on his mind, so he went up there to help him."

I was tearing up inside from the anguish I heard in Aunt Mabels' voice. "He left you here and took all the money up there to his family."

Instead of saying anything this time, Aunt Mabel turned to me so that I would see the anguish that also seeped into her face. Then she flipped the uniform over and ironed the backside.

I said "Aunt Mabel, I can't leave you here all alone to—"

She threw her hand up. "Now you know you want to go on that trip, and I am not trying to hear you claim otherwise."

"But what about you?"

"What about me? Baby, life don't always go the way you plan it. You have to sacrifice for what's best."

"And feeding Uncle Warren's family is—"

"Don't you worry about what I do, child. You just don't do as I do. Enjoy yourself." After Aunt Mabel steamed off some frustration, she laughed off the rest. She continued ironing the same leg of her uniform for the tenth time. "You just don't do as I do, baby. Be your own person. I know you want to take that trip, so go ahead and get ready. You only get to be young once, baby. Take advantage of it." The tears in Aunt Mabel's eyes gleamed like diamonds as her mouth lifted into a smile.

I went on the trip and left Aunt Mabel alone for the whole weekend. I wasn't mature enough to put my selfish ambitions aside to stay by Aunt Mabel's side, even though I knew that Uncle Warren did her wrong. Now it seemed as if I was Uncle Warren. Worried about everything and everybody else except for the one that needed me. I was probably the cause of the stroke. All the frustration built up corroded Mabel's insides, while I took pride in shopping to show off what I had outside. Left her to work on getting used to being lonely, as I held onto being young in the nightclubs. I was her only outlet to feeling alive, yet all the while, I was tearing her down.

I did Aunt Mabel's hair as the night dragged on. She hadn't awakened the whole time, but I talked to her about my day at work as if she could hear everything. All the late night shows came on and went off. I stole a chair from Aunt Mabel's roommate, and grabbed a sheet and pillow from the linen cabinet. I threw my feet up on the other chair, tossed the thin sheet over my legs, and tried my best to sleep comfortably.

"Girl, what are you doing sleeping in here?"

I jumped up, while Aunt Mabel munched on a plate off eggs and potatoes. Sun rays streamed through the cracks in the blinds, making me squint.

Aunt Mabel took in a sip of tea then set the cup down. "You ain't homeless, is you?"

"No," I told Aunt Mabel with a voice flooded with grogginess.

The tray table shook as she cut at her potatoes. "So, why you ain't sleeping at home? I'm sure you have a comfortable bed there."

I shook my head, indifferent about arguing with Aunt Mabel. "It's called support," I said. "It's what you do when you care about someone."

"Really," Aunt Mabel looked at me as if I was full of shit. "Care about who?"

"Aunt Mabel, don't start."

"I'm not starting anything. Alls I'm saying is people usually get in contact with someone that they care for."

"And I've done that. I'm here now, ain't I?"

"Hmph. Now."

"I'm sorry, Aunt Mabel, but I do work. We've already had this conversation. Now don't make this into something big. You're already as sick as it is. The last thing you need is for your pressure to go up over a stupid argument."

Aunt Mabel waved me off, went back to the eggs and potatoes. That allowed us to calm our nerves as I took back her roommate's chair. When I pulled the curtain back to cross over, I found her roommate's bed empty. At least nobody else heard Aunt Mabel getting ig'nant. I walked back over and folded up my sheet. As I went on putting everything away, Aunt Mabel was still holding on to her gas face. The tension was unhealthy for us both.

"What did the doctor say?" I asked.

"The same thing he always says. Eat like this, take these, do this, everything except I can go home."

"He is the doctor, Aunt Mabel. If he says you can't go home—"

"Yeah, yeah, yeah. I'm starting to think all of y'all are working together to bring me to my last day."

"I didn't know they were working on it," I teased. "Who can I talk to about joining up?"

"You ain't too old to receive a backslap, and I ain't too old to give one."

It was good to see that Aunt Mabel was still herself. "All right, all right," I said. "I just want to make sure that you get healthy."

"Ain't nothing wrong with me, child. This hospital is what's making me sick." She pushed her tray table off to the side, munched on the last bit of potatoes as she rest her head against her pillow.

Her comment was a trap into another argument, so I left it alone. If it wasn't the nurses, or the food, the cold air, or the doctor telling Aunt Mabel to do this, and take these, something in the hospital was making her sick. I wanted her back home just as badly. All the running back and forth and worrying had me drained.

"Child, when are you planning to open your eyes?"

I suddenly awoke from dozing off, and my chin damn near slammed into the chair's arm rest when Aunt Mabel called. I wished that she'd leave me the hell alone. It couldn't have been no later than— oh shit. It was going on twelve. I had to get my shit together for my meeting with Keith. Pick out the right outfit, get my hair done up, I had things to do.

I grabbed my cell phone and purse. "Aunt Mabel, I have someone important to call." From the corner of my eye, I saw her wave me off as I crossed over to the other side. Dammit. I was doing it again, putting off Aunt Mabel's feelings when she needed me the most. How did a meeting end up being more important than caring for my own family? My priorities were off. In the hallway, I searched for Keith's card. After only a few rings, he answered in that hypnotic voice.

"Hey, Keith, this is Sandy Reese from Dennis Porter's law firm. Remember me?"

"As gorgeous as you are, how could I forget? Are we still on for tomorrow night?"

I hesitated, trying to find the right words and use them in the right tone. "Something's come up with my aunt," I said, "and she's in the hospital. So for right now, I'm not sure. I mean, I still want to meet. Whatever's best for you if…"

I waited for Keith to set up another time but he was silent on the other end.

"Keith?"

"Yeah."

"Did you hear what—"

"Yeah, I heard. Listen, uhm…"

"Sandy."

"Right. Baby, I have a lot on my plate—"

"I'll call you later when everything's fine with my Aunt."

"Good idea," Keith said. "Listen, I hate to be rude, but business calls. You have the number. Don't hesitate to hit me up. Take care now."

"All right. I'll definitely call—

Click.

Damn. Just like that. I guess that was business. And if I didn't get with it, a lot of my calls would end up the same way; short, with no care for whatever else I had to say. Funny how to some people, I was everything, but to others I was nobody. I was going to change that. I couldn't help it. I was used to having things my way.

I went back into the room and found Aunt Mabel watching CNN. After I put my cell phone away in my purse, I straightened Aunt Mabel's pillows and sheets. She was still wearing the hard face.

"They just showed your man again," she said.

"Oh, yeah. What did they have to say this time?"

"Same thing. The police are looking for him."

"Did they say what they're investigating?"

"Child, I don't know. All I know is you're still depending on a man that can't do nothing for you."

"I'm not depending on anybody."

"Yeah, then why are you still holding on to him?"

ಬ 22 ಛ

Rachel

I t was dark out, the perfect time to get what I needed. I knew what I was doing was risky, but I didn't care. I smelled a rat in the house. A big rat named Sam, and I had to flush him out. There was something about him that I overlooked, something in his file that may not have been as detailed, but just as important as everything else, and I had to find what it was. It might cost me my job if I didn't. I had worked too hard to let one little bad ass bring me down.

It was easy getting inside. The guards would think that I had some important work to do. But the real problem was getting into Andrea's office. Only the guards had a key, and I could only approach one that I could trust. Or blackmail.

Leroy was the coolest of all the guards. He had a warm smile and a lively sense of humor. I felt he was cute too, a smooth, brown sugar complexion, and his muscular body looked nice in his little, gray uniform, but I would never tell him that. He had a crush on me, and I was going to exploit that.

I went out of my way to smile and wave when I saw him. Like a little boy when the ice cream truck comes around, Leroy ran up to me. Men are too predictable.

"Hey, Rachel," he said breathing hard. "How you doing? I never see you here this late on a Friday night."

"Got some extra work to do, that's all."

"Oh, no," he said. "I don't have a problem with that. Take your time. You need anything, just holla."

I had him. I said, "As a matter of fact, I do."

He shot me that innocent smile. "It'll be my pleasure."

"There are some papers that I left inside Andrea's office. You think you can let me in?"

His innocent smile switched into a suspicious frown. "You trying to get me fired?"

"No, Roy. Don't even think like that. I just need that small favor from you."

"Did you ask Andrea?"

Now he had me. I threw on a baby face, leaned up against the wall in a vulnerable posture. "No," I said, "because I don't want to get in trouble. It's just some work that I had to get done and I don't want her to know that I'm doing it at the last minute. It'll make me look bad."

Leroy crossed his arms and sweated me from head to toe. "Be kinda hard for anybody to make you look bad."

I placed my hand on his arm, pouted my lips. "You are too sweet."

He shot me a crooked smile. "Not that sweet. What am I going to get if I decide to be sweeter?"

"A biiiiig thank you."

"Sorry, can't do it."

I knew Leroy was playing so I played back. He may have wanted more but he wasn't getting any more than what I was already giving. That's when I placed my other hand on his arm and pulled him close.

"Please," I said.

"All right, all right. I hate to see a woman beg."

I punched him playfully in his arm, acted surprised, but laughing inside while Leroy's face glowed from an angelic smile. When the coast was clear, we strolled over to Andrea's office. Leroy stood guard as I went in. Told me hurry while he looked out. If anybody saw us we could both lose our jobs.

I had a key to the file drawer. Went about my actions quickly, but still cautious. I could feel my chest pounding, hear the heavy rotation of my breathing as I went through the names. S, s, s. Stone. Sam Stone. When I found it, I wasted no time, turned straight to his psyche evaluation. My finger ran down the page as I read most of the same things from before, like over-aggressiveness, disruptive behavior, parents died and he had been raised by a next of kin, very social personality trait, nothing that really switched on a red light. But there had to be something else. Something that I missed and somebody else saw. I didn't believe that Sam only did what he did when he met me. And once I found that evidence, I would've been cleared from Andrea's hit list.

Something told me try his criminal background. It had started back from 2000. He was just eleven years old, but had assault charges, assault and battery, assault and battery with a deadly weapon, robbery, and on. I couldn't believe it. By the time he was sixteen, Sam had committed most major crimes that should've had him doing some serious time. And his last conviction, which I completely missed before, was for manslaughter.

I almost didn't believe my own eyes. Sam had gotten off the hook for the same thing that Ace was sent up for. Hell, Sam's record was worse than all of my boys combined. He was also the oldest and—

Knock. Knock.

That was my signal to move. I wanted to read on but couldn't. The risk was not worth my job. I hurried and locked up the files, Leroy poked his head through the door with his finger to his lips.

"Don't move," he whispered.

I nodded, crouched down behind Andrea's desk. Leroy locked the door behind him. I hoped he had more sense than to leave me here alone.

"Leroy, what you doing?" I heard Andrew, one of the older guards, yell.

"Working," Leroy said, slowly walking away from the door as his keys jingled. "What are you doing, bullshitting?"

"Yeah, whatever," Andrew said. "John's looking for you. Come on."

"I'll be there."

"You better hurry up."

I heard steps quickly fade away. Then another set of feet came close and started unlocking the door. I inched in closer behind the desk, held my breath and hoped that it was Leroy coming back for me.

The person stepped in, shut the door behind them and locked it.

What was Leroy doing? Why was he locking the door?

"You can come out," I heard a voice say, but it was not Leroy's.

I knew exactly who the voice belonged to, but I was still nervous. I was certain that I was going to lose my job now.

When I stood, Darnell sat on the edge of Andrea's desk, smiling at me.

"What are you doing here?" he asked.

I dropped my head in embarrassment. "Hopefully not getting in trouble."

Darnell said, "I hope not either, but that still doesn't answer the question. Aren't you on administrative leave?"

"Yes, I am, but I just…

I moved from the corner and stood by the door in front of Darnell. "Listen, Darnell, I just needed to follow up with my group. I love my job, and I don't want to lose it. So I came here to check on my boys, and I was hoping that I can show you and Andrea that I still care by doing everything I can to show you my dedication."

Darnell stood and placed his hands in his pockets. "I've never questioned your dedication, Rachel. As a matter of fact, I have been singing your praises to everybody. You're an exceptional counselor. Andrea and those folks up in Tallahassee may have wanted you gone, but I wouldn't allow it. I know what I have in front me."

I was so grateful, I wanted to jump into Darnell's arms and kiss all over his face. "Thank you, Darnell. That's means a lot to me, and I promise that I will not let you down."

"I appreciate that. But your leave is still in effect. So that means you still have to get out of here."

I laughed. "That's fine. I'll take it."

I turned to leave. As I reached to unlock the door, Darnell's hand touched mine. He then locked his fingers between mine and held onto my hand. I was frozen as Darnell stood directly behind me. He finally moved his hand away and unlocked the door.

What had come over me? My emotions felt all mixed up. Why couldn't I walk out? Why was Darnell's presence like a magnet that stopped me from leaving? I needed to make a move. The longer I stayed, the more I would try to answer those questions, and I knew where my loyalty remained. They were for one man, and there was no question with they way I felt about him. So why was I still alone in this room with Darnell?

I turned to Darnell as we stood just inches away from each other. His gaze said he was not backing away unless I did, and neither one of us moved from the tight space that held us both hostages to this moment.

I said, "If this was twenty-five years earlier, maybe at a different place and under circumstances, I'm sure I wouldn't have this awkward feeling that I have right now. Still, I'm grateful for everything that you have done. And I will continue to do the best job that I can do, professionally. Thanks again."

I gave Darnell a kiss on his cheek. This time when I turned to leave he didn't stop me. I was speed walking out of there, thankful that I still had my job. At least I hoped so.

ಬ 23 ಚ

Deidra

It was about eight o'clock in the evening when Ronnie dropped me off around my old hood. He told me that I was to go to apartment number 13, Shakita's apartment. They had used her to bail me out. But when I got to her door, there was nobody there. I went upstairs to check on Tracy and my brothers. My mother was leaning against the railing smoking a cigarette. When she turned to me, she shot me a look of disgust, and I gave one back.

"You all right," she asked.

"I'm fine, ma. Where is everybody?"

She took a drag on the cigarette before looking back. Then she blew out the smoke as she turned to me. "I guess they're in there inside their rooms."

I nodded. I wasn't comfortable with saying anything else and walked inside the house. The strong scent of my mother's barbecue chicken seeped throughout the house and enticed my appetite. I hadn't eaten in like a day and was hungry as hell. But I damn sure wasn't going to ask for food. There were paper plates sitting at the dining table and a half of an apple pie sitting out in the open. I hurried back to my sister's room before I fell victim to mama's greatest talent.

I knocked and could hear footsteps rumble toward her door. When she opened it, Tracy's eyes lit up like The New Year's night ball.

She hugged me tight. "Dee, you're here. I'm so glad to see you."

"I'm glad to see you too, baby."

"I thought you was going away like Eric."

"I don't plan on going anywhere anytime soon."

When I looked up, Shakita was sitting on the bed with one of Tracy's books in her hand. Her face looked disturbed, almost scared. I was worried because Shakita was just as crazy as I was. Neither one of us were the type to show weakness.

"Shakita was keeping me company," Tracy said as we pulled away and walked inside. "She told me you would be coming soon. Luke and Joe are in their room. You want to see them."

"I will in a minute," I told her. As Tracy jumped on the other side of the bed, I chose to stand. "Tracy, you want to go hang out with your brothers. I have to talk with Shakita. Tell them I'll be there in a minute."

Tracy blew out a frustrated breath. "Okay. Just don't be long. I do have things to do."

I stared in shock with my mouth wide open. Tracy twisted her little hips out the door, and Shakita held down her laugh.

"You better watch out for her," Shakita said. "She's about thirty days grown already."

"I know. I'm about to smack her back into a toddler if she doesn't slow down."

Shakita dropped her head, nervously fiddled with the book.

I asked, "Did you see Panther?"

She shook her head. "One of his homeboys. Never seen him before. He gave me the grand, and another grand for looking out."

"So why are you looking stressed like you missed your period?"

Shakita waived me down. Threw on a fake smile. "Nothing, girl. I was hoping them hoes didn't fuck with you in that cell."

I rolled my eyes, crossed my arms. "Not on their life."

Shakita nodded. "Girl, everything has me spooked. I didn't know Panther was in deep like that."

While Shakita stared off into nothing, I moved towards her and made sure no one overheard our conversation. "I don't think anybody knows about all that is going on with Panther," I said. "All I know is we have to look out for each other."

"I'm trying." Shakita said. She was fiddling with the book again.

Shakita may have been shook over what may have happened if she didn't do what Panther wanted. But I was afraid of what would happen to me if I did.

"Good looking out," I told Shakita. "Trust me, you did more than most people would do."

Shakita sucked her teeth. "Girl, if I had the bread, I would've done it regardless. Can't let nobody mess with my girl. Them females in there would've tried to run a train on you."

We both had to laugh at how crazy that sounded. Shakita's seen how I broke a lot of bitches down in my lifetime. And just because I was humble now didn't mean I forgot all of my old habits. If a hoe jumped up, she could still catch a beat down.

Shakita said, "I have a feeling all of this is far from being over."

"I do, too."

There was a knock at the door.

I yelled out, "What?"

The door opened, and Luke stood behind it, his thick afro poking through with pride. "Dee, what's up? You forgot about your brothers?"

"I didn't forget nobody. Come here."

The two boys strolled in with Tracy lagging, embraced me with dap and a hug like I was one of their homeboys.

I asked, "Are you two all right?"

Luke said, "You know we're straight. You're the one we need to worry about."

"And why is that?"

"Because," Joe spoke up, revealing his four gold caps as he smiled, "all of the crazy things we heard. You need someone to look out."

"Yeah," Luke said, "and plus we still got loose lips like Raheem running around. Should've stomped his head in."

I playfully put them both in a headlock. "I don't want you two stomping anybody's head in. You hear me?"

They refused to answer.

That pissed me off. I tightened my lock on their heads. "Do you hear me?"

"Yeah, yeah, yeah."

Knowing how they were, I held on to my lock. I really wanted them to heed my word. "I want you to keep doing what you've been doing. And that's looking out for your sister, and going to school. That's how you can look out for me. Do you hear?"

"Ow, yeah, yeah," they both screamed as my lock grew tighter. I had to make sure they got the message.

Joe said, "But who's going to look out for you?"

I released the lock from their heads and gave them a much needed embrace around their necks.

I said "The same one that's always been looking out. The same one that I pray to every night. And all I can do is keep praying. Until things change, that's all that any of us can do."

ဆ 24 ೞ

Sandra

I still couldn't believe it. I was meeting with Keith Grimes. *The* Keith Grimes. That was the wild thing about the music business. You can be a nobody one day, and the next, you're having dinner with multimillionaires, discussing how you can become multi yourself. The music industry complimented my persona like a pair of new shoes.

Thank heavens Aunt Mabel's health picked up again. I felt guilty leaving though, knowing she wanted me to stay. But I couldn't be in two places at once. And I couldn't rise in the industry by canceling meetings just to hear Aunt Mabel complain about the hospital care. She had no choice but to understand my lifestyle. This was my career.

And I made sure I was dressed for the job. Red, Chanel dress that typified aggression and passion, and white, Chanel shoes and purse that said I can also be passive and innocent. Eat your heart out, Keith.

A fly hairstyle was a must. I was rocking a soft, wavy look with curls, and already got tons of compliments about how I resembled Gabrielle Union. Having Gabrielle's money would look pretty good on me too.

I was meeting Keith at eight o'clock at Redmond's, an exclusive gourmet restaurant on South Beach. Exclusive because they averaged about one-hundred dollars a plate. Exclusive because I could never afford it my damn self. But I didn't have to worry about that on this night. It was 7:55 when I arrived. This wasn't a date, and therefore, I couldn't be late. Besides, after the way Keith hung up on me earlier, I wouldn't have been surprised if at 8:01, he was out the door.

I went inside, and Keith was not even there yet. The host showed me to the table, a bottle of champagne sitting there already on ice. I was lost for words because Redmond's was exquisite. There were sixteenth century paintings on the walls, and wild orchids surrounding the edges of the doors. A hint of soft jazz lullabied the setting, and the waiters were decked out in white dress shirts, black bowties, and burgundy vest; which was also the color of the table linen.

When I checked my watch it was exactly eight o'clock. And when I looked up again, Keith was strutting my way. Oh, shit, I thought. I hadn't checked my face. Too late. He was at the table, and I stood to greet him.

After we shook hands, he took the other hand from behind his back and handed me a box of Godiva chocolates.

"Thank you, Keith." Even though I really was surprised, I threw on my sweet girl voice. "How did you know I liked chocolate?"

"By paying your boss twenty dollars to tell me."

We both laughed as we took our seats.

I said, "Yeah, that sounds like Dennis. But you didn't have to do this. I should be the one buying you a year's supply of chocolate."

"You're the one who made an impression on me," Keith said with that enticing smile. "Why should you have to pay to be sweet when you've already been blessed with the gift?"

As much as I tried, I couldn't help blushing. "Well, thank you for that, and for the chocolate, and this meeting."

Keith grabbed the champagne bottle. "No need to thank me. We're here for the same reason. Because we wanted to meet with each other. It's an opportunity for us both. What I want to know is why didn't you take the opportunity to make yourself comfortable and have a drink."

I placed my hand on my chest like I was shocked. "I couldn't do that," I said in a tone as humble as a nun. "That would've been rude. If I were to drink that whole bottle by the time you arrived, wouldn't you think I was kinda rude?"

Keith stopped in mid-poor. "No, I just would've enrolled you into some AA meetings."

This was the Keith that I was feeling. He was so cool and down to earth, I questioned if it really was him. This couldn't be the same man that cut me off short on the phone just the other day. Keith was like the perfect gentlemen. He took the initiative with ordering my food, and instead of the waiter refilling my glass, Keith did the honors. I was beginning to think that I was the one with all the money.

We spoke of my business ventures as we ate. The whole time, Keith was attentive, as if everything I had to say was of importance. A few times his phone rang. Some he ignored, and some he took right there at the table. I appreciated how he didn't make me feel like I was outside of his world. Perhaps he wanted me to see how things were. I had PrimeTime's demo with me, and I sold his image to Keith as if he was The Notorious B.I.G. reincarnated. But I really felt that PrimeTime was that good. I just hoped after Keith heard the demo, he would feel the same. He swallowed my words like he did his food.

"Why don't we go take a listen in the limo?" Keith said. "We can ride the strip while bumping to the next Notorious B.I.G."

I was hesitant, but I told Keith yes. This was my shot at something major. After he paid for our meal, he escorted me out to his limo. It felt like I was in Redmond's all over again. The soft music was playing, the lights were going, and another bottle of champagne was on ice. Keith offered me a glass. I was already a little tipsy.

I shook my head. "No, no no. I'm fine."

Keith kept on pouring. "Just a little toast."

I let out a tired breath. The alcohol was already starting to wear on me. I had to get it together because I still had to drive back home. "What are we going to toast to?"

Keith placed his glass up to mine. "To big things."

I nodded as we toasted. "To big things."

I placed my drink in the holder. "Let's listen to the next B.I.G." I said as I popped the demo inside the CD player. Turned the volume up just enough to have our heads bobbin'. It was easy for me to move because I was partially being controlled by the liquor. When I turned to Keith he was moving, too.

"You're right," he said. "Your boy is tight. I gotta hand it to you."

I was still bobbin' and boppin' as I focused on Keith's words. "So does this mean we can do business?"

Keith was boppin' too. "Maybe." He smiled easy, placed his arm around my waist and pulled me on top of him.

His hand slid down over my ass and I knocked it away. Propped myself off of him and backed a few feet away. "Keith, uhhm—this. This—is. This is not the kind of meeting that I had in mind."

Keith sat up, threw his hands out. "What's the problem? Aren't you attracted to me?"

I laughed. "I'm not here because I'm attracted to you."

"But baby, you're here for a reason. We can satisfy both of our reasons in one night."

I laughed inside while I shook my head. What started as a beautiful night had turned ugly in a matter of minutes. Any other time, I probably would've fucked Keith, under different circumstances, like if I didn't have a man, and I wasn't worried about being somebody respectable in the music industry. But now, he made a special night seem almost worthless. It was as if my pussy was the only reason he met up with me. Because if I fucked him, I still didn't have a guarantee that we were going to do business. I couldn't even trust that I would hear from him the next day. Sometimes I hated the bullshit that women had to go through.

"Keith, I'm meeting with you on business."

"I understand that." Keith inched closer as he spoke. "But I asked if you were attracted to me. Nothing else. Just if you're attracted to me."

This was an awkward position. I was being forced into playing this game when I assumed that everything would be on a professional level. "Yes, Keith, you are an attractive looking man, but—"

"And if we weren't here on business, wouldn't you have wanted to get to know me on a more personal level?" He moved in closer.

I backed away. "Yeah, but that's beside the point. I am here on business."

"Sandy, I can assure you that my decision to conduct business will have nothing to do with your decision to be physical with me or not."

I rolled my eyes. "Yeah, right."

Keith threw his right hand up. "Scout's honor."

When I looked at him again, his face was angelic, but that was just a part of his game. I said, "You weren't no damn Boy's Scout."

He looked away like he was confused. "Okay, thug's honor."

We both laughed. His smile was warm, sweet. I didn't hate Keith. It's just that he made me uncomfortable. I didn't know him. A man of his power and fortune could easily release me to the wind like a used condom.

"But of course I do know business," Keith continued. "I know how to make money. I also know how to fuck."

I was sure he did. I just wasn't sure if I wanted to find out. Our eyes locked after he allowed me to marinate on the cockiness of his words. I was flowing down a powerful river and I turned away before the strong currents pulled me in. Grabbed my glass of champagne just to have something to do other than concentrate on Keith. Dumb move, knowing I didn't need any liquor right now, but I was hoping that a hurricane would kill our hormones and blow my horniness away. And yes, I was very horny.

Keith came up on me, made as if he was about to kiss my neck, and I ducked away as if he were a mosquito. When I took another sip of my drink, he caressed my knee. I gently knocked it away, dangled the drink in my other hand. He then came at me with a double move. He placed his hand on my thigh, which was revealed from the split in my dress, and kissed the area of my neck right below the ear. I tensed up like I itched, but in reality, I was tingling. Gently moved his hand away again.

"Keith, are we going to do business together?"

My neck and thigh were caressed again. "Maybe."

I shied away, placed the drink down. "What do you mean maybe?"

"Maybe." More kisses were at my neck, strong fingers massaged my thigh.

I was getting hot. The intoxicating powers of the liquor in my system, the heat from Keith's light breathing over my neck, and the sensation from Keith's hand slowly inching between my partially open legs had me ready to get out my hot clothes. Just before his hand reached my pussy, I gently pushed it away.

"What do you mean, Keith? Maybe yes, maybe no?"

His hand crawled right back up my thighs as his lips softly ran over my neck. "Maybe, I don't know. I have to see what's on my plate."

Could it be some hot sex, I thought. My legs were pushed open and Keith outlined the edges of my panties with two fingers. I wondered if he felt my wetness. I damn sure felt it. Keith was marking up my neck with forceful, soft lips. I grabbed his head under the pressure of the sweet pain. My panties were pulled to the side as Keith's fingers ran over wetness. I jumped from the tingle that shot through me. My hormones mixed in with the liquor had me lost in Keith Grimes' world. When he used both hands to pull my panties down, I pushed myself up to make his job easier, kissed his forehead and cheeks while I got trapped in the moment. The car bumped as it made a sharp turn. We both slid to the floor, laughed as we realized what we were doing.

Keith sat back up on the seat.

I kneeled in front of him, used his knees for leverage as I kicked off my shoes. He sat there calm and patient, watching, so I allowed him to watch as I finished the job he started, still using his knees for leverage as I threw off my tangled up panties. When I straddled him, I could feel his hardness poking at my pussy.

"Why don't you take that out of there," he said.

The bounce in the car made me bounce as I reached for his zipper. Started bopping like a little child on a pony with the last song on PrimeTime's demo. I was glad because it wasn't fucking-type music. I finally had Keith's zipper down. He smiled. He knew he had me, but right now I didn't care. I wanted this dick. When I reached in to pull out his third leg, PrimeTime's demo popped out the CD player. And I pulled up a well overdue prize, long and thick the way I liked them. A news reporter's voice came through the limo's speakers and said that the police were still on a manhunt for Parish Coles, the murder suspect in the Patrick Alden case.

At that moment, I froze, undid my hand from Keith's body. The reporter's words clouded my mind when she mentioned that name. Parish Coles. What was I thinking? How could I do this to Panther while he was on the run for his life? Keith looked as confused as I felt. I slid off of him, pulled my dress down and backed away. Keith threw his hands up in disgust. I took a seat on the other side of the limo, reached for my panties and shoes.

Keith said, "What's wrong? Why did you stop? Do you know who their talking about?"

After struggling with my shoes, I stuffed my panties into my purse. "No. It's just…I have to go."

Keith rubbed his head, laughed like he was embarrassed. "You can stay a little while longer, can't you?"

"No," I yelled. "I mean I can't. I'm sorry. I have to go. Can you ask the driver to take me back to the car? I can understand if you don't want to. And that's fine. I can just get out and walk."

The tone of my voice and the expression on my face must have been enough because Keith asked the driver to take me back. He then turned around and zipped up his pants, sat there with his hands in his lap. I knew he wanted an explanation, but I didn't have one to give. I didn't have one for myself. My feelings were numb as I sat there like I was floating in space. And I couldn't have floated away from Keith and that limo fast enough.

ಚಿ 25 ಛ

Rachel

I t had been a while since I'd sat down, cleared my mind, and read a good book. And after the drama of the last few days, a good book was the perfect peacemaker. The vibe in the bookstore was always peaceful. It was also where I met Panther.

At first I played it off as if I hadn't noticed him. But almost any woman could've told you that it was hard not to have noticed Panther. His presence was magnetic. Before he uttered a word, I was pulled into his zone. His complexion was dark and beautiful, his posture, strong and masculine. The bland scent of the bookstore was sucked away by Panther's intoxicating cologne. He was so fine, I could taste him.

Back in college, I threw myself into my books, and stayed clear from throwing too much ass. But don't get it twisted; I had been with boys. The problem was I had never attracted a man. And I was always drawn to intelligent men, especially when they looked as good as Panther. I decided to innocently flirt around with him, bumped his arm and brought his attention my way. He turned and studied me inquisitively.

"Excuse me," I said looking away.

"That's perfectly fine," he said as he faced me. "And if my eyes are not deceiving me, so are you."

I pretended to be unimpressed, even though I was glad that he spoke. I said, "Thank you, but there's nobody on this planet that's perfect."

"Says who? I think there's a lot about us both that is perfect."

"Oh, really. Like what?" I said as I crossed my arms. I was interested in playing. I just hoped that he wasn't some mac daddy with corny pick up lines. That would've killed the whole mood.

"Like the place we picked," he said. "It's the perfect place to learn something new, and not just judge a book by its cover.

I nodded. He didn't sound like a wannabe Mac Daddy.

"And our timing," he continued. "If we never chose the perfect time, we never would've met in the perfect place."

Okay, I was feeling the nigga so far. But I couldn't allow him to think that he was the shit, like the rest of the little boys that I had been with. I got educated on him and said, "True, but those are circumstances. Humans are flawed, and because of it, we're not perfect."

"I don't think I'm flawed," he said.

I don't think so either, I said to myself. Panther had no problem flaunting his arrogance. It was kind of sexy. I had to see what else this sexy package came with. "And what makes you so confident?" I asked.

He smiled. "It has nothing to do with my confidence. Flaws are nothing but differences. So since we don't look like the ugly motherfucker that came up with this concept, something's wrong with us. He calls it a flaw. We've been living by some ugly nigga's opinion forever."

I laughed with a loud shriek. The other customers turned to me with angry stares, but I didn't care. It was the most intelligent joke I had ever heard.

"But in my opinion," Panther continued as if he was never interrupted, leaned in and tightened the space between us "our differences are what make us perfect. They show that the beauty of God is in everything, just like it is in this moment with us."

Right then and there, I was hooked. I fell for him like a drop of water into a stream. And I had been flowing with it ever since. Panther and I had done some of the smallest things together, like reading a book on a weekday night. But now that my nights included no work, and no Panther, I dreaded being alone. I was weary with the dragging effect that loneliness carried wherever it landed. But my career was based on teaching people to be positive, so I also had to believe in it myself. Still, I couldn't wait for the day that Panther and I snuggled under the sheets on a weekday night with a couple of good books.

Even with the excitement of reading a new book, my mind still wasn't right. As I watched the hustle and bustle of afternoon traffic I harbored a funny feeling in my gut on the way home. I took a detour and headed to my mother's house. Just needed some company for a while.

Mama was laid out on her bed with the lights off, a bowl of grapes at her side, lost in a movie on the Lifetime channel.

I reached for some grapes. "Mama, why you—"

"Shhhsh." Mama waved me to keep quiet. She was so gone in the movie she hardly noticed that I left her with about two grapes.

I walked over to her dresser, casing it out for new perfume like a thief before a bank heist. But if I had taken anything mama wouldn't have noticed anyway. The lady had a department store in her room. Just about any accessory that women used, my mother had it, even if she never used them herself. While glancing over the perfumed lotions, I spotted a picture of my brother. It had always been there, but for some reason, I studied it closer today. Felt like I could hear his voice, as if he was right there, and a tremor shot through me as I recalled how his punches hurt like hell. Funny how that feeling stuck with me after fifteen years. I rubbed the goosebumps from my arms, stared back at my mother who was still engrossed in her movie. I grabbed the picture, but when I glanced back down, I noticed that the only photos that mama had were of him and myself. I couldn't take all that she had left, especially when all she had was reduced to a few photos. But I took a bottle of some expensive perfume that I'm sure she wouldn't have missed anyway.

I stole the space between mama and the edge of the bed, forced her to scoot over as I rested the back of my head against her bosom. I wanted to be babied. She didn't care because in both of our minds, I was her baby.

"Mama", I said, staring and fiddling with my freshly done French tips, "Do you regret some of the choices you've made in life?"

I could feel mama pull away. "Chile, what are you talking about?"

I propped my head up, but focused my eyes on the beige, flower-printed sheets instead of on mama. An old habit of mine. Andrea said it came from thinking too much. "I mean… Do you ever get the feeling that you've failed, and do you regret some of the choices that you've made?"

"Not one," mama said. "We all make different choices for whatever reasons, and you shouldn't regret any of them."

"I know," I said. My chest was pounding because my feelings were trying desperately to articulate what I wanted to say. "I mean… Do you ever wish that you could've done things differently with Q?"

Mama grabbed the remote and muted the loud, annoying commercials. "Of course, I do" she said, "but I don't regret them. If I never had the heart to make choices for my family, how would I learn how to handle the situation again?" She placed her hand on my chin and turned my head around. That was her way of telling me she wanted to see my eyes. "But some things you just can't control," Mama went on. "And you can't make somebody change if they don't want to. Even if you love them from your head, down to your toenails, and holla like a stray dog looking for his home, it doesn't mean that people will listen to you. All you can do is believe that you poured and emptied out all of the energy and love that you can from your little heart, because that's where God is, and that is all that matters."

I nodded because I knew that mama was right. My eyes fell to the bed again, scanning the red roses in the sheet that seemed to lighten up the darkness of the dimly lit room. I said, "I feel you mama. I just wish there was a way to know that everything that we're doing is right before we do it. Before everything wrong starts happening."

"I know, baby," mama said. "I wish it were, too."

The volume on the T.V. was on blast again, meaning mama's movie was back on. I asked, "How long this been—"

"Shhsh," Mama said. "It's almost finished."

I checked my watch and it was a quarter 'til two. I decided to leave because I missed the majority of the movie anyway. My hands were behind me as I stood up and concealed the bottle of perfume poking out of my back pocket.

Before I left the room, mama muted the T.V. again. She asked, "Rachel, are you okay?"

I nodded. "Yeah, just got myself a new book that I'm ready to get into."

The volume on the T.V. was back to blast, and I was out the door.

I awoke the next morning with the book in my lap. When did I fall asleep? The red button on my answering machine flashed, indicating that I had a message waiting. Probably mama, I thought. I knew she didn't want anything. Something as small as shoes on sale was reason enough to call me on the spot. I was surprised when I heard Andrea's voice through my phone's speaker come off as timid as a little girl. She said that she needed me like yesterday. "Vacation's over," her words exactly. That was the only message I had, and the only one I needed to hear. I threw my book on the couch, grabbed a work outfit from the closet and jumped in the shower. This is it, I said to myself. I was back to where I was supposed to be.

When the circle of guards turned and saw me burst through the doors, their wide grins switched to puzzled stares. But I understood their confusion. I was shocked, too. No one, including myself, expected me to walk through that place for another two weeks. I threw them a happy wave. They weren't as enthusiastic with their responses. Haters. I didn't care, because *I had my job back, na-na-na-boo-boo.*

I knocked on Andrea's door a little harder than I wanted. My hand was already set on the knob when she asked me in. I thought I would have had to hide the elation over my face, but the feeling died after I glanced at the different faces in the room. Andrea sat behind her desk, tapping a pencil top against a desk calendar. And two white men were there, whose faces were just as tense as Andrea's. One sat at a corner of Andrea's desk with his legs crossed like a woman, the other stood at the other corner, twirling a set of handcuffs. My eyes locked on the one with the cuffs.

Andrea said, "Why don't you shut the door?"

I held still, kept my stare on the man that I figured was a cop.

"Oh, don't worry," he said as he smiled, placed the cuffs in his back pocket. "Those aren't for you. We just want to talk."

I could feel the perspiration building in my hands and face. The heat in the room began to circulate around my neck. "Talk about what?" I said. "I don't know you."

"Well, that's going to change today," the man with his legs crossed said with a heavy southern accent. "I'm Detective Fred Boone. That's my partner, Detective Alex Gray. If you wouldn't mind closing the door and taking a seat, we need to go over some important things."

Detective Gray moved his hands away from his pockets and pulled a chair from the corner. I reached back and pushed the door closed, but still hadn't broken my stance. The uncertainty of what was about to happen had me frozen.

"You don't have anything to worry about," Detective Gray said. "The sooner we do this, the better it will be for all of us."

Detective Gray's words relaxed some of the tension. I took the seat, but my mind raced at warp speed, wondering what these cops wanted. Had Sam juiced up more dirt to make himself look like the clean one? Was this about Ace's conviction and the choice to try him as an adult? I didn't know. I just knew I didn't like the expressions on these cop's faces. Gray was more assuring, kept his hands pocketed, and held a half-smile as if to say everything would go smooth. I still didn't know. Sam was just as laid back, so Gray could be just as corrupt. He had a lean build, clean cut face, short, brown hair, and wasn't that bad looking. His dark brown suit fit nicely.

His partner, Detective Boone, appeared to be less concerned about being friendly. He had his attention on his foot rocking off one knee. His face was harder than Gray's, but was just as clean, his hair was brown and curly, slicked down at the sides. His gray jacket sleeves were about two sizes too short, and the hole in his green, diamond print socks said that he was cheaper than I imagined.

"Ms. Baxter," Boone's voice raised an octave as he reached for a notepad sitting on the desk, "do you know a man by the name of Parish Coles?"

Oh, shit. They were here for Panther. This had nothing to do with my job. I looked to Andrea and her eyes were still glued to the pencil's tapping. I could feel my eyes water. The temperature in the room was heating up again. I couldn't speak.

"Ms. Baxter," Boone called out, almost yelling. "Do you understand the question?"

I tensed up. My palms were sweaty as I rubbed them for comfort. I couldn't get it together.

I jumped when Gray put a hand to my shoulder. "It's okay," he said. "You're not the one in trouble here, and you're not going to be. Trust me. Everything will be fine once we get the facts. But there's no rush. Whenever you're ready. Just take a deep breath."

I did as the cop said. I placed my hands on my lap and wiped the sweat away. Figured if I didn't get it together soon, the feeling would only get worse. And besides, Panther was counting on me. I had to get my mind right.

"Yes, I know Parish Coles."

Boone said, "What is your relation to him?"

I almost rolled my eyes at Boone, but rolled them towards the ceiling instead. "He's my boyfriend."

"And did you see him on October 9th?" Boone hardly allowed me time to breathe.

I told him yes.

Boone asked at what time, and I told him eight o'clock, exactly what Panther had asked.

Boone uncrossed his legs and stood up. "We would like you to come with us, Ms. Baxter. We need to discuss a few details."

"Why? What did I do?"

"Nothing," Boone said. "Certain information cannot be discussed unless there is proper police procedure. So come with us."

I looked to Andrea, but that was useless. Her eyes were as empty as her head. I turned to Detective Gray, but he looked right through me, buttoned his jacket as he held his hand out for me to go before him.

I followed Boone out the door while Gray walked behind me. My stomach turned, but thankfully, nothing felt like it was going to come up. Nothing was coming to my head either. This was going to be harder than I expected. On the way out, we passed the circle of guards that were there when I first came in. All the smiling ceased. Boone tipped his hat and they gave no response back. They were just as confused as I was.

෫ 26 ෬

Deidra

The same black Lincoln Grand Marquis with the dark boy tints had been on my ass from the time I left school. What was this all about? I wasn't feeling this right now.

At school, my professor asked if I were okay, and I told him no. My head was not in the class, or anywhere else in particular, and I grabbed my books and left class without giving a reason, the jealous eyes of the room scoping me out like, "Who does that bitch think she is?"

But I had to get away, literally, because this black car had locked down on me like handcuffs. No doubt in my mind, it was the Feds, or some kind of police. Good thing my windows were tinted, too. I searched through my phonebook on my cell phone for Dalvin's number. If he was supposed to be looking out, why was he nowhere to be found when I needed him? Just like the other night, the phone rang and rang, nothing but the voicemail answering. I was going to leave a message, but decided not to. He should've answered. Why the hell didn't he pick up the phone? Should've known I couldn't count on anybody but myself. Still, this was Panther's man. Even if he didn't give two shits about helping a bitch when trouble started, he should've at least considered what would happen to him after Panther found out. Maybe Panther heard about what happened to me and brothers, and had already gotten his hands on Dalvin. Or maybe the cops had beaten Panther to it.

Either way, I was stuck, alone, and nervous as hell. But I couldn't let this fear overpower me. Kept my focus on the road right at the speed limit. The black car was right up on me now. I could barely keep the wheel steady. My hands were jittery. My eyes were jumpy from the smallest things that passed by. Why were they fucking with me? Why couldn't they just leave me and Panther alone? Go after the real criminals, like the politicians, or the people in their own bureau.

I could feel my eyes water. Quickly, I wiped these tears before they messed with my concentration on the road. And the dickhead behind me remained on my ass. I stomped on the brakes and let up fast. The officers slammed on their brakes too and swerved off of the road. I laughed. Good for those assholes. Since they were fucking with me, I figured I'd fuck with them back. Besides, what could they say? How was I supposed to know who they were?

When I got into the lane to turn down my block, the cops got in the next lane over. Ooh, was I supposed to be skerred. They had nothing on me. And they couldn't rattle me with this Tom and Jerry crap either. I cranked up my Tupac and hoped to God that they heard every word.

Just as we were turning, a white Lincoln with the dark boys got behind me. The punk called for back up. I wasn't in the mood for this. I thought about stopping at the grocery store for like two hours just to see what these assholes would do. But my head just wasn't in it. All I wanted was to get some rest. If they had nothing better to do than watch me like a hawk, then let them. I wasn't about to crawl into some hole, afraid to live my life, ducking and dodging men in black like the world belonged to them.

As I turned into my driveway, three more fed cars blocked my entrance and a busload of hardnosed white men jumped out like I was the one who shot J.F.K. One of them opened my car door, flashing his badge in the other hand. I left my radio on blast and let Tupac cuss their asses out. When the other dicks in a suit surrounded my car, I decided to get out. I knew what time it was.

"We need you to come with us," said the prick blocking my escape.

I grabbed my purse and slung it on my shoulder. "And what if I don't."

He turned around to his other four partners who all had silly smirks across their faces. He turned back to me and said, "Then it's just as easy for us to get a warrant to search your house. Or should I say the house that Panther Coles co-signed for?"

A path was cleared for me as I walked to the open car door. They slammed it shut and I thought, here I go again. More bullshit with the law. But at least now I wasn't in handcuffs. And I didn't have to worry about big bitches named Tiny trying to run up on me. But still, I couldn't deny the truth. I knew I would be worried until I was certain that this thing with Panther was over with.

ಌ 27 ಐ

Sandra

After a while, all the questions started getting on my damn nerves. Inside that building, every woman, and every man that wanted to be a woman, had swarmed my desk today. All I kept hearing was Keith, Keith, Keith, what did Keith do, was he as fine as he is on T.V., and did I happen to see what he looked like beneath his clothes. I kept all my answers short and sweet. Short enough to have them leave it alone, and sweet enough to make them think that I never saw what was underneath Keith's clothes. Basically, my answer was something like Keith and I had a short dinner in which we talked business, and he left because he had another meeting to attend. The women would leave my desk, calling me boring, and all the gay men whispered, "I knew she wouldn't know what to do with a man like Keith".

But I sensed that Nisha had peeped my game. A few times I caught her studying me with a slick eye. Whenever our eyes met for more than half a second, she played it off with a fake smile. And Nisha was too real to be good at doing anything fake. I would throw her a fake smile back, but at least mine was a bit more authentic than Nisha's private investigator stare.

She stopped me just before I left for lunch. "What's up?" she asked, her eyes still scoping me like the police.

I said, "Girl, I'm just ready to eat. Feels like I've been working my ass off."

While I locked my cabinets, she stole a seat at the edge of my desk, folded her arms like "Bitch, you can't fool me."

She said, "No, I mean what's up. You've been walking around here with your shoulders all tight. What, you ain't had no dick in a while?"

I laughed as I snatched up my keys and purse. "If it's starting to show, then that means it's been too long."

Nisha nodded, searching my eyes for lies again. She said, "But I know that ain't your only problem."

I was afraid that she saw right through me. "Why you say that?"

"Because," Nisha pointed her head to my desk, "you locked up your cabinets, but left everything out."

I turned my head, disgusted with myself, played it off with another fake smile.

Nisha shook her head. "Don't even try it." She stood as I nervously put away all of my work, knowing she was watching my every move. "What's going on?" she whispered.

I wasn't the type to tell my business, even if Nisha was cool. "Girl, I just miss my man. You know how it is. Come on. We can talk on the way out."

That was my way of telling Nisha if she wanted to hear something juicy, she needed to walk with me. Only she didn't know that the juice was going to be watered down with a bunch of emotional stuff to keep her off balance. And to keep what I was really feeling and thinking to myself.

As we walked through the office, quiet like a couple of nuns, the stares and the whispers from everybody started up again. God, couldn't they get off of this Keith thing already? He was just a man, with a few million dollars poking out of his pockets, but my man was pretty large in his own right. And I didn't need Keith's kind of money to live. As long as my man was down to be there for me, I was cool. That's what a lot of these women didn't understand. A man like Keith could have all the money in the world, and he could still leave you feeling broker than what you were when you first jumped into his limo.

After Nisha and I strutted out of the office, talking shit and laughing at the jealous stares behind us, Dennis popped his head out of his office and called me over. Nisha said she'd wait. I wondered what the hell Dennis wanted. He knew better than to bother me on my lunchtime. Hopefully, I thought, Keith didn't tell him something bad about last night. Hopefully Keith didn't tell him anything.

But once I entered Dennis' office, I could only wish that my problems were that easy. There were two white men in suits standing in the office, and I figured that this didn't have anything to do with Keith. With my arms crossed I stood close to the door. The tension in the room already had my leg bouncing.

Dennis went and stood behind his desk. "Sandy, these men are with the—

A hand from one of the men told Dennis to shut up. "Miss Reese, we're with the F.B.I. I'm agent Downs. This is my colleague, agent Green, and we need you to come with us."

My leg kept bouncing nervously. Felt as though I could barely speak. I mean, I knew this was coming, but it was all happening too soon. Or maybe I just figured that it wouldn't happen at all. Still, I had to deal with it. I was prepared. I had no other choice. If I didn't do this right, it could cost Panther his freedom, and I couldn't have that when I wanted him here with me. I asked, "What's this all about?"

Agent Downs placed his hands on his hips. He looked like Superman, but dressed in the nerdy Clark Kent getup instead of blue tights and a cape. He said, "Your involvement with Parish Coles."

I stalled them. "What kind of involvement?"

Agent Green stepped up with his hands pocketed and stood next to his partner. He said, "The kind of involvement that would have checks from Mr. Coles deposited to your company account, Right One Management, for the last three months."

These guys are pretty thorough, I thought. I could see why Panther felt as though he had to leave. But was all of this necessary? I asked why I had to go with them.

"Procedure," said Agent Downs.

I looked to Dennis. His face was sunken as he rocked back and forth against his leather chair. He knew that I wasn't a criminal. So why were these agents in here trying to treat me like one?

My leg had stopped acting up. I was heated now. *Procedure.* They could've given me at least some credit. Hell, I worked for a law firm. I said, "Does your procedure have to succumb to taking a working woman to some, cold, stank, interrogation room?"

"Sandy," Dennis called. "It's okay. Let these gentlemen do their job. Just call me if you need me."

Asshole, I do need you, I almost said aloud. This wasn't something that I was used to. And plus Panther said that everything would be fine, but it wasn't feeling that way. He told me that all I had to say was that we were together for about two hours. Did they have to drive me off to their police rooms just for that? Couldn't they see, all of this *procedure* was not necessary?

Agent Downs went behind me and opened the door while Agent Green offered me to go before him. I turned around because I could've slapped the arrogance right off of his face.

"Thanks, Dennis," I heard Agent Green say, as if they did this type of shit all the time. "We'll give you call when we're done."

"You bet," Dennis responded. He might as well have said, "We'll have a laugh about this at happy hour".

When I got into the hallway, Nisha was still there, leaning against the wall, her face soaked in concern and confusion. But my arms were still crossed and I sensed that the anger in my face, and two, white men beside me gave away the whole story. I could feel the whispers and the stares from the rest of my coworkers. They wanted to know what was the haps. Like the two agents at my side, they wanted answers. Answers that I'd rather keep short and sweet.

ೂ 28 ೞ

Rachel

They got all the obvious stuff out of the way first. How long have I known Panther? Where did I meet him? Have I seen or ever been a part of any criminal activity initiated by Panther? And the most substantial question of all, the one that mattered right now, Did I see Panther on the day that Patrick Alden was murdered? I wasted no time telling the story the way Panther and I planned: Eight o'clock, he stayed the night, and left when I left in the morning. I wanted to ask how did they even know that Panther and I knew each other. I mean, had they been watching from a nearby window or something? It was a creepy feeling just thinking that there were men spying on my private life, like I was some animal that needed to be watched closely. And if they were watching me, how much did they see? What did they see? And how many of these assholes had seen it? My stomach turned more as those ill thoughts corroded my mind. God, when would this be over?

Sitting in this damn… interrogation room didn't make this stop any rosier. As small and cold as this room was, I felt like I was meat in a freezer. They really tried to make it seem like this was your last stop before going to jail. I was afraid of breathing in too deep, being that this room stunk like a bag of clipped toenails. And with this big, glass window beside me, I felt like I was being watched all over again.

I had been alone in the stank room for about ten minutes now, overtaken by the stankness. The two cops that brought me in had run off somewhere investigating my answers, possibly comparing them to what they already knew, or didn't know. Whatever they were doing, I didn't care. I wanted to leave. And I was sure that they could tell through the big glass. I kept fidgeting in my seat, brushing back my hair with a bare hand, as if it wasn't already tight and combed down, and rubbing away the goosebumps on my arms. Yeah, it was obvious that this was a part of their strategy, but it was also pissing me off. And they couldn't coerce me into confessing to something that I didn't know, so why hold me here? They knew the facts. Why play this senseless game with a psychology major? If I knew anything, it was my own mind, and no one could make me lose it to the point that I didn't know how to control my actions.

But maybe that's what they were trying to do. They were playing on my professionalism and integrity, hoping that somehow they could irritate me enough to forget that this was nothing but a game, and force me to slip. On what, I didn't know, but I had to be aware of everything that they might try.

And being frustrated and worried was not helping. I dismissed all of the crazy thoughts of what was going on and thought about Panther. I missed him like hell. Around the first few months that Panther and I were kicking it, I remember coming home one day to a note on the door, a card stuffed in an envelope between the knob and the crevice of the lock. It intrigued me enough to open it right then and there. And it read, "Go behind the apartment complex, right next to the star apple tree, and you'll see how deep my attraction to you is." My high heels weren't made to move as fast as I did, but my heart was too jumpy to be patient. When I reached the tree, I glanced all around, overhead between the branches, and at my feet as I brushed through the brown, crisp leaves. Nothing was popping up. I was missing something about this riddle. I read the note again, searching for clues within the words. Right next to the tree, I thought, deep attraction goes. So giddy and excited, no wonder I missed it. Next to the star apple tree was a bench and a picnic table. It felt as if time stood still and like I was moving in slow-motion. I marveled at the hand carved, heart-shaped message from Panther that read, 'Parish and Rachel, the beginning of our forever'. I was so much in awe and amazement at Panther taking the time to carve these words into the earth, I almost missed the nail half-hammered into the bench, right where the heart dips in, and a string tied around it, falling through one of the spaces in the bench. I followed its path down, washed my feet over the dried leaves, and found another card. This one read, "At our favorite spot, you can find me again, resting where the green is like a part of my skin". I raced to the car, revved up the engine, skipped the drive gear, and threw the car into haul ass. And that's what I did, en route to our favorite spot, Dave and Buster's.

If the police saw the way I had zoomed through traffic, I would've been arrested for driving while crazy. I didn't allow anyone to slow me down. When I made it to D&B's, the doorman was there as always, but inside was completely empty. Soft jazz lullabied the stillness of the dining room. I stole another peek of the note, hoping this next clue would lead me to Panther already. The anticipation was killing me. While I was doing a Dale Ernhart through evening traffic, I was certain that by saying the green being a part of his skin, Panther meant the little miniature golf area on the other side of the dining section, but I searched every inch of that space, and found nothing. I went up and down the dining tables, kept my eyes alert for anything with a piece of green on it. I was hoping that it meant some money, but I came up empty on those greens, too. Until I ran into the last table on the floor. On the white, table linen, there was a handful of red, rose petals sprawled over the table, falling onto the seat, and guiding along a trail that lead to what I had missed; A plant right next to the table, covered with green leaves. I searched the plant thoroughly, and on its stem, I found another hand carved message. This one read, "The beauty that you hold inside compliments all the beauty that I see on the outside."

I couldn't take this.

Another note was peeking up from out of the soil. Before opening the letter, I brushed it clean. What was Panther doing? I was so anxious to know what else he had planned that I almost tore the card in half. Blood was rushing through my veins like a waterfall. In this letter, Panther wrote, "There's a beauty outside that grows within. And your beauty helped me to grow, so in return, that's what I'm giving." My heart was in in the clouds, but I had to control myself. Had to find the clue to my next journey. I read the message over and over again, trying to hold back the emotion of feeling like I was in heaven. Concentrate, I told myself; Beauty outside growing within. Beauty outside growing with... Outside! That was it. My surprise was somewhere outside. But where? I had to move. I dashed down the aisles filled with flashing lights and audio playbacks of cheering crowds and angry villains from Midway, the enormous gameroom setting at the rear of the D&B's. The lone exit sign would've been easy to miss if I hadn't been looking for it. My heels were clacking down the dark hallway as I raced for the doors. I pushed one open so hard it clanged against the outside wall. Embarrassed that someone noticed, I held still in the doorway. But a slight laugh from outside told me that someone had noticed, and I knew who the laugh belonged to. I stepped down the walkway, where the orange rays of the setting sun had my eyes squinted. And to the left of me, lounging in the comfort of the shade was Panther, sitting Indian-style over white table linen, two plates of food on each side, a bottle of champagne on ice, and roses forming the shape of a heart in the middle of the linen. I kicked off my heels, strutted over like I was so calm and cool, but as excited as a child at Chuck E. Cheese, glad and relieved that I had found my surprise.

I sat on my side of the linen as Panther offered me a glass of champagne. "I thank you, my dear," I said. "But you make a sister work for love."

He gave me that magical smile. "I'm just glad I have an intelligent woman to understand what I was doing. Or else I would've had two plates of food to myself."

I giggled softly as I lifted the glass to my lips.

Panther reached over and stopped my arm. "Not yet," he said. "You're not finished. You still had one last clue."

I set the glass down. "Yeah, and I found you."

"But it's not me that you're looking for."

I blew out a playful, frustrated breath, letting Panther know that I didn't mind the hunt, but right now, I'd just rather enjoy him. I said, "So what else am I looking for."

Before answering we both laughed at my irritation. Panther knew it wasn't easy to upset me, and it was funny to us both for me to even pretend like I was angry.

Panther pointed his eyes to a spot on the linen, and I followed them. Just where the heart dipped in, there was no rose, but a budding plant about four to six inches long. I looked at Panther in confusion.

He said, "I planted that for you about 6 weeks ago, and it's obvious that it wants to continue growing."

I leaned over and asked Panther to come to me. Our faces met right where the heart was. And for the first time, I told him that I loved him. We drew in closer, slowly, as if it was the first time all over again. And it felt that way when our lips touched.

The click from the doorknob turning snatched me out of my daydream and back into the reality of why I was in this room. The stankness shot back at me like a boomerang. Goosebumps flooded my arms as I sat frozen from the cold, rigid air, anticipating what these cops had to say now.

Detective Boone walked in with his tacky ass suit. His hard stare hadn't changed from back when we were in Andrea's office. And a poked out beer belly took the place of his flat chest as he strutted in my direction with that police arrogance. While a manila folder bounced against the side of his leg, the tapping of his feet echoed through the silence as he came to the table and took a seat.

I braced myself for what was to come. I could feel the perspiration building against the edges of my ponytail, and I wondered if detective Boone had noticed. He threw the folder down on the table and dropped his hat over it, slid it back and forth as if he were performing some kind of magic trick and would surprise me with whatever was underneath the hat. The folder and hat finally held still as Detective Boone crossed his legs and clasped his hands over his knee.

He said, "Feel free to start talking whenever you're ready."

Boone's demeanor was too relaxed for a man trying to close a murder case. What did he have on Panther to make him so confident? Was he playing a game to shake me up? Or was there really a surprise inside that manila folder? Either way, I was in this room for a reason, and I might as well swallow my fear and meet the inevitable.

I said, "Sam informed you about me, right?"

Boone extended a half-a-smile as his leg bounced back and forth. "I knew it wouldn't take long for a smart girl like you to figure it out."

"Is that why Ace was sent up to the men's facility?"

Boone shrugged. "I wouldn't know. I don't deal with juveniles too often."

"No, you just make them informants while innocent sixteen-year-olds get tried as adults."

Boone turned and faced me, his face flushed red. "Look, Ms. Baxter, your friends in the juvenile system is not my concern. Your boyfriend, Panther Coles is. Now is there anything you want to tell me?"

"I've told you everything." I almost didn't notice how my voice raised until my echo sharply shot back at me as if there were someone else in the room. I even had Boone surprised. He nodded and relaxed his hard stare.

This time he showed off a full smile. "8 o'clock, right?"

I also toned myself down. "That's what I said."

Boone began fidgeting with his hat again, picking it up and dropping it down as if his words were stuck inside. "And did you know that the crime took place at about seven?"

I shrugged. What was Boone trying to get to? "I don't know. Guess I do now."

"And did you ever ask yourself what Mr. Coles was doing then, before he made it to your house?"

"Panther's a business man, so usually he's handling his business."

"What kind of business might that be?"

"Panther owns a clothing store."

"Ms. Baxter, please. You and I both know that Mr. Coles cannot have plans to run a whole T.V. network by owning some neighborhood store. The truth is Mr. Coles is involved in a lot of illegal practices, which he is yet to be tried for, and the fact is—"

"Panther's business practices are not in question here, Detective. Mr. Alden's murder is, which Panther did not commit."

"Are you sure of that, Ms. Baxter?"

"Yes."

Detective Boone leaned back in his chair and faced the wall as his crossed leg rocked back and forth again. "And what makes you so sure, Ms. Baxter? Were you with him around seven o'clock?"

I folded my arms. "No."

"So you can't be sure."

"But I am."

"How?"

"Because I know Panther."

Boone's dry laugh circled the room and bounced off the four walls. "It's good to feel like we know people," he said. "It gives us a sense of fulfillment, like nothing can ever go wrong because you know a person, or because you think you know them. But you're a psychology major,

Ms. Baxter. I would think that you of all people would know better. You've seen enough ugliness to know that someone can have two, or three faces that you have never seen. And that's when you realize that there is so much about people that you don't know. And that's when things can get scary. Tell me, Rachel, do you know much about the law?"

The feel and smell of the interrogation hit me in a flash. Again I was feeling uncomfortable, out of place, and tired of dealing with all of this shit. I said, "I know you have no right to hold me here. And anymore questions would mean that I need a lawyer present."

"I thought so. I guess that means you also know what perjury is?"

I shook my head out of frustration. "Detective, can I go now?"

"Of course you know what perjury means?"

"Do you know what a lawyer means?"

Boone forced another smile, threw his hat back on. "No need for a lawyer, Ms. Baxter," he said. "Everything you need is right in there." He slid the manila folder my way.

ஐ 29 ര

Deidra

W hatever was in the folder, it couldn't be good. Detective Boone
was smiling like he just nabbed everybody on the F.B.I.'s most
wanted list. He was waiting on me, and I didn't want to touch the thing.
But then again, I was curious to know what they had on Panther. I
played it cool when I grabbed the folder, trembling inside as I opened
it.

A batch of black and white photos. They were of Panther with
another woman, and another, looking romantically comfortable, at
restaurants and parks. Some even looked like the spots that Panther had
taken me to. I wasn't sure. I didn't care. I was fuming.

Detective Boone pretended not to notice, smiling at the ceiling and
walls. A fresh look of arrogance flooded his face.

But this was what he wanted. To feel like he had won because he
figured these pictures would make me sell Panther out.

I threw the pictures down on the table. "So what?" I said. "That
doesn't prove that Panther killed anybody."

Boone propped his hands behind his head. "You're right," he said.
"Because of your alibi, Panther couldn't have done it, right? Even
though your alibi doesn't account for 7 o'clock."

I rolled my eyes, tired of dealing with all of this crap. "Listen,
officer, if this is all you have then you don't have much. So you might
as well let me—"

"Oh, I have a great deal more." Boone's voice rose. "Like either you tell the truth about this alibi, or Dalvin Shorter goes to the D.A. about how you may have killed a sexual offender by the name of Henry Jones."

I was stuck. No words would leave my mouth. And the tension clouded my head to a point where I couldn't think straight.

"I—I—I didn't do—"

"Don't tell me you didn't do it, Ms. Williams. You were about to be raped. Dalvin Shorter tracks Henry Jones down, and Mr. Jones is found by the river with a couple of bullets in him. But the bullets didn't kill Mr. Jones. An allergic reaction to some chemical caused him to asphyxiate. And this chemical is found in mace. A fine woman like you has to protect herself, Ms Williams. Do you have mace? Did you use any on Henry Jones?"

I was shaking in my seat. That motherfucker, Dalvin, set me up. "It's bullshit, Detective."

"If it's bullshit, then why is everybody from your old neighborhood saying that you were almost raped. Old friends like Audrey Wilson, whom you assaulted because she knew the truth."

"Fuck Audrey," I yelled. "I didn't do shit."

"Tell us the truth, Ms. Williams."

"I just said I didn't do anything."

"Ms. Williams." Another cop busted into the room, surprise and concern is his eyes. "Ms. Williams, please calm down. It's okay." He walked over to Boone and whispered in his ear.

Boone nodded. His face was flush red. Before he left the room, he exhaled slowly, fixed his hat in place, and pointed at me.

I responded with a middle finger back at him.

"It's okay," the other cop said. We watched as the other dickhead left the room.

The cop introduced himself as Detective Alex Gray. He held his hand out and I left him hanging. Didn't his dumb ass know that I wasn't in a friendly mood?

"Is there anything I can get you, Ms. Williams? A cup of coffee, some water, soda…"

If my "don't fuck with me" look didn't get through to this man, then I was sure that cops had to be the most aggravating people on earth. And since my stare was not getting through, I decided to mumble clear enough for him to understand exactly how I felt about them. "Stupid motherfuckers."

Detective Gray forced a smile. With his hands pocketed, he sat at the edge of the table. "Ms. Williams, I can tell that you're frustrated."

"I guess that makes you the smartest of the stupid motherfuckers."

Gray ignored my comment. Picked up the photos and stacked them neatly on the table. "I'm not the enemy here, Ms. Williams. And I'm not trying to be. Now considering the facts of this case, I can understand why you're upset. Forgive us if we may not appear to be the most sensitive group toward your situation, but we still have a job to do, Deidra. A man was killed, and our job is to bring the perpetrator to justice as quick as possible. All we ask is your cooperation."

I couldn't believe this asshole. I was ready to throw a chair at him for trying to play me like I was stupid. "Fuck your cooperation, detective. Five minutes ago, your partner was all over me about going to the D.A. on some bullshit that I had somebody killed. Now you strut in here with your slick tongue, asking for my cooperation. Too bad, so sad. I don't have shit for ya, except what I already told you."

"And that's enough for you, Deidra? An alibi is enough. We have witnesses that say otherwise. If your boyfriend goes to jail, there's a good possibility that you will too for the murder of Henry Jones."

I bit down on my lip. My head was ready to explode. I made an effort to be as calm as possible. "Once again, detective, like I told your partner, I had nothing to do with anyone getting killed."

Detective Gray nodded. He rubbed the sides of his face as if he were searching for more to say. "Do you know who might have, or why a lot of people are saying that you did?"

"No, I don't, detective. I guess a lot of people don't like me."

"What about Dalvin Shorter. He was one of Mr. Coles' soldiers. Any reason why he would say that you did?"

"Probably to set me and Panther up. You just said he was one of Panther's soldiers. Why would one of Panther's soldiers sell him out, unless of course he was getting something out of it? Like the state cutting him a deal for some other shit he may have gotten into. Or maybe Panther was not the black man that people claimed they saw at Mr. Alden's house on the day he was murdered. Maybe it was Dalvin Shorter. Think about it. Doesn't it sound sweet, detective? Dalvin claims that I, Panther's girlfriend, had somebody killed, knowing that I was Panther's alibi, and if I were lying about the times that Panther was at the house, then I would have to make a choice between me, or my man going to prison for life. Dalvin Shorter skates off as free as the wind. It's the perfect crime, detective. For Dalvin Shorter, that is. I mean, 2-3 sounds a whole lot better than life without parole."

Detective Gray's eyes rolled off to the side, as if he was contemplating my statement. I succeeded in getting some of the heat off of me. But just how much of my answer would stick, I didn't know.

"Not bad, Ms. Williams," Gray said. "If you were on trial here, you would raise a lot of doubt in the minds of the jury. Scary thought."

"Mr. Officer, I'm serious."

"I know you are. But I'm not a member of a jury. I'm also not a lawyer. I investigate all the clues that I have to bring forth as evidence against the suspect that is charged for the crime. If you had something more solid for me to go on, then maybe it would make a difference. But unfortunately, you don't. And right now, I have enough clues, enough evidence, enough witnesses to charge your boyfriend, Parish Coles, with this murder. And all that you and Mr. Coles have as a defense is your alibi, which doesn't even account for seven o'clock. So, I'm sorry, Diedra, but it looks like Panther is going down for murder, and you just might, too."

I closed, my eyes, shook my head, disgusted at how naïve I was. Detective gray almost had me convinced that he was on my side, and then spun my statement from a rock solid argument to nothing but a whisper in the air.

I wondered how Panther got caught up in this murder thing anyway. And why did he involve me? Why use me as an alibi if the murder took place after he supposedly left my house? Could Panther really have done it? He never said whether or not he did. And I never asked. I didn't think I had to. But now the police were asking me, and were ready to throw me in jail if I didn't tell them what they wanted to hear. Yet if they were counting on my four-to-six alibi, they probably didn't have much. Or maybe they did. Maybe they had something that Panther missed. Goddamn you, Panther. I just knew that he loved me too much to ever put me in a situation like this. But that still wouldn't change my decision. I agreed to stand by my man, and I was also keeping my word.

"And I'm sorry, too." I told Detective Gray, "but I can't help you. I saw Parish Coles the day that Mr. Alden was killed. Mr. Coles came to the house at four and left at six o'clock." I could hear the tension in my voice as it took over me. Felt as if it was crawling all over my skin.

"Ms. Williams," Detective Gray said, "you ought to know that you don't have to lie."

"I'm not lying."

"Do you know that you could go to jail for murder? You killed someone the other day."

"That's not true, Detective."

"Dalvin Shorter says it is. Even though I'm sure it was accident, we still have someone that says you did it."

"Then I guess it's my word against his."

Detective Gray shook his head, gathered up the photos on the table and showed them to me. "Look, Deidra. Is this worth fighting for? Is this worth going to jail for? This isn't love."

"Please, detective. You do not know Panther. I've been with him for two years now, and he has been very good to me."

"Does it look like he's being good now?"

"Those could've been taken years ago. I don't even know if these women even exist in his life anymore. All I know is you're accusing him of a crime that he didn't commit, and you're trying to get me to lie on him because you have some rumor that I had somebody killed, and pictures of my man with other women that were probably taken before I even met him. And with technology the way it is today, you all could be the ones that are lying."

Gray dropped the photos back down on the table, a look of disappointment spread over his face. "Very good again, Deidra. We could be the ones lying here. And that's why I hate the could be's and should be's. I love facts. Because the facts are the truth. So why don't we see what the truth is."

Detective Gray walked to the door and held it open.

ജ 30 ○ঃ

Sandra

The anticipation had me holding my breath. I didn't know what this cop had to show me, but I was afraid that it might kill me. As I sat at the table trying to dry the perspiration from my hands and regain my breath, the detective called for someone to come in the room. The last words he uttered were haunting, "Why don't we see what truth is". What was the meaning behind that? What did he have that was so crucial to this case? And was it enough to…

My worst fears were staring me in the face. They walked into the room and stood by the door, the two women that were in the pictures with Panther. I looked at the photos, and looked to them. Looked at the photos, looked at them. They were the same ones. My eyes weren't playing tricks on me, but I was hoping that my head was. I shut my eyes tight, dropped my head and shook it back and forth, praying that this was only a dream. But the two women just stared back like I was crazy. I wasn't for all of this.

We all took turns rolling our eyes at each other. I couldn't believe this. Couldn't believe Panther. After everything we've—Stop. Get it together, I told myself. My eyelids grew heavy with tears. I tried drying them, but more kept coming. I should've known that this was the case. I couldn't understand why I acted so surprised. All the times that Panther was gone, the refusals when I asked him to move in, the lies, they were all signs, but I chose to keep myself blind. Now I realized what the truth looked like. Still, I was not ready to face it.

"We might as well get this over with," one of them said. She must have been the bold one. Her ghetto attitude was seeping out of her pores.

"I'm Deidra," she said. "Yes, I am Panther's lady, and have been Panther's lady for two years. Now…who are you two?"

The other one cracked a self-serving smile, walked into the middle of the room like she was the shit. Her head was high, glasses, arms folded, shabby ponytail, and was fake as her chipped fingernails. "I'm Rachel," she said. "Panther and I have been together for about nine months now."

Pshhh. That wasn't shit. What did Panther see in her boring ass, anyway? She was probably one of those intellectual girls that were crazy for thugs. Smart enough to balance the budget in America, but would give all of it to a man.

I had nothing to say to them, so I didn't respond. They watched me, waiting, wondering. I knew they were anxious to match the name with the face, but it felt good to have this little bit of control over their emotions. Especially since they had me wondering also. It sickened me to think that Panther was not with just one, but two other women. And doing God knows what. The same way he held me, he would hold them. Love… no. He fucked them, and possibly right before he fucked me. I was now convinced that he never made love to me. How could he love me and lie? Cheat. Everything that I gave him he took for granted and used my body as if I was another number on the scoreboard. A piece of ass whenever one of his other women weren't around.

And Aunt Mabel warned me. She begged me to open my eyes, yet I chose to remain blindfolded, walking down a path that I thought was love. Seeing false images of a big wedding, extravagant house with several rooms, divine children. How could I see all of that when Panther couldn't decide which piece of ass he wanted to have on a Friday night? Or whose arms he would rather wake up in on a Sunday morning. It must have been hard for him when he had three choices. I wonder if it was hard for him to imagine how I would feel if and when I found out. Or how the two women who stood in front me would feel. I looked at them, thinking that this was not their fault. We were all blindfolded, going down the same path, following the same voice, the same smell, the same touch that we thought was reserved for only one of us.

"I'm sorry," I said to Deidra and Rachel. I told them my name, and how I had been with panther for a year. They both refused when I offered them to sit at the table. I'm sure they were just as uncomfortable about this situation as I was.

"So now that we know the truth," Deidra said, "where do we go from here?"

I said, "Nowhere, but out. As much as I love Panther, I don't think I can trust him anymore. In fact, I know I can't. You two can have him."

I watched Rachel's tears roll down her cheeks.

Diedra rolled her eyes at me. She said, "Whatever, girl. Don't try to act all proud and righteous now. You've been kicking it with Panther for a year, and you expect me to believe that you don't want him anymore?"

"That's right," I said. "I couldn't trust Panther again. I don't know what else he could be lying about."

"And I can't trust you," Deidra yelled. "How do I know that you're not just screaming out 'fuck Panther', just so you can throw us off?"

"Because I can't love a man that I can't trust will be there for me."

"But where were you for a whole year?" Deidra came back at me. "Do you live outside of South Florida?"

"No, I don't. I live in Pembroke Pines."

"And did you see Panther every night of the week?"

"No, I can't say that—"

"Then you can't act like you didn't think that Panther had another woman."

"Of course, it went through my mind, but I—"

"You never asked because if you asked, it would make you seem weak. You would look insecure. And with a man like Panther, you couldn't be that way, because you thought that he'd walk all over your ass. So don't act like this is some big surprise. Truth is you were thinking the same things we were. You hoped that Panther popped the question one day, and praying that your own paranoid questions would never be answered. Truth is you would rather have stayed in the dark just like us."

Deidra irked my nerves. She made it seem as if I was guilty of wrongdoing. As if I was the one that lied to everybody. I said, "Deidra, I'm not going to argue with you, especially over something like this. What I think doesn't even matter. I mean if you're going to stay with Panther anyway, why worry about me?"

"I'm not worried about you."

"Then why are you on me like I took your man? I didn't take anything from you. He took us. He took all of us for a ride. I don't think I can deal with that for the rest of my life. I don't know how you could."

I must have finally had Deidra convinced. She studied me with wincing eyes, but didn't have a come back this time. Then she stepped up close to the table, her arms folded and hips poked out with attitude.

She said, "I don't know much of your experience with black males, Ms. Reese, but let me tell you mine. See, my father was never around. I can't even remember when I last saw him. My older brother is doing twelve years. When I was sixteen, my boyfriend was killed by the boyfriend of another jealous bitch that wanted my man, and there a several times where I've come close to being sexually assaulted, some of them were men that I knew. In other words, if you haven't noticed, Sandra, it's hard to find a good man, and there is no such thing as a perfect one. Do I want my man to cheat on me? Hell no. But yes, I do want my man. And I do love him. You couldn't imagine the things we've been through."

I said, "Yeah, and he could also give you aids."

"Oh, bitch, shut up."

"Look who's calling who a bitch."

"Wait, wait, wait a minute, ladies," Rachel butted in. "I don't mean to break up the party, but look at where we are. There's a reason that we're in here, and it's not because the cops want to know who's gonna be the one to marry Panther."

Deidra and I were still staring each other down. She wouldn't back down, but neither would I. I didn't like this bitch's attitude.

"What do they want with us?" Rachel said. "All of us. That's the real question. I'm here because on the day that Patrick Alden was killed, I was Panther's alibi from eight o'clock until the next morning."

I heard Rachel's words clearly, but Deidra responded in confusion. "You were Panther's alibi from eight o'clock until the next day."

Rachel nodded.

Deidra said, "I was his alibi from four to six."

I answered before they asked. "And I was six to eight."

Deidra clapped her hands together and shook her head. "That's why they wanted us here. They wanted to find out the truth."

I said, "But what's the truth?"

"What do you mean what's the truth?" Rachel spoke up. "Your alibi is all the truth that they need."

Yeah, right, I thought. The alibi. After everything today, I wasn't sure what the truth was anymore. And after Panther's lie about me being the only woman that he loved, I didn't know what my claim to be his alibi would do to me. I no longer trusted him, so how could I trust that lying for him would keep me from being thrown behind bars? And how could I live with myself, knowing that I allowed it to happen?

ಬ 31 ಡ

Rachel

There's a reason for everything. There's something behind everything that you see, or hear, or go through. And right now I was trying to figure what this was about.

First the police. Why would the police put us all in an interrogation room together? They were up to something. They were hoping to get something out of us three together that they couldn't get when we were on our own. They were hoping that one of us would break down and snitch.

It had to be. That was the reason for the pictures. The police figured if the pictures were shown, it brought the notion of betrayal. And by feeling betrayed, we would give up on Panther in a heartbeat. Another form of divide and conquer. They wanted to turn us against each other. They hoped that we would forget what we believed, which was sticking by our man, because after seeing those pictures, we realized that neither one of us had a man. Like Sandra said, "Panther took all of us for a ride."

And now the police were watching through the glass. Waiting patiently as we grew impatient. They were probably laughing, while we grew sick of the sight of each other by the second, tortured by thoughts of what Panther was doing to the other two women, actions that we trusted were only shared between the man we loved and one of us. All of our faith in Panther was torn down by paranoid illusions of sexual positions, sacred words of love, and precious memories of time that was shared with someone else.

Yes, we all were hurt by Panther now. Even Deidra. I read it on her face. Her words may have said otherwise, but there was something behind that also. No woman from here to Mars wanted to share the man that she loves for the rest of her life. There were some deep, psychological things going on with Deidra. Yes, I understood her loyalty to Panther, and I applauded it. But what scared me was just how much of it would she be willing to take.

Sandra was scary in her own right, but more so to Panther than to herself. I wasn't sure about her. She acted as if she cared nothing about Panther or the alibi, yet her alibi was the most important one. Her alibi was the one that corresponded to the time of Patrick Alden's murder. And more importantly, to Panther's innocence.

And I didn't know if her and Deidra's alibis were real or not. I doubt if any of us knew whether or not any of our alibis were true. But one thing was certain. It could not be discussed between the three of us in here. Just the hint of a whisper and the cops would bum rush us. They had us where they wanted. Cold, frustrated, hungry, feeling betrayed, and no way to communicate what it would take to get Panther off. And that's all that mattered.

I had to find a way to do it. Convince these women to help our brother out when he needed us most. We were all that Panther had. Deidra may not have been so hard, but you could never be sure. Sandra was definitely the key to this whole alibi thing, but at a time like this, we all had a job to do. We all had to remember what was most important.

I stepped to Sandra first. I had to. We had no clue of when the cops would bust in and separate us. I played it cool as I took the seat at the table in front of her. Deidra was leaning against the wall behind us, facing the other way. She and Sandra shared too many harsh words to stand looking at each other much longer. But while Deidra was still hot with rage, Sandra was drowning in despair, the corners of her eyes slowly sinking.

I said, "I can sense your strength. I can tell that you are very independent."

Sandra laughed. "And what, are you, a psychologist?"

I clasped my hands together. "Yes, I am."

Sandra shot me a fake smile. "A thousand points for me."

This would be a little more difficult than I expected. I had to get straight to the point. There was no time for bullshitting. "Panther got us good," I said.

I wish I could've taken those words back. I got a 'shut the fuck up' look from Sandra. "I meant to say that Panther sure knew how to treat a woman."

After taking in a deep breath, Sandra propped her hands underneath her chin. "That was a part of his game. And he played it very well."

Tears flooded Sandra's eyelids. I thought she might have been embarrassed, but she allowed them to tumble over her cheeks and splash onto the table.

I feared that I was losing time because it seemed as if Sandra was losing hope. I asked her, "Do you know what he was like as a child, or what he might have been doing?"

With the back of her hand, Sandra dried the tears away. "No, but I can only guess that he was chasing little girls in little skirts, until he grew older, and was able to cruise around in his car, chasing grown women in little skirts." The corners of Sandra's eyes were sinking again.

I ignored her sarcasm and went on. "Panther once told me when he was thirteen his mother had a man that she was crazy about too. He said that the man was smooth, tall, dark, strong, and prideful. His mama was falling all over herself for this man. He spoiled the shit out of her. Would come by right after he got paid and bring flowers, take her out to dinner, and devout his whole weekend to pleasing her. Eventually he asked Panther's mama to marry him, and that was all it took. He was at the house every day. Panther didn't mind. The guy was cool. Gave Panther a few dollars on occasion, and every now and then would take him to the movies. But after a while, it was Panther's mother that started acting funny. She would snap at him for no reason. Food wouldn't be cooked, claiming that she was eating out with her boyfriend, yet only bologna and peanut butter would be in the refrigerator, the same things he would eat for lunch. Panther approached his mother about it, and she broke down. Boo-hoo cried over his tiny chest, saying that she was sick and had been stressed. She wouldn't say why, but Panther figured it was because of her boyfriend.

He came around less often. And when he did come, it was around three in the morning, then getting up at seven o'clock for work.

"A month later it was Panther's fourteenth birthday. His mother surprised him with a gold bracelet that he had been asking for. She was back to being the mother that he knew. They grew close again. But then one night the boyfriend came in late as he normally did. He started shouting at the top of his lungs. 'Where is it? Where's my stuff? I know you took my stuff.' Panther's mama screamed out that she didn't, and begged for him to let her go. When Panther rushed to defend his mama, the man pushed Panther down. Panther's head hit the edge of the nightstand and he was out cold. A few hours later, Panther awakened, rushed to his mother's room and found her sitting at the edge of her bed, facing a mirror and lighting a crack pipe. Before she could breathe in the smoke, Panther ran to her and knocked the pipe out of her hand, shattering the glass pipe against the wall. His mother screamed, 'What did you do that for? I need that.' Panther said, 'No, you don't mama. Don't you remember? You said that all we ever needed was each other.' Panther's mama yelled, 'Boy, are you stupid? We need money. I just lost the rent money to the man that I thought loved me. All of it, Parish. So we don't have shit. But I need my stuff, Parish. That's all I have, and I want it.'

"At that moment, Panther grabbed the baggie of rocks. He rushed out of the house and sold the rocks to a known drug dealer. All he got was a few dollars, not nearly enough for the rent. He went back home to find his mother sound asleep. She should've left for work, but Panther knew that it wasn't going to happen that day. Money was already tight, rent was due, and the refrigerator was bare. Panther planned to sell the bracelet he had gotten for his birthday. But the bracelet was not in his drawer. He shook his mother awake. 'Mama, Where's my bracelet?' Panther's mama broke down crying again. She told Panther that she didn't take it. She admitted to being sick, but she did not take his bracelet. Panther didn't give it a second thought. He believed his mother because he knew that someone else had to take it. Someone that his mother thought was loyal to her.

"A few days later, they were evicted. They moved in with Panther's aunt, a one-bedroom apartment that was already crowded. Panther and his aunt had checked his mother into rehab, while Panther got to hustling. He said he did everything. Did what he had to do, including cutting grass. By the time he was eighteen, Panther had thousands of dollars in the bank, and at age twenty-one had opened his first business. Said the first thing he did was buy his mama a house. She had been clean for seven years, and was able to look after herself. When she asked Panther why he did all that he did for her after what she put him through, Panther said it was because he stood by what they believed. That all they had was each other, and that was all they needed."

Sandra looked up, her eyes no longer drunk with despair.

I said, "I know that Panther hurt you. He hurt all of us. And he basically took away the trust that we gave him freely. But I have never been with a man that has loved and inspired me spiritually, creatively, and intellectually like Panther has. Yes, he's given me a lot of physical things, too. But I know that we loved him for more. I know that we love him for everything that he's been to us."

I kept quiet after that. Allowed Sandra to marinate on my words for a moment.

Deidra came to the table and stood next to us, her eyes set in confusion. She said, "Are you sure about that?"

Before I could answer her, the doorknob turned and Detective Gray came in. "All right, ladies. That's enough of the chit chat."

Sandra said, "Are we free to go?"

"In a minute," Gray said. "We need everybody in their rooms so we can—"

"The hell do you mean in a minute," Sandra yelled. "I need my lawyer. All of this is not necessary."

"This is necessary, Ms. Reese. We need to take a written statement from—"

"I don't want to do this anymore today. Speak with my lawyer."

"Ms. Reese, please. I promise you, after today, after we take the statement, we won't need anything else, and everything will be fine."

"Fine for who? You? Or Ms.-I think I am Mrs. Parish Coles, over there?"

"Goddamn right," Diedra yelled, "because we know you won't be."

"Ladies, that's enough," Gray said. He took Deidra's hand and she pulled away, walked to the door mumbling motherfuckers, assholes, and all kinds of curse words at everybody in the room.

"Let's go, Ms. Baxter," Gray said.

I didn't want a fight. I just wanted this to be over with. But as I got to the door and turned back, I saw Sandra's face and felt like this might end up being a fight for all of us. And one that was far from being over.

ೞ 32 ೞ

Deidra

How long would the bullshit go on? When would it end? These cops would've done anything to stick Panther with this murder. Smart move on their part, bringing all of the women together, hoping they might get one of us to snitch. They were just wasting their time with me. But that other bitch, that Sandra. She was as shaky as one of those bobble-head dolls. I couldn't figure what Panther saw in her to be with for a year, other than a piece of ass. Rachel, too. They both looked like the dumb type that did nothing but throw money and pussy in between his lap. Money and pussy. Money and pussy. They wouldn't have known what being true meant if they looked it up in the dictionary. They were just a couple of young girls that fell head over heels for a man like Panther. I felt sorry for them both, thinking that they had found their true love, like Shrek and Princess Fiona. And one of them was so dumb that she felt for some bogus story about—

The bump against the door pulled me away from my thoughts. What was it now? The only words I cared to hear was that I was free to go. And even if it weren't those words, the only ones that could've replaced them was Panther was innocent. I'd stay in this torture room all night if I was promised to hear those words in the morning.

Detective Boone, with his punk ass, strutted in the room, shut the door behind him, and stood far back as if his breath was too harsh for him to come any closer. I didn't mind. The smell of coffee and cigarettes mixed with Old Spice was as appealing as roach spray.

Boone said, "Deidra, you have one last chance."

I looked at him as if his stink breath actually reached me. "One last chance for what?"

He took a few steps forward. "To come clean of course."

"Come clean." He almost made me curse, but I relaxed, thinking that was what they wanted. To shake me up. To watch me slip. All of their moves deliberate, calculated, even as he stood back, it was all some sort of trick to fuck with my head. I recalled the other day when I was in jail and that old lady, Ms. Eleanor, tried schooling me. And I understood now. In confrontation, blowing up and throwing hands was not always necessary. People were going to talk shit at times just to test me. And they could say whatever they wanted, so long as they respected me. That was what I had been blind to, with Audrey getting me locked up, with that carpet muncher in the jail cell, even with killing Henry Jones. I could've waited. I could've gone to the police and had them handle Henry Jones. But instead, I may be spending the rest of my life in prison for being impatient. And afraid.

At that moment, I was hot with Panther. Why do this to me? Why use me as an alibi. There was no need. The murder took place around seven. And I didn't see him for that whole day. Up to this point, I never thought that Panther would hem me up. But now it appeared as if I was going down. Down for killing some sick bastard by accident, and trying to protect my man from the nasty hands of the law. And yet he couldn't be around for me in the craziest hours of my life. I was facing some hard prison time to protect my man from a crime that I wasn't even sure that he was innocent of. Was he really at Sandra's between six and eight, or was that just a lie, too? Did he kill that man, ride off in the same truck that witnesses on the news said they saw him in, and spend the night at Rachel's as if it never happened? Did her fuck her that night, too. Was he fucking her at the same time that I was being—

"Yes, Ms. Williams," Detective Boone said, breaking through the fiery tension of my nerves, catching the flames before they balled up and exploded in my chest. I was prepared to let all of it out with a scream.

"The way this ends," Boone continued, "is dependent on you."

Obviously, Boone was talking about the killing of Henry Jones. My alibi didn't mean much because the murder of that white man didn't take place between four and six. Boone was trying to strike up a deal. He wanted me to give Panther up in exchange for what I did to Henry Jones. In exchange for my freedom.

I asked Boone, "What would it take for this to have a happy ending?"

Boone finally sat down, leaned back in his chair, crossed his legs and exposed the white skin poking through the hole in his socks. A smirk of relief sprung from the corners of his mouth. He said, "For you to tell me everything, Ms. Williams. About the alibi, and if you had any clue that Mr. Coles killed Patrick Alden, that would be even better. It would make for a terrific ending for us both."

I nodded as Boone's words from earlier came back to me. I said, "I thought you already had everything you needed to convict Panther."

Now Boone was stuck. An embarrassing laugh took the place of the smirk. "True," he said, "but the more evidence against him, the easier things are."

Easy. How could Boone use that word so freely? I was convinced that these cops cared nothing about the victims or the perpetrators. It seemed more like a game to them, in which one person, or a department could say that they had more points than another because of the bodies that they placed behind bars. If I actually had been raped, this system may not have given a shit. And if it were to happen to my sister, a twelve year-old girl, they still would come after me for killing Henry Jones, rather than try to prevent another Henry Jones from being produced.

"Things will never be easy for me," I said. "Don't you know? Panther's a powerful man. How would you guarantee my safety?"

"Witness protection," Boone said with delight in eyes. "Believe me, Ms. Williams, you will never have to worry about Parish Coles again."

"And what about my family? Can you promise their safety? My little sister, my brothers, they cannot live with me because my mother uses them to get her aid."

A smirk sprang up again. "There are ways around that also."

I didn't doubt that.

"What about my brother that's locked up."

Boone leaned forward, clasped his hands together. "You mean Eric?"

"How did you know—"

"Eric is a special case. One where the powers that be have made sure that he serves the majority of the term he's been given. To make it short and sweet, Ms. Williams, Eric has to worry about his own safety. And I know that you want your brother home, but it is not a part of the deal. There's nothing I can do for him."

Sounded like rehearsed lines from a page of bullshit.

I asked, "Who's giving me the offer?"

"The D.A. You know everybody, including the mayor, wants this over with as soon as possible. And the more we have on Mr. Coles, the quicker this thing will end, for the families, the detectives, and for you and your family. Trust me, Deidra. It makes everybody's life that much easier."

There it was again. That word, easy. It was used so loosely you would think that it was as natural as air. A phenomenon that existed for every living creature at any time of the day. I thought about the word again, and about the detective's last statement. If everybody's life should've been that much easier, then why was I almost raped? Why did the person that saved me from being raped turn against me and finger me as the killer? Why did I have to sell my man out just to give my sister a better living environment? And why weren't the powers that be powerful enough to get my brother out of prison? The truth was they didn't care because they didn't need my alibi. To them, my brother was just another black body in prison. He was supposed to be make things easier for everybody else, yet nobody cared about how life for him was very much hard.

I decided to get it over with. I knew where my heart was. And besides, I hated playing games. I said, "I have told you everything, detective. And there is no more to tell. Parish Coles was with me the day Patrick Alden was killed, between four and six o'clock."

Boone turned as red as a beet, his jaws tight as they trembled. "You're trying to save some lucky criminal from going to jail, what are you going to do when Dalvin Shorter starts singing to the D.A.?"

I leaned in close so Boone could see that there wasn't pinch of fear in my eyes. "Then I guess I'll see his bitch ass in court."

"And I bet you wouldn't get too far with that."

I nodded. "Maybe so. Maybe not. But I could never take the word from a man whose cologne is stinker than his breath."

Boone leaned away from the table and back into his chair, finally getting the hint. He cleared his throat as if he had gotten stuck on what he wanted to say. "And I'm glad that I can get two other women's word about these alibis."

I dropped my head in thought. For a moment, Boone had me stuck on what to say. It was true that the other two girls were still out there, and I had no idea of their agendas. All I could do was control mine. And after reciting the serenity prayer to myself, I said to Boone, "Then I guess you'll do what you have to do. I've already done my part."

A knock came at the door, caused us to break our stares on each other. Boone left the table and strutted to the door. Detective Gray was the one knocking and called Boone out into the hallway with him. They left the door open and allowed me to watch. As they whispered to each other, I tried reading their lips, knowing I had zero lip reading skills. Boone seemed confused, his eyes screwed up as he pocketed his hands. Was it good news for Panther? The conversation was hard to decipher from so far a distance. Whatever they were saying had Boone blood red again. That was enough to force a smile out of me for the moment.

Boone came back inside and shut the door behind him. The stink of the room and Boone's cologne took turns jabbing at my nose. With his hands pocketed, Boone moved up to the middle of the room, his face looking as if he was lost for words again. My heart fluttered prematurely as I daydreamed of this being the end. I could hear everything that Boone was going to say. What he wanted to dismiss, but couldn't. What he had no choice but to say. "Panther is innocent. You're free to go home". And the redder that Boone became, the more I felt as though I would hear those words. Finally, I thought, this was about to be over.

"I don't know how this has happened," Boone confessed.

I nodded with excitement.

"But somehow," he continued, "it has."

Of course it has.

He shook his head. "I should've known."

Yes, you should've.

"Like you said, Panther's a powerful man."

You should've listened when I said that, too.

"And somehow he's managed to get you off the hook."

"What?" I said aloud. I was confused. "What are you talking about? What do you mean get me off the hook?"

Boone turned away, paced back to the door with his head lowered. "I'm talking about Dalvin Shorter." When Boone reached the door, he turned and faced me, his eyes tight with tension. "He's dead."

I almost didn't believe what I heard, but the truth was written all over Boone's face. The man that was trying to frame me had been killed. All kinds of emotions, happiness, fear, and confusion all at once came over me. Right now it didn't matter how Dalvin Shorter was killed, but rather who the hell was he? How was he convinced into coming after me? And was it worth him losing his life for? This was the craziest moment in my life. In two days, I was involved with having two men killed. But in no way did I feel guilty about it. I knew that my family and I never had to worry about those two ever again. The chains of the pressure around me had loosened. On the outside I let out a sigh of relief, while inside, I told God thank you.

Now happiness was the only feeling I had when Boone opened the door. He said, "You're free to go, Ms. Williams." Before he exited into the hallway, his eyes locked in on mine. "But don't fool yourself into thinking that this is over."

As I rose to leave, I studied Boone and his words.

A crooked smile spread over his face. "Let's just say that I'm glad that this case is not dependent on you. Like you said earlier, Ms. Williams. You've done your part. Now it's time that I do mine."

As Boone walked off, I wondered how much did Sandra care for Panther? And with everybody, especially Panther, counting on her alibi, was she going to help in making this thing easy for us all?

ಐ 33 ಞ

Sandra

The door was pushed open and pulled me from my daydream, from paranoid thoughts of Panther behind bars, questioning whether or not I would visit him, and if I did, would I have forgiven him for forsaking the love I thought we shared. I didn't know what made me think about such things, but I knew that I would have to face them if, and when the time came. At this point, I was ready to get out of this room. And ready to get on with my life.

Detective Boone walked over to the table, opened the manila folder and spread out the pictures of Panther with Rachel and Deidra as if I hadn't already seen them. As if I wanted to remember that I had been dating a lying son of a bitch.

"Fact," Boone shouted, poking his beer-pregnant belly out in arrogance, "Cameras show Ellen Alden, the late Patrick Alden's wife, leaving their house at approximately 7:03. The cameras at the drugstore show her arriving there at 7:10. She picks up a few trinkets, moisturizer, paper towels, maxipads, what have you."

"Question," I said, breaking Boone's flow, using lawyer tactics like I was in the courtroom, "Why isn't Mrs. Alden a suspect? How do we know that Mr. Alden wasn't dead before she left?"

"Because home cameras also show him coming from the pool and into the house once she left."

I never said I was that good in lawyer tactics, so I kept my mouth shut.

"Fact," Boone continued, "The cameras at the drugstore do not have Mrs. Alden leaving, or speaking on the phone, or looking suspicious in any way during the time that she was there. The only person they show that she spoke with was the cashier, and she hardly said hello to him. She gathers all of her bags by herself, and exits the drugstore at 7:57."

Still, no lawyer techniques were coming to me. I just absorbed everything, praying that something good would come out of this for Panther.

"Fact," Boone went on, "Home cameras have a gray S.U.V. pulling up to the house at approximately 7:21, a black man with the size, build, height, and skin complexion matching that of Panther Coles. Eyewitnesses, neighbors from across the street, and an El Salvadorian gardener all have made claims that they saw the same thing."

"But that doesn't say anything. Did anybody see his face?"

"Don't play yourself, Ms. Reese. You're a smart woman. You work for a law firm. The evidence is right in front of us."

Boone pointed at the pictures of Panther with the other girls, blatantly trying to tug at my nerves. "Don't try to play me, detective," I said. "All you have is a black man that has the same physical characteristics as Panther. What is this, a case of all black people look alike?"

"Ms. Reese, it was Panther Coles."

"Nobody knows that. It could have been somebody else."

"Patrick Alden has not had any black person other than the chief of police and Parish Coles to his house in years. And I'm sorry, Sandra, but just because you're a racist, it doesn't give someone the right to kill you."

I was flaming now. The police were saying that Panther killed a man in cold blood. And would probably be going to prison for it if they caught him. Tears rolled down my face with a vengeance. I didn't want to believe that Panther could do this, but I no longer knew what to believe. Deep within my heart, I still believed that Panther was a good person. For a year now, he had taken me into outer space. I fell in love with the reality that he was giving me.

But now that reality had drastically changed, and a nightmare haunted me. Locked and cornered me within the depths of its darkness. A darkness so thick that it caused me to doubt that I ever knew Parish Coles. Or that a man named Parish Coles had ever existed.

"Believe me, Sandra," Detective Boone said, his eyes soaking in desperation. "Panther was the man at Patrick Alden's house. And I know you don't want to hear me say this, but Panther is also guilty of murder."

My blood was so hot with hate I could feel my veins reaching out to choke Boone and his words. The dark side of me wanted to come out to the light. I couldn't...

Wait a minute.

"You don't have anything on Panther," I told Boone. "It was too dark to know that Panther was even in the truck."

"Inconclusive evidence, Ms. Reese."

"Inconclusive evidence my ass. You know you don't have him. Panther is innocent."

"But what about you, Ms. Reese?"

"Don't try to play games, detective. What about me?"

"Are you sure that Panther was at your house at seven o'clock?"

"Why wouldn't I be sure?"

"Because you live in a gated community," Boone said. "And cameras are on every car as soon as they enter. License plate numbers are on tape as we speak, Ms. Reese. Do you know which car Mr. Coles drove when he supposedly came to your house at six o'clock?"

I couldn't allow myself to get jammed, but Boone had me and he knew it. His face was as cool as an ice cream cone.

I wasn't sure if Boone was lying about the cameras or not, but I couldn't test him either. My mouth wouldn't move. I was stuck in fear of uttering the wrong thing. Perspiration soaked my hands. Anxiety held my heart hostage and quickened its beat. And although I tried my best to stop them, the tears came crashing down my face like a rainstorm. How could Panther do this to me? Why? I only wanted a good man. A man that would treat me right. A man with goals, ambitions, and dreams. A man that would love me as if I was the only woman in the world. As if his soul depended on it.

"It's okay," Boone said, his tone distant and patronizing. "I understand how this may feel, but you still have your life to think about. You still have to do what's right. Listen to me, Sandra. Panther is no good for you. He never was."

The heat in my eyes must have been enough to tell Boone to shut the fuck up, because he did.

"Obstruction of justice," Boone went on. "If you lie for this man, you can go to prison, Sandra. Is this worth it? Your life. Your reputation. Your freedom. Is it worth it?" Boone grabbed two photographs from the table of Panther kissing each of his other two women. Two pictures of Panther romantically involved with Deidra and Rachel, and all the while, betraying me. Boone said, "Is he worth it?"

I dropped my head to escape those images of Panther with his other women. Goddamn you, I cursed Panther in my head. How could he fuck with my life this way? If a mirror were near, I would've tossed it against the wall, disgusted with myself for being so dumb. For being so fucking blind. And if Panther and I had a house together, I would've destroyed everything in it. Burned that motherfucker to ashes like Lisa 'Left Eye' Lopes did. All of the hate and anger that he created, I would've taken out on everything that pissed me off. On everything that had anything to do with Panther. No, my tears were not falling out of sorrow. I didn't feel sorry for Panther anymore. I didn't feel anything.

I had to be real now, and say whatever I needed to say, despite the agony that tore at my heart. I could no longer hold this pain in. "Working for a law firm," I told Boone, "I've seen a lot of fucked up things that you may or may not know about. I've seen lawyers, and their rich clients laugh at how they have stolen from people that are poor already. I've seen cold-hearted killers up close tell us to our faces that they would kill again if they were out on the streets, only to see them set free in a matter of months, possibly moving to another state to claim their next batch of victims. I've seen doctors, police officers, politicians, get away with crimes that the average man would spend the rest of his life in prison for. And after I saw women being locked up, their children snatched away from their arms because they were trying to protect some man, I thought I had seen everything.

"Then I began to watch the news and have seen in the last couple of days how they have tried to crucify my baby. The love of my life. The way they spoke of Parish Coles, he may as well have been the antichrist. There wasn't a good deed done by this man, according to all these journalists, and so-called law experts that get paid to give their shitty ass opinions about everyone and everything. Some days, the coverage on Panther was the only coverage that they had on any black man, or any black person period. And after all of this news, and all of these expert opinions, if you didn't know Panther Coles, you would've thought that the man I loved was the craziest man alive. And something like that, I wasn't able to stand. But not as much as seeing a woman forsake her life, her dreams, and her family, and go to jail for a man that probably doesn't even lover her."

A twinkle gleamed in Boone's eye as a slight smile began to spread over his face. "What are you saying, Ms. Reese?"

I couldn't answer Boone's question. My soul felt empty, my heart was fed up.

"Ms. Reese, are you saying that Panther was not at your house between six and eight o'clock?"

As a tear fell from my face, my eyes followed, examining the mess I created over the table. I could see myself in the thick puddle, the despair in my face as deep as the hurt I felt inside.

"Ms. Reese," Boone said. "Did you see Panther Coles at all on the day that Patrick Alden was killed?"

I could no longer look at the pain in my eyes. There were saying that I had been through enough. I looked up and allowed Boone to see all that I had been through. And my confession to him sailed out lighter than the softest whisper. Still it felt as if the whole world heard me when I said no.

The elation on Boone's face made me despise him even more. His face burst into a smile, the air he released from his chest signaled his sense of relief.

I had never felt such heartache in my life. Never felt so drained. So weak. My mind kept trying to persuade me to believe that I did the right thing, but nothing else inside of me would respond. I felt like there was nothing in my seat but a woman's body, lifeless, and void of the one thing that makes us human. A heart. The woman I knew as Sandra Reese ran off and left her responsibilities behind, just as Panther Coles did to me a few days ago.

Boone said, "You're a brave woman, Sandra."

My eyes showed Boone that if he were the last cop on earth, I wouldn't have called him.

The door flew open. Detective Gray leaned against it, held open for Dennis to walk in. Both their faces were wrapped in concern.

"Something's come up," Gray said. "The chief wants to see us now."

Boone hesitated, his face in confusion. "Yeah, fine. Good. I've gotten what I needed."

As Boone stood up to leave, Dennis blocked his path. "Yeah, I bet you have," Dennis said.

Confusion flooded Boone's face again. "What's going on here?"

"Let's move," Gray said. "Chief wants us now."

Before Boone left the room Dennis stared him down as if he was ready to beat him down. I had seen Dennis run from roaches. Something was up with him.

Dennis wore a gray, flannel suit, his hands pocketed as he stood near the door. "I tried calling you," he said. "Hoped that you would've been home, or on your way by now."

With the back of my hand, I wiped my face. "Yeah, I thought so, too. Obviously, they had other plans for me."

Dennis removed the handkerchief from his jacket, came toward me, and a look of surprised sprung up in his eyes as he examined the photos on the table. He took a seat, handed me the handkerchief, and shook his head while he gathered the photos and moved them to the side. "I'm sorry," he said. "I didn't know."

I responded with a giggle, appreciative of Dennis' kind words. "It's okay," I told him. "It wasn't you."

As if he was trying to find the right words, Dennis' eyes tightened. "I just want to know if—"

"I'm fine," I said. "I'll be—"

I paused as a shiver of hurt ran through my blood. "I'll be okay."

Dennis did not look convinced. His hands were clenched, shoulders tight as if he was nervous.

I managed to smile at his silly behind. "Are you gonna be okay?"

He cleared his throat, took the handkerchief away, placed it aside, and firmly held my hands. "I was calling you because I got an emergency call from the hospital."

Out of instinct, I pulled my hands away from Dennis. My mind raced a mile a minute while my heart beat in fear, hoping whatever my senses were telling me were wrong. "What is it, Dennis?"

He paused. His mouth was wide open as if the weight of what he wanted to say held down his tongue. "They said they tried reaching you at home, and I when I didn't get you, I came straight here."

"What is it, Dennis?"

"I spoke to the doctor, Sandy," Dennis said, "and he assured me they did everything that they could."

A stream of tears rushed over my face and landed in between my mouth. "Dennis, just say it," I pleaded. "Just tell me."

"They said it was a stroke, Sandy. Worse than the first one. And they exhausted all of their options, but Aunt Mabel just didn't... She just couldn't..."

"Dammit, Dennis, just say it!"

"It's your aunt, Sandy. Your Aunt Mabel... She passed about an hour ago. She passed, Sandra. I'm sorry."

The feeling in my chest would not allow me to speak. The only thing that came out was a shudder of pain. Loud shrieks of hurt that were too strong to be held down by my fragile heart. I trembled as I stood and walked in the direction of the wall, hid myself and my tears in the corner of the room, fought off all types of demons that were messing with my head by pounding my little fists against the cold concrete. The tears kept trying to convince me that this was my fault. That if I was with Aunt Mabel then this wouldn't have happened. My heart refused to let my mind tell me that. No, no, no, I kept telling myself. I wasn't to blame for Aunt Mabel's—I wasn't to blame. I wasn't...

Dennis came close and wrapped his arms around my waist, whispered all kinds of sympathetic things that didn't make a difference to me right now. But his touch was secure and comforting enough for me to rest my head against his chest, his suit thick enough to bury my cries.

I couldn't believe that Aunt Mabel had lost her fight. It seemed as if it was all she did. As if fighting was what her life was about. And I never thought I'd see the day when she would stop. Her husband, Uncle Ray, was relentless in his verbal and mental abuse, and she just kept taking it. Kept letting him mess with her mind, which in turn ended up messing with her body. By the time she realized what he had done it was too late. He was already gone, and she had frequent visits to the hospital. She spent the next four years preaching to me about how I should live my life. And how a man should provide for it. If a man claimed he loved me he was supposed to show it. My talk of independence was nonsense to her. Because in her eyes, man and woman would always get together, but if a man wasn't around to provide, then he didn't care for you two to be together for too long.

After my heart accepted the truth for what it was, I pulled myself together, strolled out of the room with my head still against Dennis' chest and his arm around my waist. And while we walked out of that place, I could say that Dennis' touch put me at ease. He dried my tears away and held me tight, close, as if I was the only woman in the world that he cared for right now. As if his life depended on it. And I needed that. Did I miss Panther's strong, gentle hands? Yes, I could say that I did. But right now, he wasn't around, and I didn't know if he would ever come back. He abandoned me for his freedom. He placed us both in a position to make a decision, but I refused to allow that decision to dictate my freedom. I still hoped for the best for Panther. I wanted him to be free. I couldn't blame him for doing what he felt was right. If it were my freedom on the line, I might've done the same thing. And I would hope that I loved at least one person enough to stand by my side.

❧ 34 ☙

Rachel

A uniformed cop entered the room and released me. Thank God they didn't give tickets for hauling ass while walking. I couldn't move out of that place fast enough. And I prayed that I never had to come back. If everything went smoothly for Panther, then my wish may have come true, because I did my part. I held it down, and refused to allow the law and the injustice system to play me.

As I made my way through the reception area, Deidra was also on her way out. We both paused and looked at each other, the agony of defeat flooding her eyelids. I went towards her, extending as much as a smile as I could produce, and offering her an outstretched hand. To my surprise, she gripped it firmly, a hint of genuine respect for me had settled in her eyes.

"While we were in that room," Diedra began, "I watched you closely. I watched both of you. Listened to what you two were saying with your mouths and your bodies, and I could tell that you were going to do whatever you had to do to make sure Panther was free."

I smiled at Deidra's words. "And I felt the same thing about you."

Deidra said, "But it's the other one I'm worried about."

Before I could form my own opinion about Sandra, a breaking news message flashed on the T.V. screen. Deidra and I both watched in curiosity. A concrete stare and the slim mouth of an anchorwoman greeted her audience and said there was a new update in the Patrick

Alden investigation. For a second, I almost forgot that Diedra stood beside me. We both were fixed on the T.V. screen.

The camera cut to a press conference. Snapshot flashes flickered off the wall as police officers, and other important looking people stood at the podium. One clean-cut, baby-faced gentleman stepped up, tested the mic with a tap, and welcomed everyone gathered in the room. He introduced himself as John Abel, the lawyer representing Mr. Pedro Vila, the man that worked as a gardener at Patrick Alden's estate. And Mr. Vila was holding this press conference not to gain any kind of special favors, but only to clear his conscience by doing the right thing.

Mr. Abel stepped aside and allowed Mr. Vila to take the mic. Mr. Vila was a small man in weight and height, with short, slicked-back hair, and a tanned complexion. His timid eyes jumped from the papers he placed on the podium, to the awaiting audience in front of him. After clearing his throat, Mr. Vila greeted the crowd good afternoon in a frail tone, and slight accent.

"Members of the press, esteemed ladies and gentlemen, I thank you for holding this press conference. I am Hector Vila. I was Patrick Alden's gardener for four years, and have been employed longer than anybody else on his staff. Mr. Alden always say that he like me. He treat me especial. He give me days off, take me fishing with him, and he promise to help bring my brother and my mother to United States. Which is why I have come forward today. I owe it to Mr. Alden to be brave, and tell the truth."

Mr. Vila scanned the crowd. He stuttered trying to get out another word, the crack in his voice just as embarrassing. Before going on, he stopped and pulled himself together.

"Mr. Alden give me a video camera for my birthday last year. He say he give it to me to use for my family when they come to United States. Mr. Alden always say there is nothing like family. All that we have is family. All we have is the people that love us. He show me how to work the camera. When I learn how to use, I record everything. And the day that Mr. Alden was murdered, I had the camera. It was 7 P.M., and I finish work for that day. I remember coming inside the house, and inside the den, the black man, Mr. Parish Coles, was argue with Mr. Alden about the money. Mr. Alden saw all the workers looking at him, and he tell us to leave. Everybody rush to the kitchen to eat, but I grab my camera from my room on the other side of the house and sneak back to the den. But they stop argue. I press record on the camera, and I watch Mr. Coles speed away in a silver S.U.V. I walk to the kitchen, but only the workers were there. They play around with the camera and ask me to make a movie with them. After five minutes, I walk around the house again. I find Mr. Alden in his room sleep. He snore very loud, with his mouth wide open. I go close to him and record him sleeping with his mouth open. Then I hear the front door open. I hear high heels click, and keys jingle. I know it's Mrs. Alden coming. I know she fire me if she see me inside the room, so I hide under the bed. I see Mrs. Alden high heels shoes come close. Then she turn and walk out. I hear her in the kitchen. She tell all the workers to go the guesthouse and don't come out until she say so. I hear her ask for me. Then I rush from under the bed, but I hear the high-heels coming back. I run out the room before Mrs. Alden see me, but I did not grab the camera. When I come down the hallway, I see Mrs. Alden. She say where was I coming from. I told her from my room. She say if I see Mr. Alden in the last five minutes. I say no. She ask me if somebody come to see Mr. Alden. I say yes. The black man, who we know is Mr. Parish Coles, leave fifteen minutes before. She ask me if I see anything, I say no. She tell me to go with all the workers to the guesthouse and don't come until she say come out. I say yes ma'am, and I leave. A half hour later, the police come to the guesthouse and say that Mr. Alden was murdered. They ask us if we see what happened and everybody say no. We tell the police that Mr. Coles was fussing with Mr. Alden, but we did not see how Mr. Alden die. The next day, Mr. Baker, the police commissioner tell me that my fingerprints were on the camera. I get scared. I tell him I did not kill Mr. Alden. Mr. Baker say everything okay. He play the tape, and one of his men, Detective Boone, shoot and kill Mr. Alden while Mr. Alden was asleep, and Mrs. Alden stand right there with Detective Boone and watch him. I will testify on behalf of the prosecution against Detective Boone and Mrs. Alden. That is all. Thank you."

A barrage of questions was thrown at Mr. Vila. Cameras and microphones collapsed in on him as each reporter bullied their way up to the podium. Two policemen and another gentleman grabbed Mr. Vila and rushed him away from the relentless crowd.

"Ladies and gentlemen, please calm down," shouted Mr. Abel. "All of your questions will be answered in due time. Just please calm down."

When Mr. Vila was out of sight, the hungry crowd turned to Mr. Abel for answers. And it seemed as if Mr. Vila's leaving only intensified their craving.

After pleading with the crowd for several moments, Mr. Abel finally succeeded in settling them down. "I want you to know ladies and gentlemen, that we also have good reason to speculate that Mayor Tinnerman is behind this. We have proof that the mayor and Mrs. Alden had an intimate affair, and we plan to expose that there is enough evidence and motive to convict these individuals. We shall speak again. Thank you."

Mr. Abel was hurried out the back door, and left the hostile crowd shouting and begging for more.

Shouts also erupted throughout the station. Cops ran back and forth, phones rang off the hook, and a sullen-faced Detective Boone was handcuffed and escorted back to processing as everybody looked on.

I turned to Deidra, and I could see the corners of her mouth curling up. I could no longer hold it in myself and burst out with a loud shriek. Deidra and I hugged each other and jumped around like two cheerleaders that had just won the national championship. Then we calmed our tones, and embraced like two old friends reunited, the heavy breath leaving our chests confessing how relieved we were to see this day. To see that our Panther was free. It was funny to think that two women messing with the same man would be on each other's side. To be on the side of a man that cheated on us both. But we shared a common goal. And in the end, that was all that mattered.

"I guess it's over," I said.

Deidra nodded. "Guess so."

I asked, "What are you going to do when you get home?"

A sigh was Deidra's first response as her eyes went up in thought. "Pray," she said, "and take a long, hot bath."

"I hear that. Sounds like I should do the same, especially considering I don't know if I will have my job tomorrow."

"Yeah, this situation may have cost us a lot of things that we thought would never leave us." Deidra leaned on one hip, her eyes still concentrated in thought. "Listen, Rachel, I'm sorry about all of this with Panther. I didn't—I don't want—"

"Don't worry about it," I said. "Something tells me that it may be a long time before I see Panther again. I'll definitely miss him, but I'll be fine. If I ever get an urge to send him a message, I can always try to look up his mother in West Palm Beach."

Deidra shook her head and laughed.

I was confused. "Why are you laughing?"

"Where did you get that from?" Deidra asked. "And where did you get that wild ass story about his mother being a crackhead?"

"What do you mean? I got it from Panther. Didn't he move his mother to Palm Beach so he could get her away from everything?"

"Girl, Panther's mother ain't even alive."

My mouth dropped open. "What?"

"Panther's mother and father have been dead for some time. They both died in prison. His father died first. For a while, Panther was able to deal with it, but then his mother was also murdered inside after a riot. Story is a guard bust her head open with a nightstick and she never recovered from the blow. She fell into a coma, and within a week, she was dead. Ever since then Panther has despised the prison system. I heard that he has a little brother that he's trying to help get out. And after my brother was locked up for murder, Panther said that he would do everything in his power to get him out, too. That's why I can never leave Panther. Even if I wasn't to see him again, something tells me that Panther will keep his word."

I didn't know what to think. I couldn't understand why Panther felt he had to lie to me. It was crazy, but the more I learned about Panther, the more I realized that I didn't know him at all. I asked Deidra, "But how could Panther do all of this?"

"He knows a lot of people. I don't doubt what he can do. My brother believes that Panther can do it, and that's good enough for me. From the time I met Parish Coles I knew that I was dealing with a very powerful man. The type that you know can help bring you the things you need in this crazy world. Who wouldn't stand by a man like that?"

"You're right," I told Deidra. "Who wouldn't want a man like that on their side?"

"And who wouldn't want a couple of women like us on their side."

"I know that's right, girl." We gave each other five.

"Girl, I'm ready to go," Deidra said. "I'm hoping my mother cooked a big meal and left me some. I could eat for today and half of tomorrow. You want to roll?"

"No, thank you. I'm going to enjoy some much deserved quiet time."

"I hear that. But maybe someday we'll meet again, hopefully under different circumstances."

We embraced one last time before leaving the station and going our separate ways. "Yeah, girl. I hope so, too."

ಬ 35 ಛ

Deidra

I hopped on the next metro headed to mama's house. Invited Rachel to ride with me, but she called her mama to scoop her up. And I didn't want to be a burden to anybody at a late hour. The bus ride home was cool, though. I was treated like a regular person. The bus driver greeted me with 'hello, beautiful, black sister,' and an elderly woman smiled at me as if I were one of her grandchildren coming to visit. No police officers harassed me with annoying questions. And no threats of jail time were tossed my way. Finally, I was able to rest my head.

The silence of the bus allowed me a chance to reflect on what I had been through in the day. Allowed the opportunity to evaluate myself, and my life. I acted stupidly. I had a man killed, and even though it was not my intentions, it almost cost me my life. My brother, Eric, is an intelligent man, but I should've known better. Prison was a vulnerable place for anyone to be, including Eric. He only wanted to help, but his perception was seen through a reality behind bars. And I couldn't blame him for giving me the advice he gave. Everyday he had to make decisions based on that reality. A reality I could hardly understand. He wanted to show me that although locked up, he could still be of some help to his little sister. But at this point, I was just grateful that he was still around to listen.

A cool breeze ran over me, but another sweet compliment from the bus driver warmed me as I strutted off the metro. Although well past eleven at night, the hood still moved with the pace of a go-getter and the spirit of a hustler. My steps were just as quick. The only way a gazelle survived in the lion's den was to act as though she were a lion too. And I was no fool. I wasn't trying to get caught up. Again.

A mirage of red, white and blue lights bounced off the project walls. Police cars surrounded the front of the building while onlookers stood close by and peeked through their windows. I was inching up to a neighbor for the scoop, when I noticed that the officers were standing in my mother's doorway.

I rushed up the stairs, shoved a few nosey folks out of my way, and broke through the fake police wall.

"Ma'am, wait outside," one officer yelled as he reached for my arm.

I spun around and swung his arm off of me. "This is my house. What is going on here?"

He and two other officers came close and encircled me. "Who are you?" he asked. "What's your name?"

"Don't worry about my name. Where are my mother and sister?"

"Miss, I asked who are—"

"Where are my mother and—"

"Dee." Tracy raced around the corner and threw her tiny frame into my arms.

I swallowed Tracy up with a tight hug as she buried her cries deep within my shoulder. I said, "I'm here, baby. I got you. It's okay. I'm not going nowhere."

"I was so scared, Dee." Tracy said. "I thought he was—I thought—he was gonna get me. I thought he was gonna get me, Dee."

"Nobody's gonna get you, baby. I'm here. You're safe now. I promise."

"Please don't leave me, Dee. Please. Don't leave me."

"No, no baby. It's okay. I'm here. I'm always here. I can never leave you. That's a fact, baby. I can never leave you."

A tear forced itself from behind my eyelids and ran down my cheek with hot anger. I had to find out who was crazy enough to put his motherfucking hands on my little sister.

At that moment, mama came around the corner with a slow, heavy stroll. The bottoms of her bedroom slippers glided across the floor as she moved closer to where Tracy and I stood. Her face was flooded with guilt and sorrow. She could barely look me in the eye.

I said, "What is it mama?"

Still, mama's eyes bounced from the officers behind us, to the ground, to the walls, and away from me.

"Okay," I said with irritation. "Then tell me who was it."

"Ma'am," one of the officers spoke up. "The accused has been handcuffed and is in the squad car. He has been accused of attempted sexual assault and attempted sexual battery."

"Thank you officer, but I don't want you to tell me. You tell me, mama. Who was he?"

"Leave it alone," mama said as she turned away. "The officer said he is being charged."

"I know, but I want you to charge him mama. I want you to accuse him of trying to rape your twelve year-old daughter. I want you to confess to all the bullshit that you have brought around her for all of these—"

"All right, Deidra. He was a man that I was seeing. Okay. Shit, you think I wanted this to happen?"

"No, but you didn't do much to stop it, either. If you were watching who you were bringing around here, this might not have happened."

"And I'm sorry, all right. Is that what you want me to say? I fucked up, Deidra. You happy now? Is that what you wanted to hear?"

"You damn right, mama." I pulled Tracy away from my shoulder and had her face mama. "But I'm not the one you're supposed to be apologizing to."

A stream of tears tumbled down mama's face as her lips quivered. "And I did," she said. "Just before you got here, I hugged my baby, told her that she was beautiful, and told her that I was sorry. And that it will never happen again"

One of officers stepped up in between us. "I'm sorry, Ms. Williams, but we've got to take you and Tracy down to the station for a statement."

"Give her some time," I said. "Does it look like she can do this right now?"

"I understand, but we need to—"

"Leave it alone, Downings," another officer said. "It's late. Getting a statement tomorrow or tonight won't make much of a difference."

"But sergeant, I don't think—"

"And I think I'm still your sergeant, Downings. You boys get that perp down to booking. We can speak to Ms. Williams tomorrow."

The other three officers slowly made their way out as the sergeant stayed behind. "I understand that this is a tough time for all of you," the sergeant said. "I want to give you a card to one of the best counselors in the county. She can help. And also, we are going to need a statement if we're going to charge the accused with the crime, and we are going to need it by tomorrow."

"Thank you, officer," I said, "but I don't know if she can do this so soon."

"No." Tracy said as she turned to me. "I want to. As long as you're with me, I think I can do it."

Through her tears, Tracy's eyes showed signs of that joyous innocence that I was so used to seeing. I was surprised by her strength, even though I shouldn't have been. She grew up watching her big brothers and sister stand firm in the face of hard times. And like all of those situations, this too would pass.

Mama took the card of the counselor as the sergeant left. She walked up to us and handed me the card. "You're going to need it," mama said, "since Tracy is going to be staying with you."

I held the card with confusion clouding my brain. "What do you mean?"

"I mean for good," mama said. "If that's all right with Tracy."

A sparkle sprung up in Tracy's eyes as she grinned from ear-to-ear. "Yes, yes, yes. Can I, Dee?"

"Baby, that's not something you have to ask me. I want you to be with me. And that's a fact."

Tracy threw herself into my arms again. The hurt disappeared and we took advantage of this moment of comfort. She then turned and hugged mama, too. Mama's face glowed with surprise. She let out a long, deep breath. I could not remember the last time I saw mama with so much peace in her face, but I knew it always existed.

As mama and Tracy slowly pulled away from each other, Tracy got slick and tried pushing mama and I close. Tracy stood between us and rested her head over both our shoulders. It had been a while since I looked at mama with affection. And it had been a while since my heart confessed that I loved her. But I did. And there was no better time to show it. We all hugged like a bunch of long, lost sisters that had found each other. I was grateful for them. Grateful that my family was coming back together. And I knew that soon enough, there was going to be the day when all of us, including Eric, would embrace each other this way. I still had all of my hopes and belief in one man. And when I got home, I planned that the first thing I would do was get on my knees and thank him.

೧ 36 ೦೮

Sandra

The next morning, I woke up with Aunt Mabel on my mind. I realized how much I missed her. In the last few years, just before she started to get sick, I took her life and her love for granted. I became detached from our relationship and clung to a greater need for money. My security, my lifestyle, my career, were all that mattered. Spending time with the only person that truly loved me was put to the side like a worthless piece of jewelry. Yet Aunt Mabel glowed like the morning sun whenever I came over. She would act as though she was hot with me, but never held a grudge. I explained how school and a good career were important to me. She would tell me to also make time for love, but accepted my aspirations and never judged me for having them. I was indifferent to her pleas of us spending time together, and excited only when I was getting a raise in pay. Before long I wasn't visiting at all. Spending most of my time shopping and club-hopping, the only time that Aunt Mabel and I shared were five-minute conversations over the phone no more than twice a week. That's when the bitterness began kicking in, and the sickness began to take hold. The hospital became Aunt Mabel's home away from home and she would let me know just how uncomfortable she felt there. I took notice of my selfishness, felt guilty about it, and at least tried calling everyday if not going to visit. But in the last few days, I had slipped and shirked my responsibility. I took an undying, unconditional love for granted. And like most of the fools in the world that did the same, I didn't appreciate what I had until it was gone.

But this time I would make it up to Aunt Mabel by honoring her life to the fullest. I planned to go all out. Have it feeling like a celebration rather than a funeral. Everybody that ever knew Aunt Mabel would be invited. Old men to little children would swarm the old house like a family reunion. Food would include nothing but the best. Greens, catfish, cabbage, and the cheesiest macaroni and cheese, anything that Aunt Mabel loved. Everything done with class, and everyone would've remembered Aunt Mabel's day of celebration; not because I went all out to make it that way, but because everyone there would know that she deserved it.

My mind was at peace now. I didn't need Panther to make me feel that way, but man, did I miss him. I couldn't help but wonder where was he now, or if he was coming back. And if he were to come back at this moment, what would he think of me? Would he still want to be with me after what I had done? And after I had broken free from the trance that I constantly fell into from staring into his sleepy, brown eyes, would I still want to be with him?

I was never one to live my life on what ifs, though. I was always about action. About moving. About placing myself in the positions that I wanted to be in to get me what I needed. And today was no different. With or without Panther, I still had a life. I had needs to fulfill and goals to accomplish. Sandra Reese was just getting started, and was not willing to sit around moping and crying over one man. He may have been a good man, but he wasn't here now. Dennis was. And from what he had told me, he planned to stay. He entertained my selfish rambling about all the things that I wanted, yet agreed to provide them. He asked about my needs, and promised to fulfill them. But most importantly, he was here. Here at a time when I needed him to be.

This may not have been what I spent countless nights dreaming of from the time I was a little girl, but this was about real life. My life. And I was determined to live it the best way I could. I started by wrapping my new man's arm around me as he lay beside me on the bed. And I cuddled up into a feeling that even if Panther were to come back, he could no longer give me. And that was peace.

෨ 37 ෬

Rachel

My time in bed was short, but I didn't care. It was time to go. I jumped up and moved like the Tasmanian devil. And even though my rest was brief, it was still rewarding. I followed Deidra's advice and served myself a long, hot, bubble bath last night. After I steamed away the tension of yesterday from my pores, I called mama. We talked for hours about everything. We laughed as much as we could about the past, tried making sense out of the present, and spoke optimistically about an otherwise, uncertain future. By the time we were talked out, we realized that all we had was each other. And that was more than either one of us could ask for.

In our two hour long conversation, mama reminded me of the first time Q was shot. I was in school at the time when mama came and pulled me out early. We arrived at the hospital and all of Q's homeboys surrounded his door like bodyguards. Mama told me that it was only a shot in the leg, but I was still unnerved and thought he might've died from loss of blood. T.V. shows like *E.R.* was a big influence on me at the time.

Q's boys respectfully granted us privacy. I was in awe of Q. Besides Martin Luther King, he was my first experience of a strong, black man. He acted as though it was another day. As if a bullet had hardly whispered in his direction. Upbeat like always, he had mama and me in tears with jokes about his homeboys crying louder than I ever did when they heard he was shot. He even bragged about the nurse's assistant that was feeling him, and had a love letter she wrote him and phone number to prove it. It seemed as if mama and I were in more pain than he was.

Then the conversation turned serious when mama asked Q about who shot him. Q said everything was cool, that he had it taken care of, and there was no need to worry about it anymore.

"No need to worry," mama asked. "Quincy, this boy put a hole in your leg, and you're telling me not to worry. Where's he gonna put that hole the next time?"

"And that's why I don't want you to worry," Q said, "because I don't want it to be a next time."

Mama's face turned rigid. "So you know the boy that shot you. Is that why you don't want me to worry about it, Quincy? Because you're already planning to take care of it."

"If you're thinking it's like that, mama, then you got it wrong."

"Okay," mama said, "then you're gonna to identify this boy to the police."

"No, mama. I've been shot. That means it happened for a reason."

"And it means that it could happen again," mama said.

"You're right," Q yelled, "but I don't want it to happen to no one else."

Mama had confusion in her eyes. "What you mean by that, boy?"

"I mean if I did wrong to this cat, then I did him wrong. Not my homeboys, not my girlfriends, and definitely not my family. Do you hear me, ma. If I respect the game and leave this thing alone, then maybe it would be left alone for good. For everybody's good. But if I don't play by the rules and go to the police, then not only am I a target, but so are my homeboys and my family. And I don't care what you have to say about it, ma. I've made up my mind. And I'm not having anybody or anything come anywhere close to touching the most beautiful women in my life. I wouldn't be able to live with something like that."

Q was shot and killed four months later. To this day, the killer has never been found.

Someone as lovable as Q. Someone as cute, and funny, and kind as my brother, why would somebody want to kill him? That question had poked at me for years like a thousand needles to the brain. But instead of allowing it to rip me apart, I embraced it. I encouraged it to take on a life of its own, and it did. That same question was my soul's desire. It woke me up early, and drove me through the late hours of the night. It gave me the hope of knowing that my brother did not die in vain. It was the reason that I put my heart and soul into helping every young, black man that was just like Q.

A call from Darnell had me filled with hope again. He said to come prepared for work. There was no more to be said. I raced through morning traffic like I was the culprit of a high-speed chase. My heartbeat bounced like a pinball machine, but my mind was focused on work like I had never left.

When I walked into Darnell's office, he was in the middle of a call, and quieted me with a finger to his lips. I remained patient, although anxiety was swirling all around my stomach. I couldn't wait to hear those words from Darnell; I want you to come back to work.

Darnell hung up the phone, smiling as he looked to me.

I said, "Darnell, I came as soon as I could get here. Is everything, all right?"

"Everything is great," he said as he made his way around the desk. "Especially for you."

I was jumping inside. "Really? What's up?"

"Congratulations," Darnell said. "Looks like you are going to be supervisor of this facility."

I was confused. "What are you talking about, Darnell? I don't understand."

"I'm talking about Andrea's position, Rachel. She's retiring at the end of the week, and I have recommended you to take her place."

"Wait, wait. Andrea. This is crazy. How can she make a life decision to retire in a week?"

"Don't question it, my dear. I know how much you care for the boys. That's why it wasn't hard for me to consider you to be the one to fill her place."

"But why is she stepping down so quick? So soon?"

"This isn't quick, Rachel. She's been here for ten years."

"And what if I'm not ready to take the position?"

Darnell shrugged. "Then that is your choice."

I looked at Darnell like he had escaped from a cell herself. A mental facility cell.

"What do you mean that is my choice? Words like that, it's like you don't care if you placed a serial killer in that position."

Darnell laughed. "If I didn't care I wouldn't have asked you to fill the position. I know you can do this job." Darnell looked at me like a father giving reassurance to his daughter for doubting herself.

"The D.A. will be here in a few minutes to congratulate you," Darnell went on. "That is why I wanted you to come in today. After that, you take the remainder of the week off, come back Monday morning, fresh and prepared to be the next supervisor of this facility."

"But Darnell, I haven't even had time to learn about—"

"And that's why I'm giving you the week off. If you feel you need more time, just say so. You don't have to worry about having a job anymore. Now you make those kinds of decisions about others. Now, relax. I'll get us some coffee so we can be awake when the D.A. arrives."

Darnell left the room, and left me dumbfounded. Why was Andrea retiring, and on such short notice? And why did Darnell recommend me for her position? Did he want something from me in return? But why would he promote me after I made it clear that I wasn't going there with him? Just what the hell was going on?

But if this was going to happen, and it seemed like it was, what did I know about being a supervisor? I was a counselor. A rookie counselor at that. Who was I going to supervise? From what I had seen with Andrea, there wasn't much to do except make sure that everyone else did their job. Most people would've killed for this position, but I adored being a counselor. I shared something special with my boys. They looked up to me like a big sister, and confided in me like a friend. Being a supervisor, I wouldn't have that. And there wouldn't be a reason for me to be here at all.

Then I started thinking. Supervisors did what they wanted. I could sit in on sessions and give input. I could coach other counselors to be just as dedicated to the boys as I was. And the boys would be able to confide in me at any time of the day. That's right. My boys. They were the reason for everything that I was doing, and everything that I would continue to do. Especially as a supervisor.

I took a sneak peak at my boys' files to see what they were up to lately. To see if everything was the same, or if one of them may have fallen off track. To my surprise, there were no new changes. Everything about the same as when I left.

I was going to miss Ace. I opened up his file. How could the state try him as an adult? Didn't they even read everything in his file? He was a good kid. And he was young. How could they put him in the prison system with older, grown men that were killers, drug dealers, and...

Sexual deviant. Wait a minute. Was this Ace's file? It couldn't be. There were complaints from some of the younger inmates of how he sexually molested them in the year that he had been there. I even found reports from other counselors, citing him for carrying a home-made knife into their sessions. One claim in his file was from a female counselor, 24 years old, stated that she trusted Ace, felt bad for his situation and tried to get him to open up. One day when they had a one-on-one, she said that Ace pulled a knife from his side and sliced her across the face. Who was this lady? Did she leave before I started because I had never heard of her, and I knew all of the counselors there? And the last claim in Ace's file was a report by Andrea, citing Ace for carrying a knife in Rachel Baxter's class, the day he fought with Sam Stone.

What?

I turned to Sam's file. Sam Stone. Everything about his file read trouble. All the arrests, charges, time spent in the hall, it was a miracle that he wasn't sent to the adult population. I read over his mental background, self-explanatory. His health, strong. His family background, parents deceased. His mother and father were—killed in...

Oh, my God.

Mother and father killed in prison.

Deidra's words came to me when she revealed the truth of Panther's family history. "Panther's mother and father have been dead for some time. They both died in prison."

Oh, God. This couldn't be. I read on. Father murdered when party was eight years old. Mother killed during a prison riot when party was ten. This couldn't be real.

In my head, I could hear Deidra's words again. "Story is she fell in a coma, and within a week she was dead."

I rushed through the file, looking for those key words. The title that would let me know whether or not I was crazy for thinking what I thought. And there it was, at the end of the file. I almost fell back, but instead the file slipped from my fingers and landed at my feet. And the last page was staring at me. The title of the page read next of kin. And right next to it was the name Parish Stone. A.K.A. Parish Coles.

A piercing echo of Deidra's voice invaded my mind again. "I heard that he has a brother that he's trying to help get out, too."

Then Sam's voice took the place of Deidra's. "Parish Coles. I've heard that name before."

The voices of the truth kept haunting me. Letting me know that I was a part of Panther's plan from the beginning.

"You play the game," Panther's voice said from the dream that I had, "but you don't show your cards."

Sam Stone was Parish Coles' brother. And they planned all of this. And their plan also saved my life.

I remembered Deidra's last words to me. "Panther's a powerful man," she said. "The type that can help give you the things that you need in this crazy world. Who wouldn't stand by a man like that?"

A chilling thought. But I had no choice but to agree.

The last nine months of my life ran through my mind like a favorite movie that I could've watched over and over again. I adored me some Parish Coles. And I was going to miss him. Even though he was nowhere near me now, and chances were he'd probably never be again, he would always be with me. He would always be near to my heart and share a piece of my soul. My man, Panther.

Epilogue

Through the passenger window of a midnight blue Mercedes-Benz, Panther watched the man in the tailor-made, dark suit approach. The gentleman's walk was smooth, easy. That was a good sign for Panther. He let the window down to complete the transaction. Before the briefcase was passed, Panther showed the contents inside. The man smiled. Panther was sure that the man wouldn't take anything less than what was agreed. A small price to pay for freedom. The briefcase was closed and slid through the window.

In the darkness, the chief's eyes lit up with genuine respect for Panther when he grabbed the briefcase. He said, "You played the game quite well."

Panther smiled. "I don't know any other way to play it."

"Just one question," the chief said. "Why use the women? Why take a chance on the testimony of three women that would probably hate you after they found out about each other?"

Panther shrugged. "Because we were all focused on one thing. One thing that was going to bring us closer to getting what we wanted out of this whole situation. And that was love."

The chief chuckled. "You can't tell me that Panther Coles actually believes in that."

"Everybody does, chief. We all need someone to love. And whoever that might be, we do what we can to find that person, and keep them. Even if you don't believe it, there is something worth having that's greater than what's in this briefcase."

The chief nodded. "If that's the case, then I should've have gotten more out of it."

Panther smiled easy. "But I didn't say that I was stupid either. How's Mr. Vila?"

"Happy. His family will be here by the weekend. I'm sure he's grateful."

"And my brother?"

"Your brother is smarter than you think" the chief said. "He knew something was up so with Mr. Colon so he followed his instincts. It worked out well for everybody. My men got a big arrest and shut down Mr. Colon's men, and your brother prevented you from getting touched. You can't blame him for looking out for you."

"I don't want him to look out for me. I want him stay clear from all of this."

"He'll be home in twenty-four hours," The chief said.

Panther nodded, and then faced the front. "What about Eric Thomas?"

The chief let out a slow, hard breath. "Sorry, Panther. There wasn't much that I could do for your friend."

"And there's no way you can get me to believe that, chief. You all can do pretty much whatever you want. If you want to."

"Yeah, Panther. But—"

"But you can get Eric out, too."

"It just wasn't in the works, Panther. I tried, but they figured that you got everything you—"

"Not everything."

Panther's point must've gotten across to the chief. For a moment he was lost for words. The chief finally said. "I'll see what I can do. But of course that means—"

"I know what it means," Panther said. "Believe me. I know. Everybody has their love. And yours doesn't come cheap."

The chief smiled. "I'm sure I'll be in touch soon."

They shook hands again before going their separate ways.

"What's with you and this super-hero stuff?" The chief asked. "You on some kind of mission to break all of the brothers and sisters out of prison or something?"

A vision of Panther's parents crossed his mind as he thought, what if. What if he had just a little bit more time? The outcome may have been better for them. He looked at the chief and said, "Somebody has to help them. And I'll make sure I do my part."

When Panther rolled up the window, the chief turned away. Shorty threw the car into drive and crept back onto the I-95.

Panther popped in a CD and reclined in his seat. After this battle, he wasn't sure if it was the power of money, or the power of love that set him free. He would figure it out some day. Before the sun set for good over the cold and unyielding city streets, the answer would come to him. But one thing was certain. In the end, everybody got what they wanted. And others got what they deserved.

This was just one small battle, though. Panther was sure that there'd be many to come.

The night sky was clear. The ride was smooth. Panther could breathe easy for a moment. The vultures had been burned by their own fire. Now everything was settled. Quiet. Peaceful. Deep within the rhythms of the Charlie Parker that played, Panther felt as free as Bird himself. He had won. It was time to go and claim his prize.

Panther hopped out of the car as Shorty dropped him off. He snatched his keys from his pocket, excited about finally being able to come back home. But before Panther could unlock the door it was opened. Panther's woman grabbed him close and kissed him softly on the lips. Then Panther grabbed her hand. He shut the door and led the way. This was it, he thought. No more hiding. No more games. He was complete. He and the only woman for him made love in their home, and in their bedroom. It was the one with the heart-shaped waterbed.

Reading Guide Questions
for "All That I Got Is You"

1. While reading the novel, did you believe Panther committed the crime or did you think he was innocent the whole time?
2. Were you surprised by the outcome of the novel?
3. Who do you think was the perfect woman for Panther?
4. Were you surprised when Sandra "squealed" toward the end of the investigation?
5. Was Panther right to use his women as decoys?
6. Was Sam really looking out for Rachel's safety or did he have an ulterior motive?
7. Did Diedra go over Panther's head when she agreed to have Dalvin handle the situation with her almost-rapist?
8. Did the absence of Panther throughout most of the novel add to the character's persona?
9. Would you have slept with Keith Grimes to advance your business career?
10. Which male character would you consider dating?
11. How did you feel when you found out Ace was truly a dangerous criminal and not caught up in the system as Rachel first assumed?
12. Would you have created an alibi for the person you love, even if you weren't convinced they were innocent?
13. Which woman did you relate to the most: Diedra, Rachel or Sandra?

A conversation
with The, oc

1. How long did it take you to write the book?
It took about three months to write the book. The story was already inside me. I just had to put it down.

2. Did you base any of your characters on somebody that you know?
Sandra is loosely based on a female manager that I once worked with and Aunt Mabel had some of grandmother's characteristics. That's why Aunt Mabel sounded so authentic. My grandmother was just like her.

3. Do you plan to make this novel into a series?
The book definitely has potential for Panther and Sam's back story, and I feel that a series based on them will make for great stories. I'm currently putting that together as we speak.

4. How long did it take to come up with the idea for the novel?
It was all inspiration. It literally hit me all at once as I sat with my wife discussing my writing. I told her how I was amazed at how Eric Jerome Dickey was able to write from women characters perspectives, and my wife enlightened me on how the goal of an artist is to challenge themselves to do things they've never done before. And at that moment, *All That I Got Is You*, was born. I can truly say that I was hit with inspiration at that moment. It was crazy.

5. Who would you date if they were a real person: Diedra, Sandra, or Rachel?
(Laughs). All of them are beautiful in their own way. And I'll just leave it at that.

6. Do you consider Sam a good guy or bad guy?

I don't believe any character is good or bad because I don't believe humans are good or bad. We are who we are. Some people are misguided. And some people are plum dumb, crazy. I feel like Sam was just misguided. Still, his heart was in the right place by looking out for his brother, and for Rachel. And we will learn more about Sam's character in books to come.

7. What is your favorite scene in the book?

My favorite scene has to be when Sandra was in the limo with Keith Grimes. Because it showed how Panther was still there, while not actually being there. It added to his mysteriousness. Even though the whole story was told through the women's eyes, Panther remained the central figure of the story. And at that moment, even Sandra couldn't deny him.

Learn more about The, oc, and all he has coming up at www.theocbooks.com

www.ingramcontent.com/pod-product-compliance
Lightning Source LLC
Chambersburg PA
CBHW032038240626
47154CB00003B/972